The Peruvian Notebooks

Camino del Sol

A Latina and Latino Literary Series

The Peruvian Notebooks

(a novel)

Braulio Muñoz

The University of Arizona Press   Tucson

Contents

High Noon   3

One O'clock   59

Two O'clock   119

Three O'clock   185

Three-Thirty   237

Seven O'clock   269

The Peruvian Notebooks

High Noon

July 5, 1989

Mr. Aniceto Gutiérrez Bayle
Correo Central
Canto Grande
Lima, Peru

My Very Esteemed Uncle,

I hope that the present letter finds you in good health along with all the family. As for me, as usual, I'm without much to report and thinking about all of you.

After greeting you I go on to tell you that I am very sorry not to have written as often as I would have liked. It's because I have been very busy. I have had to travel abroad frequently on account of business. It's a pity, Uncle, but it seems that the more successful I am in business, the less time I have to dedicate to the more important things in life. At this very moment I am preparing for another trip. So this huge house, with all the amenities I have mentioned in my prior letters, is going to stand empty once again. How I would like for the family to be here! The thing is, Uncle, I miss Peru. I miss everyone. If someday any one of you would ever come to visit me in the USA, I promise you'll have everything. You have my address. My house really belongs to the family. I promise to write as soon as I return from my trip. I would like to make plans to visit you all in Canto Grande.

Meanwhile, hoping everything is well with you and all the family, I say goodbye with a warm embrace.

Your nephew who esteems you greatly,
Antonio

1

The mail arrives unusually early today. It is Saturday, high noon. As if in a dream, Antonio Alday Gutiérrez hears the postman stuffing the row of mailboxes on the front porch of the old house. He pictures the old postman talking to himself as he works, complaining about something with deep resignation. Perhaps the weather. When he finishes, he clears his throat. Moments later, his tired footsteps begin to die away down the cement driveway. Meanwhile, inside 209 Rogers Lane, in Lima, Delaware County, Pennsylvania, Antonio Alday Gutiérrez is trying to discover the patterns of his past to ease the remorse-smeared bewilderment that keeps his eyes blurry, his hands trembling, and his stomach churning. He focuses on the old postman's dying steps as he lies prostrate on his yellow vinyl couch, facing the wide west-facing windows. Absorbing Lima's winter light, white and soft on his face, he asks himself again and again why his life changed so suddenly and why nothing will ever be the same again.

Hoping for the soft winter light to warm his limp body, Antonio Alday Gutiérrez considers the possibility that *al fin se me haya roto el cascarón,* that at last his thick shell has cracked. There seems to be no other explanation. The protective armor he has built with utmost care over twenty-two years has finally failed him. And for the thousandth time this Saturday in December, he curses the ineluctable fact: he is now a murderer. Yes. El Azar has gotten the best of him. It seems he only fooled himself into believing that he could exorcise the ghosts of Tacora.

Or was it, perhaps, a mere accident; a dismissible misstep in his otherwise successful journey; something that in some way he can still explain, defend, even fix? Snared in a feverish fatigue, with his desire to go on already waning, unable to stop the shaking of his hands or the churning of his stomach, Antonio Alday Gutiérrez makes one last attempt to review his steps from the beginning, if only to carry on picking up the mail, dressing in Cerruti trousers and Armani jackets, missing Hannah, imitating Robert Wagner, writing in his Peruvian notebooks—brittle paper, blurry red lines, scent of dry lemon peels—and living, perhaps, with what he has done. Yes. He manages to sit up straight: I must relive everything. It is my only hope of saving something of who I once was, before they knock on the door.

2

Anthony Allday adjusted his belt and felt the dead weight of the Smith & Wesson .38 against his right thigh. He rested his hand on the grip and sighed almost inaudibly, ready to begin his rounds. He cleared his throat, straightened his tie, and moved toward the door. Nearing the threshold, he turned to look in the square mirror on the back wall of the security office, as he had done for almost eight years now. But on that evening, December 9, for the briefest moment, he did not recognize himself. As if touched by the ghostly image reflected in the mirror, he sensed he had changed, though not how or why. He was startled by a diffuse yet real feeling of panic. He felt something important was oddly amiss. But he managed to shake off these feelings by taking comfort in his routine: He checked his weapon by lifting it out and putting it back in its leather holster. He straightened his cap with one hand on the black plastic brim. He checked that his white shirt was well tucked in under his navy blue pants. He patted his light brown hair with soft, long, white fingers. He synchronized his wristwatch with the metal clock hanging on the back wall of the room next to the mirror: it was exactly 10:30 P.M.

Now, of course, seeing everything in the light of day from the perspective of a defeated man sitting on a vinyl couch, it is clear that it was not a run-of-the-mill 10:30. It was, in fact, the eve of a cursed day, one different from all the others Anthony Allday had anticipated with that routine. There is no doubt now that at 10:30 P.M. on December 9, 1995, he had a premonition that something was about to change in his life, that something was pulling him back into a dreaded past, which in turn was thrusting him into an obscure future. But, of course, Antonio Alday Gutiérrez thinks at high noon, Anthony Allday no longer knew how to appreciate such sensations. He had been in America for too long. He had lost the Peruvian ability to fear the future and hence to read the power of the past in the slightest change of mood.

Anthony Allday opened the security office door and was momentarily blinded by the garish lights that flooded the festive halls of the Springfield Mall. The first store on his left was Stonebridge Coffee Co., a gourmet coffee bar. It had opened only six months earlier but had quickly become one of his favorite stops. In fact, Anthony Allday had come to see his brief visits there as something of an extension to his rights and benefits as a night watchman. He greeted Karen, the Dominican woman who worked the early-morning and late-night shifts, and asked for the usual, a strong double cappuccino. She treated him to her pleasant smile: rows of beautiful white teeth set in a dark and friendly face. 'Nother day, 'nother dollar. Whaddya say, Mr. Allday? *Parece que va a nevar*, it looks like it's going to snow; I can feel it in my bones. And he, *que va a ser,* can't be. And, in any case, it's better to be in here than outside, right?

Anthony Allday turned around, leaned both elbows on the faux granite countertop, and let his big, light brown eyes wander among the throngs of shoppers that crisscrossed the mall. They looked happy. The multicolored lights bathed them in a carnival atmosphere. And Anthony Allday thought that he had never seen anything like it in the Peru of his youth. Not even in downtown Lima, the capital. Not even when he managed to get to the posh places on Plaza San Martín or Jirón de la Unión—full of apprehension, simulating and dissimulating for the Peruvian watchmen—or climbed the escalator in places like La Escala, the newest and fanciest department store in all of Peru. Nah. Anthony Allday clicked his tongue impatiently on that cursed evening. By comparison those stupid lights were feeble.

In fact, at 12:05 P.M. on this cursed Saturday afternoon, Antonio Alday Gutiérrez distinctly remembers that during his first round, Anthony Allday thought that everything Peruvian was anemic next to what he had found in his new *sitio,* his new place: Lima, Delaware County, Pennsylvania. Yes. He had long been filled with disdain and hatred for the land of his youth. He had long wished to distance himself from its polluting influences.

Anthony Allday recalled that when he was still in Peru he could not perceive the difference between the two worlds. One has to live them, he said to himself, taking a slow sip of his cappuccino, his tired eyes panning the row of stores on his left. Only by living can one balance them and find solid ground from which to judge. Those who have never left their barrios, their rags, their inherited masks and thick shells can never have a justifiable opinion about the differences.

And Karen, smiling again: It'll snow tonight. I can guarantee you that. I feel it in my bones.

And Mr. Allday: I guess you're right, Karen. You're always right.

On the other hand, he thought to himself again, someone like Mr. Anthony Allday, a night watchman at the Springfield Mall, had the right to judge. He could choose between the two worlds. And he could construct a life based on that choice. Someone like Mr. Anthony Allday had the right to take full advantage of all the opportunities that the clash between the two worlds afforded. He had the right to use the dust and chaos cast up by that clash as cover to advance his own designs. *A la mierda*, to hell with it! He had made the right choice. And he had no regrets. He was at peace with himself.

And so, to Karen: they're always predicting bad weather. Don't believe them. They just love to invent things. . . .

But, of course, Antonio Alday Gutiérrez remembers at 12:05 P.M. on the day of the sinful deed, once Anthony Allday embraced the full measure of what he had done, it also produced in him the distinct sensation, the certitude perhaps, that his construction of a world according to his own measure had entailed a fundamental loss of memory. He figured that from the moment he chose to become someone else, he had lost a clear sense of who he had really been before his departure from Peru, before Antonio Alday Gutiérrez became Mr. Anthony Allday.

Nothing like my island, Mr. Allday, Karen said, with a hint of sadness in her smile. Palm trees. Warm water. Blue sky. The air comes and goes as it pleases. In December, like right now, it's so hot we can only dance at night, with the breeze.

And Mr. Allday: in Peru, too, it's hot. But on the coast, where I come from, it's very dry. A desert. The garbage stays around for years. There used to be thousands of buzzards, but they've gone north on account of the stench. Mine is a cursed country, Karen. And he smiled back at her, to excuse himself for the bitterness he had let slip.

His name change had not been premeditated. When he was still in

8

Peru, Antonio Alday Gutiérrez did not know that in the USA people could change their names as easily as they could change their shirts in Tacora. In truth, he did not become Allday until years after sneaking into his new sitio, by crossing the Rio Grande. He did not become Anthony Allday until much later still, in the mid-eighties, after he saw an Italian American movie with a title he no longer remembered, at the International House in Philadelphia. He liked the hero's name, because . . . well, first of all because he was the hero; but also because it let Antonio retain something of what he had been in Peru, a Peruvian Antonio, while giving him something else, something, one could say, American.

Yes, Antonio Alday Gutiérrez says to himself, feeling the soft white light of winter against his trembling, guilty hands: the name change had not been premeditated. Given his starting point in life, such a thought would have been beyond his wildest dreams. No question about it. The opportunity to change his name and become someone else altogether— a process that at the beginning was imperceptible but in the long run turned out to be fundamental and irrevocable—did not even enter his mind while he was still dealing with the world in Tacora.

Anthony Allday was thinking he had come to America to escape from Peru, because there he was suffocating in the daily misery that was his life. *¡Carajo!* Damn it all! He threw himself into his journey and embraced the empty and gray abyss that was his possible future because, in a moment of utmost despair and anger, of hatred for everything that surrounded him, he managed to shut his eyes tight, carajo, and see himself free from everyone and everything there. And I do not regret it, Anthony Allday convinced himself, now for the first time on the cursed evening of that cursed day feeling the diffuse but persistent throbbing in his left big toe, which was by now a loyal companion during his rounds. I do not regret a thing.

The trip to the USA was easier than anyone in Tacora would have supposed. And it was cheap. Five hundred dollars in cash, for everything. Of course, in Peru and in 1973, that was a great deal of money. Even so, thought Anthony Allday as he turned the corner by Aldo's shoe store, still flooded by the multicolored holiday lights, it was quite cheap. And Anthony Allday remembered the day La Loca Pedro Lorca, the *maricón,* the fag, from La Parada, had thrown him the possibility, his future life jacket, almost as an afterthought: they're going to Gringolandia, Toño. Through Mexico. We need one more *güevón,* one more shithead, to fill our quota. If you're interested, let me know. Five hundred dollars. Cash. And not a word to the *güevones* of Tacora. When? In a week.

Toño Alday Gutiérrez thought about the prospect a thousand times over. He found it both unreal and terrifying. He made subtle inquiries among his friends: Did they know anything about Mexico? Had they heard of the coyotes? Did they know anyone who had gone to the USA illegally? No one knew anything specific, but they all advised him against even thinking of getting there through Mexico. They had heard the coyotes were a gang that made a living by robbing and killing foreigners near a place called Río Bravo, that the border was mined, that many travelers ended up as slaves for rich gringos who liked young men. . . . Funny thing, thought Anthony Allday, checking his wristwatch at 10:35 on the cursed evening, instead of dissuading him, those comments only egged him on: already at eighteen he sensed that the easy fear of his friends and acquaintances rode the waves of envy.

Those were different times, Anthony Allday said to himself, pausing briefly at a natural foods store. Now people come to America *como si nada,* as tourists, without fear. Like Genaro, his cousin. Lucky son of a bitch. In 1973 Toño still had the fucking Peruvian fear coiled up in his heart, in his soul. *¡Carajo!* How to leave behind the smell of mother, father, brothers, uncles, friends? How to escape the fear of the police, of the unknown, of the future? How to escape Tacora's smell of darkness, of dampness, of rotting flesh?

Fortunately, our family had just arrived in Lima. Fortunately, the old man was never afraid to make us go on long trips, to take us on adventures born of hard necessity. In a way, we were immigrants in our own country. Still, Anthony Allday remembered, Toño said nothing about his own impending adventure. Neither to Ricardo nor to Carmen. Not even to his mother. In part he did not want anyone trying to dissuade him with talk of real or invented dangers. But also he did not want his mother to try to tie him down with her tears. Toño already knew, but did not wish to have it confirmed, that his mother's tears no longer amounted to very much. And so, before the week was over, Antonio Alday Gutiérrez had sold his small Suzuki motorcycle, his AGA radio, and the '57 Chevy that his father had used to move his family, like a happy gypsy, across the length and breadth of Peru, until he died in Lima, blind, shaking, and sweating, confounding himself and the doctors, in Loayza, the poor man's hospital of last resort.

No one knew how to drive that stupid car, Antonio Allday Gutiérrez mumbles to himself, feeling the soft white light of winter in Lima, Delaware County, Pennsylvania, remembering that first fateful decision he made with premeditation and embraced with a sense of inevitability. The damn thing was just going to rot!

3

It was going to rot just like the old man. Anthony Allday felt an unexpected trace of bitterness in his heart on that cursed evening. It was going to rot like everything else he had left behind, for good, when he ventured out to find his new sitio, his new place in life. But, as a premonition of things to come, Anthony Allday faced the fact that he had not yet left everything behind. In the very instant of justification, urged by something reaching him from the depths of his being, Anthony Allday remembered the face of his father. He remembered him through a thick mist of hatred and longing—feeling the need both to acknowledge and to bury a part of himself.

Anthony Allday lingered on the memory of the old man's wrinkled face and tired eyes as he walked through the throngs of festive people. He pictured the old man distracted, looking deep into himself as if searching for something elusive and mesmerizing. In his last days Don Juan had had the habit of going away like that, for hours. And Anthony Allday felt compelled to connect those tired eyes with his more recent memories. And he remembered the bittersweet moments when, back in the early eighties, at the Elmwood Avenue branch of the Providence Public Library, he had written down his musings, his divinations, about the old man's last days. Yes, Anthony Allday remembered, he had kept the Peruvian notebooks with him, even after saying goodbye to Alex Sosa, his Portuguese friend in New Bedford, Massachusetts, and coming to Philadelphia, leaving everything else behind once again. ¡Carajo! Don Juan Alday Alzamora had been a strange man.

Antonio Alday Gutiérrez walks to the old credenza next to the front door, opens a narrow drawer, and takes out the four Peruvian notebooks. Loose letters and newspaper clippings are tucked between the pages. He brings them to the yellow vinyl couch and begins trying to decipher his nearly forgotten words, recorded in diminutive handwriting. But he is very tired, his eyes are failing him, and his mind wanders off so freely that he finds it difficult to read everything he has written down. With much effort he finds the page where he set down his thoughts about his father and starts to read, haltingly, filling in the gaps from memory and emending the text to conform to his desires.

4

Peruvian Notebook No. 1
August 1, 1983

On an ordinary morning in August of 1973, don Juan Alday Alzamora sat up slowly in his old bed. His bones ached. His limbs needed coaxing to wake up. He set his swollen feet on the cold, damp cement floor, thinking, It really does not matter that, after all I have done for her, she still throws everything in my face. Shapeless old hag, with dried-up breasts, dried-up insides. He scratched his sweaty armpits and cursed the fleas. She had refused to give him more than one child. And to top it all, el cojudo, the fool, had come out a weakling. A cojudo without ambition, without well-hung balls—wasting his time in that stupid theater full of black people, practicing poses in front of the mirror, moving his hands like a maricón.

Sneaky old hag. Despite her daily complaints, despite her tiresome fake scorn, she continued to stick around, rolled up under the damp blankets. She didn't even get up to make him breakfast. Even though it was already seven in the morning and he had to go out there, to see if he could find something, anything, to bring home. Sneaky old hag.

The room was as small as a matchbox. ¡Carajo! Windows sealed with flattened-out cardboard Gloria Milk boxes, walls covered with quivering spiderwebs, corners reeking of flea shit. Don Juan Alday Alzamora scratched his head. It was no use waking her up. She would just grumble and huff. Stubborn as a mule. He would have to find something hot to drink in La Parada, that rotting lair of thieves. But what else could he do? He had to make a living. And so, performing a long-established ritual, don Juan put on his only pair of pants. He tied the waist string with three knots. He pushed his swollen feet into his narrow, brown shoes. He stood up straight and felt his weight. He blessed himself, kissing his thumb with intense feeling. He approached the largest window in the room and pulled away the flattened-out Gloria Milk box. It was drizzling outside. Tacora's winter was especially nasty that year. Don Juan stood by the large window for a moment, peering into the mist, picturing the narrow corridors of La Parada, slippery and treacherous. He sighed. What the hell! There was nothing to be done about it.

On his way to the door he picked up the white enamel washbasin lying in a corner—all chipped, dented, and rusted. ¡Carajo! He then collected the brown soap that the old hag used to wash clothes, the rusting Gillette razor with its week-old blade, and the blue-and-white checkered wash towel/family napkin. He opened the door and stepped out into the callejón, a muddy, narrow, roofless hall-way flanked by the unfinished brick-and-mortar walls of adjacent apartments. He felt Lima's drizzle like the mist from an unseen waterfall. Holding the washbasin against his right side, don Juan looked at the only water spigot, at the end of the corridor, near the main entrance to the labyrinthine compound that was La Estrella.

He was thinking that el cojudo Antonio would not wake up for hours yet. Where had he been last night? With the black whores of the damn theater, for sure; doing sabrá Dios qué, God knows what, after the performance. That boy was heading for disaster. He felt it in his gut, but what could he do about it? He barely had the energy to bring food to the table. Don Juan Alday Alzamora took his place in the growing line in front of the water spigot.

He was in line after don Gustavo Paez, a huge black man who told everyone he was a porter at the El Augustino market nearby. A por-ter! That black man was a thief! It was written in his bloodshot eyes; on the thick, black lines of his enormous black hands. Don Gustavo was born a thief, just as surely as his own wife was born a hag and Antonio born useless. He then realized that doña Esmeralda had taken a place behind him. She was the wife of Sato, the Japanese flower vendor. No one really knew how in God's name he had arrived in Tacora or managed to catch such a woman. Because, truth be told, doña Esmeralda was woman enough for at least four men. The entire situation between them was a mystery.

It was not his fault that Antonio didn't want to go to school any longer. . . . Good morning, doña Esmeralda. . . . What a woman, carajo. . . . He had never discouraged the boy, as the old hag always accused him. On the contrary: here are a few soles; go and buy your-self some books. Besides, el cojudo always got the best grades. That

14

was a mystery, too. He never saw him studying. El cojudo was happy to carry his dog-eared scribbling notebook in his back pocket. No, definitely not. It was not his fault. To find someone to blame, one would have to look among the people at the theater. So many black whores drooling over him. They must like his meekness, his maricón manner, his affected gestures. But thank God for small blessings: Antonio had not turned out to be a real maricón. Had that happened, he might even have blamed himself. After all, Antonio was his only real son, flesh of his flesh.

The boy was not stupid. What does one get from going to school? After all that bother and hard work, one ends up the same anyway: selling trinkets on street corners, washing, ironing, and sewing for the rich pitucos from Miraflores. Trying to make a living, or just passing time kicking stones in Tacora, La Parada, El Augustino, Vitarte. Wherever.

As in my case, thought don Juan Alday Alzamora, hanging his head with resignation. He had a high school diploma. He had worked his tail off for that, against his own father's wishes. He had even thought of attending the university. To study what? It didn't really matter—so long as it was at the university. But then life happened. And now here he was, standing like a fool with his little washbasin and his soap, waiting for the fucking line to move.

Antonio seems filled with resentment. He's hiding something. Yesterday he was on the corner of Elías Aguirre, arm in arm with the black whore Cecilia, the one who until recently was the pet of sambo Chumpitaz, the mugger. I hope he's not getting in over his head. He thinks he's so smart. He doesn't know who he's dealing with. Those people are to be feared. Take this don Gustavo Paez, for example—always throwing money around, always making deals with Quispe, the cop who lives at the foot of the hill, and yet here, in La Estrella compound, he acts like a corderito, a little lamb. And don Juan decided he was tired of telling Antonio to be careful.

There were only three people ahead of him now. Don Juan shuffled his feet the requisite two steps. He was getting colder. He could almost feel his beard getting harder. And he thought the Japanese Sato was taking too much time. Who did he think he was, the hero of a novel?

And to don Gustavo: They should put up another water spigot. What do you think, don Gustavo? They charge us enough!

And don Gustavo: You said it, don Juan. You said it! But then they think we're gonna be so greedy we'll be expecting them to throw out the garbage every week or to put a roof on this shit hole! It ain't gonna happen, don Juan. It'll never happen.

Don Juan lapsed again into reverie. Maybe I should speak with the boy again. Ask him about things, just in case. Not that don Juan worried too much. Life had taught him that worrying too much about other people's lives ended up lightening their loads. In the long run, such acts of kindness could be deadly. They ended up making people either lazy or weak, or both. Not good. People have to learn to make their own way in life. Still, for better or worse, el cojudo was the only flesh of his flesh. Even though he was always siding with his mother. They say sons are like that—always looking out for their mothers.

Two more to go: Perico Huanta—the cholo, the highlander who lived at the end of the callejón—and Gustavo Paez. At least ten more minutes. And don Juan thought that Perico Huanta was a truly rare bird. He had arrived from Junín alone but loaded down with weird things. The largest brass bed in the world, larger than the ones used by the whores of Tacora, with canopy, frills, and everything. A wicker lounge chair he had to leave out in the callejón, summer and winter, because after innumerable tries he had finally admitted to himself that it would not fit through either the door or the largest window of his apartment. Two huge, white talking birds that no one in La Estrella knew what to call. And, weirdest of all, a mechanical music box that could only play two 45 rpm records, which he kept wrapped up in separate red flannel towels. He used to crank up the music box now and again, mostly when he got drunk—when he dared everyone to come and even try to touch his contraption—or when a full moon rose over La Estrella.

Perico Huanta first arrived in Tacora on the hottest day of January in 1966, the hottest day in anyone's memory, the day when grown men, fat women, and small children took turns sleeping, even if only for two minutes, under the open water spigot, a day so hot that no memory other than the feeling of exhaustion should have

16

survived. That day Perico Huanta made a mistake. Perhaps overcome
with an exuberance brought on by the heat, he told everyone with
much glee that his wife of many years would be joining him soon.

Over the following days, as the heat wave subsided and children
were allowed to walk barefoot in the callejón again, the entire
compound community had been full of expectation. Stories were woven around the yet-to-be-heard sound of the music box and the huge
bed that, no doubt due to the earlier heat, had appeared to many to
be made of solid gold. This impression was so widespread that three
days after Perico Huanta's arrival a delegation of residents of La
Estrella, including don Gustavo Paez, had gone up to the newcomer
to offer their services as guards in exchange for a small piece of
the bed. Undeterred by Perico Huanta's refusal, the delegation sat
at his door day and night for almost a week. They withdrew their
sensible offer only after a desperate Perico Huanta took a brick to
one of the legs of the bed frame to prove it really was made of brass.
In the face of such proof don Gustavo Paez—by then the tacit leader
of the delegation—acknowledged with marked disappointment and
even sadness that he had known all along the bed could not have
been made of gold: I say so, he told his followers, mostly because no
one in their right mind would bring gold to Tacora.

Soon, as was bound to happen, some residents of La Estrella began to place bets on the arrival date of Perico Huanta's wife. The
usual entrepreneurs gave two-to-one odds that it would be before
the end of carnival, but don Juan knew better than to take those
odds. He knew that people do not leave their palaces or their hovels when a carnival party is going on. He would sooner place stock
in those who swore that Perico's wife—whose name no one knew for
sure—would turn out to be one of the whores they had known in
their travels up to the central highlands.

As always happened at La Estrella compound, thought don Juan
with a twinge of sadness, after a few days of gossip and curiosity,
people moved on to other things. Only some two years later did everyone in La Estrella realize that Perico Huanta's wife was never
coming. And not long after that Perico Huanta felt the full force
of communal pity. His most distant neighbors greeted him with studied affection. They turned to gawk at him as he passed: poor man,

Perico guessed they were thinking, he must feel so utterly alone. No one looked him in the eyes again, and they all stopped complaining about the music he played when the moon was full. By a twist of fate and circumstances, Perico had become the embodiment of a pitiful existence.

Don Juan thought there was nothing worse than for a man to be pitied on account of a deceitful woman. Since the neighbors could not put a face to the cause of his suffering, in time their pity turned to overly sweet scorn. That was why don Juan had always kept his distance from Perico Huanta. He would see him in the callejón— lying in his lounge chair through drizzle and heat, reading his newspapers, as if waiting for good news—and he would only shake his head: some people just gather up all the world's free-floating bad luck.

What most impressed don Juan about Perico Huanta was that he never seemed bothered by the hellish noise of rabid dogs, drunkards, and sick babies that filled the enclosed compound with a constant buzz of despair. He is a true cholo, a damn highlander, don Juan said to himself, fixing his eyes on the flattened hair at the back of Perico Huanta's head. He has inherited the stoicism of his Indian ancestors. He is not normal, carajo. At least I'm not like him. Not at all.

Don Juan couldn't even read a comic book in the callejón. To do that, he had to go all the way to Latorre's kiosk, near the police station. He had to sit on those little chairs Latorre rented, like a newborn babe from the Andes. ¡Carajo! Never mind reading the newspaper! Damn it all! Even if he went out early to the kiosk, he had to content himself with reading La Última Hora, that filthy rag. La Crónica, El Comercio, El Expreso, they didn't arrive until about nine o'clock. By then, if he was lucky, he would already have found some work. By then there would be too many snot-sucking bastards fighting him for a seat anyway.

El cojudo Antonio is always reading, thought don Juan. And not only the best newspapers, like El Comercio. He reads novelas ejemplares, lives of the saints, and real novels, too, and comic books and books about the history of the world and about the Bronze Age and the Iron Age. He reads everything those people at the theater put in his effeminate hands. Because, don Juan had to admit, intelligent black people must exist. Before their performances they dance the paso doble and the tango; at intermission they sing and recite poetry. They even claim don Luna, the director, has been to the university, that he is known by the pitucos in Miraflores and Barranco. He must be doing something good there. . . . And don Juan Alday Alzamora remembered with unexpected pride the only time he had gone to the theater to see his son, the actor.

He went there anonymously, just in case. Because one never knows about those black people. And there Antonio was, dressed in a charro outfit, reciting God only knew what verses, walking on the stage along a low wall illuminated by a dying streetlight. He seemed happy—even though he was supposed to be suffering from the pain of misunderstanding and a lover's rejection. Antonio was so different. He walked on the stage with long steps, his head held high, his eyes full of light. I'll be damned! don Juan had murmured to himself: in this world Antonio is a winner.

Maybe because of what he had seen on the stage that night, don Juan never again tried to stop his only son from going to the theater. Not in earnest, anyway. Besides, don Juan thought now, shifting his weight in the line, feeling the washbasin hard against his ribs, how could I have prevented him? Nah. To hell with it! He has to learn to make his own way in life. At least he has someone to warm his cold nights and, at his age, what more does a person need? He has to become a man.

I'll be damned! This man is fucking solid! Don Juan stepped back, suddenly noticing don Gustavo Paez's torso up close. Black people are strong. Strong enough to be bodyguards. How could one stop them if they were to come up with a knife? And, averting his eyes with suppressed embarrassment, don Juan remembered that, like all black people, don Gustavo Paez knew how to fight. He remembered how he had once toyed with Adrian Coishco, the sweet potato vendor who had confronted him with his machete. Don Gustavo had let him live only because sweet Alicia, Coishco's youngest daughter, had begged him to. . . . ¡Concha su madre! Fuck! Luckily they're all Antonio's friends. They greet me, don Juan thought, noticing again the hard edge of the washbasin against his body. They even seem to respect me. Having a son like Antonio is worth something, I guess. . . .

If only I had at least two children, don Juan Alday Alzamora lamented. But the old hag had not wanted more, since she already had two others. I'm tired of getting up at night and washing diapers, she had said when, for the only time in his life, he had begged her to give him another. He had never felt so humiliated. So resentful, too. Such open rebellion gave him the excuse to beat the living daylights out of her. To hell with all of your excuses, damn hag! Pum! Pow! . . . But he knew better now and controlled his temper. Was it because he pitied her for being an old hag, as everyone pitied Perico Huanta for being alone? Was it because he was afraid of something she might do, like put a curse on him? It was pity, carajo! Sheer pity.

Besides, he was also tired of worrying. Antonio had turned out malucho, a weakling, and there were no guarantees another child wouldn't be worse. Where would he get the money for the milk, for the doctors, for the medicine? No. ¡Carajo! Now looking at the situation with calm, the old hag had been right. . . . It wasn't because he was afraid of her or of any curse. He had given her a few slaps now and then, just to keep her in line. He wasn't afraid. . . . But yes, as he waited for Gustavo Paez to finish brushing the white teeth in his black mouth, don Juan accepted that it still bothered him not to have had another child. Antonio no longer paid attention to him. He had lost him to the black whores of the theater.

And don Gustavo Paez: It's all yours, don Juan. Water is damn good today.

And don Juan: Thanks, don Gustavo. As I said, they should put in another spigot. And, good luck with your work. . . .

The water was damn cold. Brrr! . . . And him with a full beard. Why wasn't he like Perico Huanta? That man had hair only here and there. He could be finished washing in the blink of an eye. None of this torture. . . . Have to change the blade one of these days. . . . In any case, don Juan thought, hurrying to finish, it was time to go out there and make a living. Today, he would go all the way to Vitarte. The old Chevy could still make it, even though it sometimes didn't like the climb up to the Andes. What else could he do? Now there were pickup trucks that could cart things over longer and longer distances for less and less money. People were desperate. Too much competition. . . . Still, he was cheap and quick. Besides, he had a steady clientele among the newly arrived vendors from Tarma, Huancayo, Junín. Those cholos were always willing to make a deal with a paisano. Don Juan dried his face with the towel that was also a napkin, taking in the distinct aroma of onions.

5

That smell has not gone away, Anthony Allday said to himself feeling enveloped by the din of the people and the lights of the mall, remembering. It is the smell of damp desert, wet dog, dirty sheets, morning breath. A Peruvian smell, carajo. It was only 10:40 P.M. and Anthony Allday was already tired of the happy sounds of Christmas. He felt the air of offensive superficiality during those days. He much preferred Mother's Day or Valentine's Day. The mall was filled with people then, too, but the mood was different. It did not get under his skin. And Anthony Allday went on to think that, despite his many attempts to enjoy the holidays, he still found the Christmas season depressing. Over the years he had tried inoculating himself against the seasonal letdowns. He had ridiculed the holiday's spiritual value. He had railed against its materiality. But nothing ever worked. Americans, he would complain to Hannah, were truly naïve when it came to having a good time. You want happiness? Let us have some carnival!

Yes, thinks Antonio Alday Gutiérrez at 12:10 P.M., the soft white light of the winter sun caressing his trembling hands, perhaps Anthony Allday was caught in the invisible web of jealousy that night. But even as enveloped as he was by the cloying sounds of Christmas, how could he possibly have imagined that, only a few hours later, he would be sitting on this yellow vinyl couch in this ugly apartment, in Lima, Delaware County, Pennsylvania, trying to remember his past, so filled with fading colors, lingering smells, and murky deeds—trying to shed some light on the dark recesses of his thoughts and feelings? How could he possibly have imagined what was coming? He had no reason to see the world differently then. Anthony Allday could not have prevented anything.

Sometimes the future is not only the result of the capricious designs of El Azar—that playful, unforgiving, and unpredictable demonic force which don Juan Alday Alzamora believed lords over the world and which one might possibly influence, though only under certain conditions and with adequate propitiation. Sometimes the future is already written and visible in the most casual act or the smallest thought, but we are usually too busy dealing with life to notice.

Of course, thinks Antonio Alday Gutiérrez, disheartened, the future and its possibilities were always in Anthony Allday's mind. That man never had time for anything else. And now, no matter how closely Antonio Alday Gutiérrez tries to remember his actions and thoughts on that cursed evening, he cannot discern a hint of the coming disaster in his consciousness.

Anthony Allday continued on his first round caught in the din of happy people and the airy-fairy lights of the mall, remembering, turning over the dislocating nature of his new situation: His cousin Genaro would arrive the next day at ten o'clock in the morning. The lucky bastard was coming to America with everything prepared and smoothed out for him. He would arrive with the wind on his face, with light steps, smiling, like a tourist. Not like he himself had done, wading and hiding, his stomach in knots, hardening his shell.

Some people are born with all the luck in the world, Antonio Alday Gutiérrez remembers Anthony Allday thinking that cursed evening. Some are just too damn lucky. And yet he cannot say that Anthony Allday was blindly jealous or envious of Genaro. He was filled with something stranger and more complicated. Within him anger and hope were braided into a seamless white coil that was choking him. Anger because el cojudo Genaro was tumbling out of the shadowy past to ruin his life and bring down the world he had managed to create for himself with so much effort and pain. Hope because if Genaro could understand the difference between the two worlds—night and day, death and life—he might decide, of his own accord, to stay with his cousin in Lima, Delaware County, Pennsylvania. Maybe then Anthony Allday would at last have someone with whom to talk and to share. Because deep down Antonio Alday Gutiérrez knew that Anthony Allday still wanted to have someone who might reconnect him, if only as a tangent touches a circle, with a past made ever more unrecognizable by the recurrent cropping up of faulty memory and eager fiction.

It is not envy, Anthony Allday murmured to himself, passing by Macy's perfume section, glancing at the solicitous attendants looking for homely and lonely women willing to submit their faces to their expensive and ineffective products. These women do not even see me, thought Anthony Allday without bitterness. They come only to show their stuff; mostly in winter, when gringo faces wither in the wind. They come for Christmas, when everyone is expected to put on a happy face. They follow the seasons. Always smiling. Even when no one is watching. They are like the Mexicans so used to crossing the frontier running that they no longer care about the road they travel or the partner beside them. *¡Puta madre!*

And Anthony Allday remembered what Coyote Padilla had yelled at the twenty men and women squatting around him in a mud hut with a tin roof: You have to cross when I tell you to, *chingones!* Mother fuckers! It doesn't matter where or with whom. Understand? If any one of you chingones doesn't want to take the risk, let me know now, 'cause once we begin, there's no turning back! . . . Some were drawing their worries in the dirt. Others were looking up at the roof, trying to figure out how those rusty round holes had formed. Antonio Alday Gutiérrez kept his eyes on the coyote. The man licked his thin black mustache with the tip of his red tongue. He had his thumbs hooked over a black leather belt with silver studs. He swayed back and forth, planted in a pair of tall cowboy boots stitched with wavy blue lines. In the silence of that eternal moment, he looked at Antonio Alday Gutiérrez with dark eyes and winked. Antonio Alday Gutiérrez looked back to let Coyote Padilla know he had no intention of turning around.

Anthony Allday remembered that journey across the frontier—an odyssey only he adequately valued and remembered in all its weight and importance. Whom could he have told of the marrow-sucking feeling of impending doom that accompanied him on that journey? With whom could he have shared the sense of warmth he drew from his dreams, forged and reforged on that journey, through the hunger and the cold? And now perhaps he could not share those things even with Genaro. He comes as a tourist. He has been spared the knowledge of such ordeals. But Anthony Allday was proud of his *gesta,* carajo. In the twenty-two years after meeting Coyote Padilla, he had come to value his odyssey correctly. He had come to see it as a rebirth. That is the truth, Anthony Allday said to himself: I was born at the very moment when Antonio Alday Gutiérrez blessed himself and jumped into the waters of the Río Bravo, leaving behind fears, regrets, smells, memories.

24

And yet, Antonio Alday Gutiérrez thinks at 12:16 P.M., watching the oblique rays of the winter sun trying to warm his trembling and guilty hands, he cannot forget how convoluted the labyrinths of his past really are. Did Anthony Allday remember it all correctly? Did Antonio Alday Gutiérrez not wish for a rebirth well before he met Coyote Padilla, even before he climbed the metal stairs to board the Braniff International Airways flight to Mexico City, in December 1973? Hadn't Antonio wanted to be reborn in Tacora itself? Of course. Antonio Alday Gutiérrez recognizes those old feelings even now. He had wanted to become someone else even back then. Was it out of hatred for his life? Was it the sheer desire for adventure? Or was it because, in the depths of his being, he felt as strange and unknown then as he felt on that cursed night as he made his first round at the Springfield Mall? Antonio Alday Gutiérrez has to admit that he has always felt like someone whom no one really knew, like someone who does not even know himself. No. It was not envy at all. Or hatred. That night Anthony Allday only hoped Genaro would understand him, knowing that he never could.

Oblivious to the Christmas spirit around him, Anthony Allday clenched his teeth and accepted that from the very beginning he had decided to kill himself, to remake himself, to reconstruct himself, alone. That was the reason it had never bothered him to know that he was forlorn, cast away, forgotten, and forgetting those whom he had left behind. Puta madre, motherfucker. In that initial flight from his old sitio, leaning against the window with his arms crossed over his chest, listening to the muffled sound of the plane, Antonio Alday Gutiérrez had steeled himself, carajo, to face the fact that he was burning all the bridges leading back to the putrid world of Tacora.

There was no doubt about it, Antonio Alday Gutiérrez accepts: even in Tacora, in a moment of absolute honesty, looking in the cracked mirror beside don Juan Alday Alzamora's bed, he had sworn in the name of his old man's soul that he would become a different man; that if he did not make it to the USA, he would at least stay in Mexico, carajo, if for nothing else than to live somewhere else, as a stranger. That was why, to Antonio Alday Gutiérrez, the crossing of the Río Bravo was not only desired and premeditated. It was also final. In that crossing he learned

25

that, to fulfill his desires, he had to embrace them irrevocably. All his decisions in his new sitio had been made the same way.

At least until today, Antonio Alday Gutiérrez corrects himself, wringing his still cold and trembling, guilty hands. Did he kill with premeditation? Were the braided anger and hope reason enough for that? Antonio Alday Gutiérrez offers his face to the winter sun. He sighs deeply. The sinful act does seem irreparable.

6

Peruvian Notebook No. 1
August 1, 1983

On another routine day, in the summer of 1972, don Juan Alday Alzamora woke up with a marked lack of interest in the world. He did not feel like getting out of bed. He decided to remain under the covers a little longer, with his eyes closed, guessing at the goings-on of the world around him. The sky was probably ashen gray. La Parada market would be filled with the sounds of shoppers, victims, police. The factory whistles in Vitarte would take turns calling the shift changes. Traffic would already be snarled for miles around. Closer to home, he heard the usual sounds of the people within La Estrella. He pictured the line in front of the water spigot—already long, twisting, made up mostly of young children and old women by now. The old hag is probably standing there, he thought. Gossiping. Complaining. Always complaining. And with that thought, he decided not to give her any more reasons to nag him. He opened his eyes.

To his surprise, he found the small and dank room pitch black, even though surely it must have been at least eight in the morning. Not a hint of light was coming through the window. This was unusual. He had always had so much trouble fending off even the slanting rays of Lima's weak winter sun. Antonio's idea of using flattened-out cardboard Gloria Milk boxes with little cutout windows to regulate the amount of light coming into the room had been a stroke of genius. The boy was strange, carajo! . . .

Don Juan shook off his puzzlement, swinging his aching body to the edge of the bed. He lowered both feet onto the cement floor. It was cool, familiar. He remained there, thinking: Why weren't things going his way lately? Why did he no longer feel like a real player, even in his own life? Why was it that for quite a while now the world around him seemed to have lost its sharp edges, its aggressive smells and happy colors, and felt instead like wet cotton, heavy and dense? Such sensations came upon him even in the plain light of summer, when it was so hot and wild in Tacora that even the shadows went around looking for some shade. Very strange, indeed. ¡Carajo! Don Juan Alday Alzamora appeased himself by noticing he could still feel the uneven planks and the metal strips of his bed frame under him. That at least was something.

The fact of the matter was that the old man was not yet ready to admit that something was terribly wrong with him. Feeling the uneven planks under him that morning, bewildered by the changes in his world, he nevertheless refused to take a closer look at himself. For months already, whenever he had felt dizzy and disoriented, he claimed indigestion. Don Juan was a very stubborn man. He was a man determined to cling to the routine of living in Tacora. He was a macho man, carajo. The world wouldn't get away from him just like that!

But that summer day in 1972, when he tried to get out of bed, the room spun like a silent and colorless top. He lost his balance and fell back. ¡Carajo! The bed's uneven planks and the sharp metal strips that held them together went soft, liquid. It was then that don Juan Alday Alzamora finally realized that not only the hard edges but the very substance of the world around him was escaping his grasp. He also noticed at last the wild thumping of his heart and the odd sensation in his mouth: his tongue limp, dry, numb, as if it had been dabbed in smooth white chalk. He panicked. He could not breathe. He thought he was losing his mind.

It was on that ordinary morning, in the summer of 1972, that for the first time don Juan Alday Alzamora was shot through by an undeniable, fear-laden insight: what had been assaulting, disorienting, crushing him of late had nothing to do with the world turning white and cottony but with its very opposite. The world had in fact been growing darker and darker. ¡Carajo! Don Juan opened his eyes wide. He rubbed them with both hands. He shook his head a thousand times, as if to deny what he already knew. He slapped himself more than once in desperation. Nothing. Don Juan Alday Alzamora had gone totally blind.

That was the reason they took the old man to the Hospital Loayza the first time, Antonio Alday Gutiérrez makes out from his diminutive handwriting set in three tight rows between the blurry red lines of his

Peruvian Notebook No. 1, at 12:14 p.m. on the day of the sinful deed. The old man was accompanied to the institution of last resort by the smell of Antonio's oily hairspray and the doleful pain of his wife: a hum of pain, without edges, rounded by her familiar whimpering against *el destino,* against fate. And when he found himself on the hospital bed, pressed between fresh sheets, enveloped in what appeared to be the smell of clean, surrounded by walls with black echoes, don Juan Alday Alzamora made an effort to understand how the blindness, the dizziness, had overtaken him. Because, Antonio Alday Gutiérrez murmurs to himself, the old man had always believed that the only chance of escaping an oppressive present was to understand the steps leading up to it.

Don Juan Alday Alzamora had to admit that this was not the first time he had lost the sense of having a sitio, a proper place in the world. He had tucked away the growing signs simply because he feared even the possibility of going blind. He had been able to cover up his fear and its effects because—word of a macho—don Juan Alday Alzamora had never been afraid of death. ¡Qué carajo! When La Pelona, the Bald One, Death, came—he had been telling everyone who counted, for as long as he could remember—he would receive her properly: with his tie, jacket, and hat on; remembering the many women he had known and loved, the many friends he was leaving behind, the innumerable victories he had accumulated in his forty, fifty, or sixty years of life; thanking his enemies for an interesting life. Because ¡qué carajo! he did not believe in all those stories of the hereafter told by the tristes sotanudos, the sorrowful priests. When don Juan went, he would go de un tirón, once and for all, without protestation or lamentation, without hidden hopes for anything better. ¡A la mierda! . . . But ¡carajo! he was not prepared for what was happening to him now. It had never occurred to him that he might go blind first. To die unable to see the world he was leaving behind would be like being taken away by the Bald One, kicking and screaming, while still alive and aware.

Don Juan Alday Alzamora stepped away from his bed feeling the hair on the back of his neck stand up, as if he were escaping a ghost's embrace. He walked around the small, dank room with both hands extended, reaching for the window he desperately wanted to believe was still covered by the flattened-out Gloria Milk box. He felt the rough walls. He recognized the family clothes hanging on rusty nails. He felt the small broken mirror by the window. And he felt a puff of warm air on his face. Not wanting to believe the hunch in his gut, he reached out. He found the window wide open. . . . The realization overwhelmed him. He yelled like a newborn baby: Gloria! Gloria! ¡Carajo! His world seemed to be ending and the old hag was not even around. Gloria! . . .

An eternity passed until someone took the old man by the hand and led him back to his bed. Until someone rubbed his head telling him con cariño, tenderly, to calm down, that everything was really all right. . . . Of course, it was Toño. Who else? Don Juan recognized the scent of Glostora oil in his hair, the smell of Salem cigarettes on his Alianza Lima sweatshirt, the scent of the black men's sweat on his body. The old man detested Toño because of that. Even when Toño managed to take him to the hospital. Even then. . . .

At Hospital Loayza he was measured, weighed, and poked by stealthy doctors and nurses. Some came and went after only a few seconds. Others came to move things around and touch his face with plastic hands. But they seemed not to breathe and never said a word. For all don Juan knew they could have been ghosts. ¡Carajo! When at last they talked, they did so as if he were no longer there: A case for future generations to figure out, doctor. Indeed. Very strange. Indeed. Very peculiar. Indeed.

Antonio Allday wrote down in 1983 that the old man had reached out to the world with his feelings. Toño? Toño? Are you here, Hijo?

And Toño: Yes. I'm here, Papá. I'm here. And Antonio Allday wrote that all at once, at the Hospital Loayza, don Juan Alday Alzamora had been forced to learn to control himself and curse and swear only under his breath, because he was afraid of upsetting the people around him, since he could not know who was there. The old man also had to learn to cry and beg in silence. Don Juan never asked for anything, lest he would have to pay for it if and when he got better. And Antonio Allday wrote down that an overweight nurse had asked the old man, Who brought you here?

I don't know, sister.

And the stealthy doctor: Do you have family here?

I don't know, *doctorcito,* dearest doctor.

Where do you live?

I don't remember, sir. I swear. And all the while Toño was walking, *va y viene,* back and forth, in the main hall of a hospital teeming with sick people, his hands in his pockets, his moist eyes lost on the floor's shiny checkerboard of yellow tiles, not knowing what to do or what to hope for.

They kept the old man between fresh sheets for several days. A torment, Toño, he would tell his only natural son days later, after he had overcome the muteness brought on by his immense embarrassment. I had to learn to eat, sleep, defecate, do everything in spurts, Toño. He had to learn to detect the slightest shift in the air around him. What else could he do? Everyone knew that in the Hospital Loayza people often lost their good organs. They would fall asleep and pow! a cornea for a pituco from Miraflores or a kidney for a gringa from Chicago. Everyone knows it is the worst fate to arrive here alive, Toño.

And Toño: I'm sorry, Papá. I didn't know. I'm sorry.

On the fourth day of his ordeal, like a miracle, the old man regained his sight. He could then see what up to then he had only intuited.

The sheets really are white and the nurses really are fat, Toño! Dolores, the oldest nurse, looks almost unreal. It is as if she just stepped out of a Humphrey Bogart movie, Toño! She has this little hat perched on her large head and she walks bouncing from side to side. ¡Caramba! . . .

The old hag went to see her husband on his last day at the Hospital Loayza in the summer of 1972. The old man found that she had lost neither her nagging, high-pitched voice nor her annoying breathing that resembled a cat's purr. Here are your blue pants, your pajamas, your razor, Juan. Ohh! Thank God Toño ran up to the theater to find help, Juan. And thank God that, don't ask me how or why, we don't have to pay for anything. Can you imagine that? Better hurry out of this place, before they discover the mistake, Juan.

And the old man: I survived the ordeal, Gloria. They weren't gonna fool me. I kept my wits. And Toño, at the foot of the bed, a bored fool, looking for God knew what along the white walls. Until don Juan Alday Alzamora said it was time to go, he had suffered long enough.

7

Antonio had jumped into the gray abyss that was his future with fists tight and eyes shut. None of the invented obstacles and chilling stories of his friends from Tacora made a dent on his hardening shell. Not even when they, squinting and gasping in concern, would whisper, You'll never even make it across the river, Toño. La Migra is controlled by bastards. They say they're plugging all the holes along the frontier. They rake the riverbed at night with helicopters. They have dogs specially trained to sniff out Peruvians. They have a sonar that works like bats' ears that they use to find illegals even if they hide under the brown water of the Río Bravo. They use an infrared light that cuts through cement walls. That's the truth, Toño. And if they catch you, they implant a tiny tag in the back of your neck, to keep track of you and make you docile. All you can do after that is watch them put you in a covered truck bound for a prison in Texas, where you'll spend the rest of your life weaving baskets for the gringas of Chicago. Some say that in a few of those prisons, in places called Houston, Dallas, or Galveston, they take out your marrow to make perfume for bald men. You'll spend the rest of your life smiling like an idiot because you have no *tuétano,* no marrow. They think they're at war, Toño. *Por Dios.*

And Toño: It must be tough. ¡Carajo! It must be horrible. . . .

But in his heart, Toño was not a bit scared. He let the stories roll over his shell. Maybe, Anthony Allday thought, continuing his first round at the Springfield Mall that cursed evening, maybe it was because since the day his father died, but especially since he had talked to La Loca Pedro Lorca, Toño had begun to change, to become someone else. Maybe, while still in Tacora, he had been beginning to leave behind, to tear out from his insides, that snakelike fear that had coiled up in his soul over eighteen years of routine life in Tacora: watch out for the cops, Toño; they can send you away for no reason at all. Watch out for the pitucos, Toño; they can fuck you over and over and over. Watch out for the judges, the pimps, the soldiers, the whores, the blacks, the cholos, the men in all the corners of all the bars. . . .

Maybe that was why, when he jumped into the Río Bravo one night with his little bundle on his neck, Toño was no longer afraid. On the contrary: he felt the cold waters as a kind of baptism. ¡Carajo!

And Coyote Padilla: Crouch low everyone! Push that fucking chest into the water! Lower! Lower! And Toño looked through the murky waters to the other shore. There was his future, carajo. And he made it. He survived. He made it across. By the time he climbed out of the brown waters of the Rio Grande, he was in possession of a promise to himself: he would become another man. No fear. No pity. No looking back. ¡A la mierda! And he had made it all the way to Lima, Delaware County, Pennsylvania. He had become Mr. Anthony Allday.

For an instant, Antonio Alday Gutiérrez feels pride swirling in his heart. But he does not let the feeling linger. What is the nature of such pride? Is it based on having survived hunger and disdain long enough to become a night watchman at the Springfield Mall? Is that feat sufficient to indulge in such feelings? . . . Remembering his first round caught in the festive lights of Christmas that cursed evening, remembering how he tried to prepare for what he must have somehow sensed was coming, at 12:20 after the deed, Antonio Alday Gutiérrez finds the strength to excuse himself: he did the best he could, considering all the obstacles life threw in his path.

It was not easy. He had had to overcome his fear of the power of the gringos reflected in La Migra, police officers, mail carriers, clean rooms, traffic lights, exact change. And that was the least of it. Most of all he had to overcome the sporadic kindness of gringas and bosses. He had to, if he was to create himself freely. When power and kindness come together, they form the strongest bond against the possibility of freedom. The combination is worse than all the fear in the world. And so, to make his own way on this side of the Rio Grande, Antonio Alday Gutiérrez had to deny before all others, and most of all before himself, what everyone in his new sitio saw. He had to become otro, other, in order truly to be himself. He had to imagine and proclaim himself beyond the lawnmowers he pushed on the riverbanks of San Antonio, beyond the polishing machines he used in the skyscrapers of Houston, beyond the paintbrushes he shared with Alex Sosa in New Bedford: I am not a peon. I am not a painter. ¡Puta madre!

Feeling the faint but steady throb in his left big toe, Anthony Allday confessed to himself that he had been able to overcome the oppressive

34

crust formed by kindness and power only when he had managed to see himself as he wished others to see him. He had to believe in his new being. He had had to jump deliberately into that cold river of re-creation, embracing its finality. Only then did he find the key to his success in America.

Anthony Allday paused on his walk to appreciate his insight. And he remembered clearly that a few years after his baptism in the Rio Grande, shortly after meeting Alex Sosa, the happy realization that would show him the key to his success in America crossed his mind: for gringos, sincerity is truth. Honesty is the privileged password into their lives. Here, the word of an honest man is taken as truth. And an honest mistake is always forgiven. So, if he wanted to become otro, he had to do so with sincerity. And he remembered sharing his discovery with Alex Sosa: Isn't it so, Alex? All you need is to believe it with all your heart, right? Isn't that what they say? Even if it isn't true, right? As long as you believe it, right?

But Alex Sosa showed that he was already too much of an American: You cannot be honest if you lie, Antonio.

In the beginning, Antonio Alday Gutiérrez, the illegal Peruvian, did not know what to do with the key. He kept it to himself. He turned it over and over in his head. Months passed. Still pausing, Anthony Allday remembered with a vague and unexpected sadness that it was then that he was confronted with the first fork in the road of his new life. It was then, in New Bedford, that he had the first, the decisive, opportunity to choose his reconstruction.

8

Peruvian Notebook No. 1
August 1, 1983

The second time they took don Juan to Hospital Loayza was less embarrassing. He didn't cry out like a lost child, carajo. By the time they came to take him away, he did not even try to shake his head or rub his eyes. He was resigned to more poking and more needling at the hands of strangers. And as he had wished and expected, he eventually recovered his eyesight again. Only this time it took a little longer, and the doctors were even more puzzled. They gathered in small circles at the foot of his bed and tossed strange words about. Don Juan did not understand any of it. The doctors and the nurses contradicted each other, carajo, while he, like a newly unearthed mummy, moved his cowardly eyes all around, seeking in the dark for the smallest sign of light that could bring him hope.

In the end, after days of contradictions, they all left his side, shaking their heads. Even Dolores, the fat nurse with soft hands, seemed resigned never to know more than she already knew. Don Juan could always feel her looking at him with amazement and pity in her eyes: You're a rare bird, don Juan. Don't know what to make of you. You'll be the death of me yet.

And the old man: There's really nothing wrong with me, señorita; it's only indigestion.

Over the two weeks it took him to fully recover his eyesight, wrapped up in the public solitude of La Estrella, don Juan came to the conclusion that Nurse Dolores had been quite right to look at him with amazement and pity. There indeed seemed to be something very odd about his condition, and about his bad luck. How did it happen that all of a sudden the world around him was losing its substance? Why did people avoid his Chevy and hire older, less reliable trucks? Why was it that every day for the last two years an enormous buzzard had come to keep an eye on La Estrella, perched on the high, unfinished wall at the end of the callejón, facing his room? Yes, amazement and pity were right.

36

When don Juan tired of torturing himself with a thousand unanswerable questions, a simple and single answer appeared: his condition had no possible remedy because the brujería, the witchcraft, was very good and very old. It was useless to try to escape the webs of his fate with regular medicine. Whoever wanted him blind and dead, to pay for God only knew what ill he had caused, had been willing to pay for the worst curse from the arsenal of the best sorcerer. And the first thing a good sorcerer does, to make the curse irreversible, is to bind the wings of El Azar. A good sorcerer knows that the only power against fate is the whim of El Azar—that unpredictable jester in God's court.

Yes, don Juan accepted, the sickness was not in his body but in his soul. And he smiled bitterly, thinking that with all their pituco air of superiority, most of the time the doctors knew shit. Like all pitucos, they were good at convincing themselves of their powers. But all their talking and poking were impotent gestures. They failed left and right. They failed even in the face of the human will to live or to die by choice.

Take the case of Guillermo Quintana, for example: they stuffed him with all kinds of syrups and pills, they clamped his penis with plastic hoses, they poked at his ass with needles of all shapes and sizes . . . and the poor man died in a hurry. Sí, señor. Guillermo Quintana died because he no longer wanted to live! What had kept him alive after the death of María, his wife of forty-five years, was the care he received from his only daughter, Consuelo. And so, when Consuelo was raped and made pregnant by Aurelio Espinoza and Guillermo felt he could do nothing even to force him to recognize the child—being too old, too weak, too afraid—while Aurelio went on celebrating his feat in all the bars of Tacora and poor Consuelo went back to the highlands of Jauja to bury her shame, Guillermo Quintana let go of life. He died of irrelevance.

When don Juan had gone to Guillermo's dark and dank room to console him, to tell him that there were greater powers in the world and that someday Aurelio would pay for what he had done, he looked into the old man's eyes and saw he was no longer there. . . . Pituco know-nothings! They couldn't even help Guillermo. What made them think they could help him now and stop what was killing him? Their weapons were useless against la brujería.

The old man now wondered who might have served up the goods against him. Could it have been the chola Justa, whom he had convinced to make love with him, just for laughs, almost a year ago, right after the butcher Moro's birthday party? Not possible. She was too timid to look for a good sorcerer, to make him pay for reneging on his promises. Besides, she had enjoyed herself too much that night. Flora, who sells used bicycles? Maybe. She was from Chincha, and they say those mulattas do know something about the darkest brujerías. But maybe it was some jealous taxi driver from La Victoria. . . . Who knew? Besides, none of that mattered now. After two weeks of reflection, the only good thing don Juan Alday Alzamora could see in the whole affair was that the pitucos at the Hospital Loayza had thrown in the towel. What a victory. . . . And so, in the public solitude of La Estrella compound, receiving the pity of young and old, the old man became convinced that his days were numbered.

9

At 12:25, after the sinful deed, Antonio Alday Gutiérrez wonders: Could he have become like Alex Sosa and have believed all sincere stories? Absolutely. He could have become whatever he wanted to then. He knows that now, after what he did to become Mr. Anthony Allday. And had he chosen Alex Sosa's path, what kind of life would he now have? Would he have become a murderer anyway? Or would El Azar have let him be and whisked away that possibility? . . . He will never know now, of course. . . . Feeling the soft light of the winter sun on his tired body, Antonio Alday Gutiérrez accepts without regret that the life of a gringo might be boring sometimes, but it does give a good footing to achieve comfort and security. To believe that sincerity is equivalent to truth is to weave a cocoon of goodwill. The recurrent refutations against such dreamy constructions are seen as mere lapses of character.

Antonio Alday Gutiérrez, the illegal Peruvian, did not wish to end up with furrows in his brow and his soul, carajo. He was determined to heed his father's warnings. He therefore took the other path. He chose to live among the gringos without letting go of his *viveza,* that sly briskness so useful in Tacora, the armpit of the world. He refined his pugilistic stance against the world by remembering the cold nights and the cold shoulders he found in his new sitio, until that stance became his life jacket and his hard shell.

It was then, Anthony Allday remembered now clearly, still feeling a vague and unexpected sadness, it was then that he had decided to use his natural gifts and become a full-time, consummate actor. It was then, Anthony Allday recalled, running the fingertips of his right hand over the black plastic brim of his cap, that he decided to imitate Clark Gable and Robert Wagner.

With his eyes closed, feeling the hard vinyl of his yellow couch with still-trembling fingers, at 12:26 P.M., Antonio Alday Gutiérrez remembers himself remembering that, in those long-ago days and nights of *batidas,* roundups, by La Migra, in those almost forgotten sleepless hours and anxious moments, somewhere in New Bedford, Massachusetts, he de-

39

cided to perfect his American accent: Of course, Mr. Brown. It is indeed warm today, Mrs. Pierce. Do come in, Mr. Pinehurst. . . . And he spent hours practicing a slow and deliberate manner of walking, like Clark Gable, so as never and nowhere to give the impression that he did not belong. He cultivated the sophisticated mannerisms of Robert Wagner: How interesting, Miss. . . . In those hours Antonio Alday Gutiérrez, the illegal Peruvian, readied his ticket into the world of *gringos bobos* and the naïvely cruel.

In hours spent before the mirror, he imagined being dressed in a black tuxedo, cashmere scarf dangling from his neck, offering Chesterfields out of the thinnest golden case. He imagined himself conversing in elegant halls, in multicolored gardens, near pristine water fountains. He imagined himself exchanging glances with well-coifed women in summer evening gowns. They flowed in and out of his imagination like silky veils in a gentle breeze. He imagined himself in complete possession of the slightly crooked smile of Robert Wagner and the utter confidence of Clark Gable in *Gone with the Wind*. And it was all worth it! Otherwise he would not have stood a chance of becoming even a night watchman at the Springfield Mall. After all, he had entered America by wading the Rio Grande.

Antonio Alday Gutiérrez drops his face into his hands. Why did Genaro come to ruin everything? What he accomplished over the last twenty-two years might not be very much, all built on fear as it was, who knows. But, for God's sake! It was his life, made by his own choices.

10

Peruvian Notebook No. 1
August 1, 1983

The third time he woke up blind and dizzy, don Juan Alday Alzamora knew it would be his last. Father, Son, and Holy Spirit. Amen.

The faint tremor in his hands had started the day before. He had spent all that night with the premonition that his eternal darkness was coming, carajo. That was why he had called Toño to his side as soon as el cojudo had come back from the theater, near dawn. Come, Son, he called to him. Sit over here, by my side. Toño understood. He sat down on the edge of the old man's bed, facing the large red rose printed on the flattened Gloria Milk box that barely held back the coming daylight leaking into the room around the edges of the cardboard, wringing his hands, making an effort to hold his slender body upright, feeling his Elvis Presley moño, his pompadour, heavy against his forehead. Go far away from here, Toño, the old man said. Find another way to live. This callejón is really a graveyard. . . . Listen, Son—he touched Toño's right hand—listen: Don't get used to the routine of this life, like everyone else here. Don't get used to any routine in life. Routine is the enemy. Remember that. It makes the deepest furrows in your brow, in your soul. Go away. Escape. Tacora will dry out your insides. Do you understand, Son? Go, Toño. I don't want to come back from the hospital and find you still here. Know what I mean? Go away. Don't let El Azar catch and trap you here. . . .

More than twenty years later, Antonio Alday Gutiérrez reads from his Peruvian Notebook No. 1 and remembers that Toño did not answer the dying man. He did not even turn to look at his father. He kept his light brown eyes fixed on the large red rose aglow in the ever-stronger rays of daylight.

And at 12:26, after the murder, he tells himself it was the only way he could have listened to his old man's confession. For that was what it was: a confession. The old man had wanted to confess his failure to

41

escape the entangled, dragging hooks that was life in Tacora. He had never intended to die there, in La Estrella, blind and pitiful. He had traveled and seen too much for that. But now all he could do was confess his failure as a warning. A warning. . . .

And then, for an infinitesimal instant, in Lima, Delaware County, Pennsylvania, feeling the soft light of the winter sun on his face, Antonio Alday Gutiérrez wishes he too had a child, a son. . . . A strange desire. . . . Antonio Alday Gutiérrez goes on reading, divining, emending his father's confession.

The old man said that he felt the sun coming up pristine over the Andes, his homeland; that he was never really bothered by doña Gloria's intermittent snoring; that he had always dreamed of winning the lottery; that he was certain El Azar could be tricked into service—only he had not been able to find the way; that he had nothing but the old Chevy to leave behind. Take it, Toño. But don't tell anyone that I've given it to you. Take it because it's yours. Go away! . . . Toño listened without speaking as the old man went on and on: that the darkness would never leave him now; that don Sato was inscrutably sad; that he was letting himself go because he did not want to get used to the routine of being a blind man in Tacora. It boils my cojones, Toño! . . . Until the red rose on the flattened-out Gloria Milk box was swallowed up by the light of day.

Then—Antonio Alday Gutiérrez remembers clearly the time he wrote this down, sitting on the grass in Roger Williams Park in Providence, by the lake, near the Temple of Music—the old man laced his fingers over his chest and let his head sink into the pillow he shared with his wife.

Looking inward, the old man imagined his only natural son untying his shoelaces, taking off his Alianza Lima T-shirt, lying down on his damp mattress on the floor, covering himself with the woolen blanket that his father had brought from the highlands and that still smelled like Tarma, lacing his long white fingers behind his neck, and beginning to look inward, too. Poor Toño. Poor old man.

When the winter sun placed a beam of morning light squarely on her face, doña Gloria Gutiérrez Bayle de Alday woke up. Without

42

noticing anything out of the ordinary, she took off her nightgown, stained brown by the night's labor of the fleas, put on the black dress she had made for herself a year ago, stepped into her old black shoes with flattened heels, picked up the washbasin by the door, and headed for the line at the water spigot. Toño heard her shuffling steps die away. At that very moment, don Juan let go of the last dragging hooks attaching him to his routine life in Tacora. He followed his own steps backwards and revisited all his memories, all his unfulfilled dreams, knowing that it was now impossible to hold on to his regrets any longer.

11

Letting his thoughts mingle freely at 12:30 P.M. on the cursed day, Antonio Alday Gutiérrez has to admit that not having written to his mother had also been a choice. At the beginning it had been driven by fear: fear that La Migra would catch him at the post office, weighing a letter to Peru; fear that even if he did not put his return address on the envelope, even if he were lucky enough not to be seen, La Migra would show up at his front door, following some invisible thread, a betraying scent that had lingered on the envelope. . . . But he has to admit now, when he realized that his fears were at least exaggerated, his decision not to write home was driven by something even more powerful: the determination not to be crushed by nostalgia. He did not write letters then because he did not know how to do it without conjuring up the music, the food, the colors, and the smells of Peru. And he did not know how to write without thinking about Betti.

He had to cut out all the dragging hooks in one liberating slash. Of course, Antonio Alday Gutiérrez, the illegal, secretly missed the voice of his mother, so timid and mournful; he missed her smell, her presence. But in a few years, as Antonio Alday Gutiérrez became Anthony Allday, he learned to fend off and even dislike her memory. And it was not very hard, Antonio Alday Gutiérrez accepts now. She had always portrayed herself as a victim. Mournful. Cowering behind sighs and tears. . . . The illegal Peruvian came to dislike the memory of his mother because, as soon as he had crossed the river, filled with an inexplicable anger against Coyote Padilla and the world, he had sworn never again, ever, to beg or be cowed in his new sitio. He swore to live or die with his head high and never to be like his mother.

That must have been why, Antonio Alday Gutiérrez accepts now, he had avoided *el barrio* and everything having to do with *lo latino* in America. The truth is that Anthony Allday always believed they begged too much, he says to himself, feeling the oblique, soft light of the winter sun on his face. Anthony Allday believed the fear of the future had settled into the very core of their hearts.

44

Anthony Allday took off his cap, wiped his forehead dry with his white handkerchief, and adjusted the dead weight of the Smith & Wesson .38. It was 10:45 P.M. and he was ahead of schedule. He decided to stop a moment to admire a new automobile on display in the very center of the mall. A Mustang. Red. Long nose. Lowrider. But not quite like the Mustangs he had so admired as a young man, during the hot summers of Lima, as he saw them zoom by along the Carretera Central or La Costanera. Hot days. Days for dreaming of being a pituco from Miraflores. Days for imagining escapes to worlds beyond Tacora. . . . Anthony Allday shook off those memories. He did not have to envy anyone any longer. He was an American now. He lived in a world any Peruvian, even the pitucos, would envy.

American consumerism can be oppressive, Anthony Allday said to himself, continuing on his first round, watching the people gathered around the red Mustang. Everyone laments it. But few do anything to escape. Not even Hannah. She is constantly lamenting it, but she is more than ready to fall into the trap of the new and improved. Ay, Hannah! Anthony Allday wiggled his left toe in an attempt to shake off its hum of pain. She is so frivolous, even if she doesn't admit it. Always with new shoes, new earrings, new blouses, pocketbooks, hairdos. . . . Insatiable, carajo.

Maybe that is why, Anthony Allday thought as he again shifted the Smith & Wesson .38, which was beginning to feel heavy, she had never expressed the desire for a more permanent relationship. Maybe she would always be looking for someone new and improved. . . . Good thing, too. He would not have been able to please her. Especially now that Genaro was coming to ruin everything.

Or so it seemed. Because it remains to be seen what el cojudo would have to say. Who knows? Maybe he would be one of those highlanders who know instinctively what is best for them. He might not be like his father, Uncle Aniceto, who from what he remembered, never knew how to value anything and who, surely, was spending his last days stuck in La Parada, selling a few potatoes here, a few apples there, like a güevón, a stupid old man. He should be here at least, selling nice clothes, brass lamps, red Mustangs. . . . And Anthony Allday thought that maybe he could talk to Genaro, that maybe things were not as dismal as all that.

12

Peruvian Notebook No. 2
January 12, 1984

We didn't go around hiding in those years, Antonio. In those years
we were ready to face anything, as the corrido says, with a pistol in
one hand. Not for nothing I was born in Nogales, a mucha honra, to
my honor, and rode south with Pancho Villa. And don Jacinto Mora
looked into the past, the bluish hue of his old eyes shining under
the low ceiling light. Those were different times.

Antonio shifted his weight on the wobbly orange crate. He rubbed
the palm of his left hand with his right thumb. He cast down his
eyes, following the thin dark crack that split the cement floor. I'm
not hiding because I'm scared of La Migra, don Jacinto. It's just
that I don't want to be sent back to Tacora. I can't think of anything worse than being sent back there. That's like dying a slow
death. No, don Jacinto, I'm not hiding here because I'm afraid of the
German shepherds that sniff the air or of the Mexicans, muertos
de hambre, those backstabbers who work for the gringo government.
It's for fear of Tacora. That's why I'm grateful to you, don Jacinto.
Thanks for letting me stay. I won't cause you any trouble. I promise. If they find me, I'll go quietly.

In the old days things were never as black and white as today,
Antonio. Our world was full of color and possibilities. Of course,
as I said, we sometimes had to gamble a bit. Sometimes we had to
take our life in our hands. Even when we went courting. There were
open fields, shady streets, cool riverbeds where we could spend the
night, alone or bién acompañado, with good company. Not like these
days when everything is fenced in, illuminated, even mined. We
could come and go as we pleased. Day or night. But things changed.
In my opinion, it all happened because Cárdenas nationalized the
oil. That must have been around the forties. Everything seemed to
change in the forties. The whole world changed. Even Peru, surely.

That's why I had to stay here, in San Antonio, and learn to make
a living by playing and singing. I didn't have a good voice or any-

thing. I only knew a few chords that my uncle Rigoberto taught me when I went to live with him in Chihuahua, back in the twenties. But, as they say, we humans are better than chameleons. Fact of the matter is, Antonio, I decided to play and sing because I didn't want to become a gardener. After one has spent years starting revolutions, one just can't stomach going about bowing to patrones, especially if they're gringos. But, as I said, those were other times. Besides, I was already tired of running around. Tired of throwing hope to the four winds.

Don Jacinto said he very much liked to sing corridos. He liked to strum the easy beat on his Coahuila guitar and tell the stories his own way. Because that's all there is to a corrido, Antonio, a good beat and a good story told fresh. Of course, there are some stories one can no longer change. Like the story in the corrido of Gregorio Cortéz, for example. And mind you, Antonio, of all the corridos, from California to Colorado, that one is closest to my heart. I could still change the story if I wanted to, but some things are better left alone. And Antonio noticed that the bluish hue of the old man's eyes seemed to dim. I knew Gregorio's family. Decent people. Kind, normal types. His granddaughter still lives in Brownsville. She has a little taquería there. Someday I'll make my way back, just to see her. I'm sure she still remembers me.

To tell you the truth, I no longer sing only corridos. I also sing huastecas, rancheras, Peruvian waltzes, Chilean cuecas, and sambas from Argentina. As I said, things change, Antonio. Nuestra gente, our people, don't seem to want to know what's happening around them now. They'd rather imagine what would happen if things were different. You know what I mean, Antonio? The new bands, those kids who sing with accordions, electric guitars, and everything, they still sing about our experiences. But they tell their own stories in different tunes. . . . Besides, the old man said as he stroked his leathery face with limp fingers, lost in thought, since I've come to play and sing on the River Walk, I've had to adjust, like a good chameleon. . . . That is the truth, Antonio, la gente don't come here no more. Only tourists.

To empathize with Antonio Alday Gutiérrez, lonely and in hiding, don Jacinto Mora sang an old Peruvian waltz:

47

Todos vuelven a la tierra en que nacieron.
Al embrujo incomparable de su sol.
Todos vuelven al rincón donde vivieron,
donde acaso floreció más de un amor.

Bajo el árbol solitario del silencio,
cuántas veces nos ponemos a soñar.
Todos vuelven por la ruta del recuerdo,
pero el tiempo del amor no vuelve más.

El aire que trae en sus manos la flor del pasado,
su aroma de ayer,
nos dice muy quedo al oído su canto aprendido del atardecer:
nos dice su voz misteriosa,
de nardo y de rosa, de luna y de miel:
qué santo el amor de la tierra,
qué triste es la ausencia que deja el ayer.

Everyone returns to the land where we were born.
To the incomparable enchantment of its sun.
Everyone returns to the place where we lived,
where blossomed perhaps more than one love.

Under the solitary tree of silence,
so many times we set ourselves to dreaming.
Everyone returns by the road of remembrance,
but the time for love never returns.

The air that brings in its hands the flower of the past,
its aroma of yesterday,
whispers in our ears its song learned from the twilight.
It whispers, its voice mysterious as the spikenard and the rose,
the moon and the honey:
how blessed the love of the land.
How sad the absence that yesterday leaves behind.

The old man filled the cramped pantry with languid verses of departures and returns, of faraway sitios, of suffering mothers, of endless betrayals. . . . Antonio Alday Gutiérrez drank his coffee. He sighed. He longed to see Betti's face again. He could almost smell the old, muddy callejón. . . .

But his heart was also filled with apprehension: they were going to find him. They were going to send him back, and he was going to lose even the three hundred dollars he had hidden in the fourth-floor room he shared with Lucho Canales, the Chilean. He had rolled the bills tight and stuck them in the hole in the back right leg of the bed. If they tossed things around, as they were bound to do, his savings would be gone, without a trace. Even if the roll of twenties did not fall out, Señora Reid might go ahead and rent the room to someone else. She was clear about it: The rent is due every fifteen days. If you can't pay for whatever reason, I'll put you out on the street.

Everyone knew she was a woman not to be messed with. She dyed her hair flaming red and walked around like a man, with a hammer and a pair of pliers dangling from the belt hooks of her ample trousers. Everyone also knew she was not a real gringa. She had taken the name of her ex-husband, who had left her some twenty years before, when she was still young and beautiful. She had never remarried. She seldom left her large house and, so far, not one of her tenants had had the balls to try wooing her. Of all her tenants, only Lucho Canales was on familiar terms with her. You're becoming more and more beautiful with every day that passes, Lucia, he would tell her. She would then look at him with an air of playful intimacy and tell him she tolerated his antics because, like her, he was a real American. Your people, like mine, came here invited, to work in the mines. We're not like these pendejos, these jackasses, she would say loud enough for everyone to hear.

It is true, remembers Antonio Alday Gutiérrez at 12:30 P.M. Lucho Canales was Chilean in name only. He was a real American. He had never made it in life because he liked to drink, gamble, and get high. When he was really drunk, he liked to insult all the new arrivals to the big house. Some tenants even swore he had taken their money. When he was high, he would sing and dance cuecas barefoot. But he did all right by me, Antonio Alday Gutiérrez murmurs low. He left me alone. Maybe it was because I could talk with him about the Colo Colo soccer team. Maybe it was because Lucho Canales felt bad that Chile had taken a chunk of land from Peru during the Pacific War of 1879. Who knows? The fact remains that he invited me to share his little room, at a time when I could barely afford to eat.

Ten days in hiding. Afraid that the owners of the restaurant would ask him to leave, since he could not even help out around the place for fear of being seen. Antonio Alday Gutiérrez, the illegal, spent the hours picking his fingernails and trying to read don Jacinto's old comic books, in English: Batman, Little Lulu, Superman, Green Lantern, Red Rider. . . . Don Jacinto Mora would tell him that he was sharing the pantry and his food with him so he wouldn't think the entire world was full of shitheads. And Antonio swore he would never forget the favor.

Thinking back, in Lima, Delaware County, Pennsylvania, Antonio Alday Gutiérrez considers that perhaps it was in order to return that favor in the only way he could that he confessed to the old man that he was dying of nostalgia. It was the only gift he could give. . . . That was the last time Antonio Alday Gutiérrez had a reason to confess that in his dreams, he returned to Tacora, walked its dark alleys with Betti by his side. In his dreams, he would see her beautiful face, enveloped in the *garúa,* the thin mist of Lima's winter, and he would know, as clearly as can be, in the deepest corners of his heart and soul, that she would always be there, waiting for him.

   Antonio Alday Gutiérrez also remembers that he could hardly sleep in his old hiding place. He was terrified at the thought of waking up to find himself still in the little pantry. Worse still, he was terrified at the thought of waking up to the sound of someone knocking at the door. . . . Antonio Alday Gutiérrez knows that ever since those days in San Antonio, he has abhorred waiting for things to come, things as horrific as they are inevitable.

13

Peruvian Notebook No. 1
August 2, 1983

You are leaving me, whimpered doña Gloria Gutiérrez Bayle de Alday at the cemetery. Out of sheer perversity. What did you expect, mixing with that kind of people? Doing things. She looked at Toño out of the corner of her eye. The boy seemed not to be paying attention. I guess we're all born with our own destiny. But we arrived in Lima, at least. Good or bad, one can make a living around here. Not like in Tarma. . . . You were such a womanizer. And such a liar. You probably told them all you were about to leave me, that it was a matter of time. But you knew it wasn't true. We were meant to be together, you and I. And we were, a long time. Ever since you saw me with my two little children in tow. What did you see in me? You were faithful where it counted, Juan. You never lifted a hand against me. You provided the daily bread for my children.

They should've loved you more, of course. But it was your own fault. Why didn't you let them call you father? Only don Juan. And now? Fortunately, my Ricardo is already grown. We'll carry on with our lives, somehow. And Carmencita, with that face, that body of hers. Maybe she'll be knocked up someday, end up like poor Consuelo, Guillermo Quintana's daughter. Or like me. And you won't even be here to stand up for her. There will only be Ricardo. But perhaps not. Girls are smarter nowadays. What with the telenovelas, the soap operas they watch, the advice from their teachers, the things they read, everything. She takes care of herself. I am sure she gets around, but she takes care of herself. Let's hope.

Doña Gloria Gutiérrez Bayle de Alday complained that Tarma was far away. Very far away. But one had to move on, to survive. Luckily, you had family around these parts already, Juan. Of course, they didn't welcome us as they should have. But why blame them? What with so many small children of their own, dispersed among those brick factories, eking out a living, surviving in their little sitios. And they did lend us a hand, para qué; they shared what they could. We must be grateful for that. You didn't have reason to curse them for not taking us in, Juan. And doña Gloria Gutiérrez Bayle de Alday saw out of the corner of her eye that Toño was looking far into the distance. The sky of Lima's desert extended like a gray cotton blanket below Augustino mountain.

You were always trying to improve our life. And we nearly succeeded in making something really good for ourselves, didn't we, Juan? Like when we bought the Chevy. Remember? We'll sell everything we have, if we must, Gloria, you said, with that strong voice of yours, but we need to buy that car. There's nothing like mobility. In the army, I learned that without mobility one is at the mercy of the enemy. You used to talk funny like that sometimes. And we did it. We sold everything: the little cow, the little store, the little cowhides and saddles that my daddy had left me, the three long dresses with mother-of-pearl from Venezuela and real Brazilian lace that my mother had made especially for the feast of Santa Eulalia when she was still young. Everything to buy the little Chevy.

We ended up stuck here. Maybe it was something in Tacora, or in La Estrella itself, that held our heels to our endless bad luck. Because, let's face it, Juan, we didn't have to roll around the world just to come to this. You didn't deserve to end up like this, blind and alone on this mountain. Alone because, as far as we know, you are the first of our families to die in Lima. That will be your privilege: to have died first. You'll have to find your way up to heaven all by yourself. I'll go back to Tarma in a month, to pray to Santa Eulalia for help. I only hope she doesn't remember you very well. You were so unkind to that blind woman who cleaned her little chapel at the top of Goat Mountain, Juan, and you made such a fuss over my weekly pilgrimages. But now, when it's perhaps too late, you must see the value of prayer.

Stuck in Tacora, Juan. That's what happened to us. Maybe it was because you were so footloose. And now, see? Why did you mess with those people?

And doña Gloria Gutiérrez Bayle de Alday turned her head toward Toño. Toñito warned you, Juan: Don't fool around with people from Chincha, Papá, he said. He knew why. He knew them. Not for nothing does he walk with the black people from La Victoria, El Augustino, Tacora, La Parada, and the theater.

Not a theater, a whorehouse! she must really have thought. Antonio Alday Gutiérrez recoils, lifting his face from his Peruvian notebooks. She must have cursed el cojudo Toño who, to her highlander way of thinking, was up to his armpits in the sludge of sin particular to black people. He walks just like them, she must have thought—as if he were dancing, with the sleeves of his Alianza Lima T-shirt rolled up high, with fluffed-up brown suede shoes, and with that stupid moño, that pompadour bouncing and shining with Glostora oil.

You didn't pay attention to him, Juan. Oh, Juan! You really made me mad sometimes. But all that's past now. You shouldn't blame me for anything having to do with them. I don't even say hello to them. They can be so arrogant and mean. Take Toya, for example. She walks by all perky, swaying, like a palm tree in summer. Who knows? Maybe she was angry at you because—as everyone in Tacora knows—you didn't go to bed with her, even though she asked you to, during last year's carnival, when the two of you were in Domitila's kitchen making aguadillo, chicken soup, at three in the morning. Or take la samba Libertad, the one with the honey-colored eyes. She's always coming by, dressed in those obscene watermelon pants, looking for I don't know what. What did you do or leave undone?

I knew you were having an affair with her. Everybody in Tacora knew. Even the children, of course. But I didn't want to clip your wings. You might have left me. Just like you are leaving me now, with me unable to say or do anything to prevent it. Just like now, Juan. Not even my tears would have been enough to keep you. Because you had a heart made of stone, Juan, just like the song says. A heart made of stone. Because when you decided to cover yourself with silence, nothing could affect you. And I didn't want to lose you like that either. That was why I gave you a long rope and left you to roam freely. Maybe I should've done otherwise. Maybe this is all my fault. But no, Juan. No. Toya or Libertad or someone like them must have finally made you pay for all the slights you sowed in your careless roaming. I wonder who it was, Juan.

One has to accept that it was daño, witchcraft, doña Gloria Gutiérrez Bayle de Alday said to herself, looking around her, barely noticing the cement crosses and elevated nichos that surrounded her. She set her gaze on the white chapel and took in the pungent aroma of marigold, the flower of the dead, stirred by the wind. It's the only way to make sense of things. Otherwise, how do I explain what happened? The doctors had no idea what was wrong with you, Juan. They didn't even agree on what to do. Until the fattest and baldest one said, We just have to watch him and hope it passes, whatever it is.

For God's sake! I could've said that! And I want you to know that I was ready to sell the Chevy to spare you. I had already talked to Aparicio Valderrama, the guy from Ecuador who sells bananas in La Parada. Toñito gave me courage: Sell the car, Mamá, he said, so long as the old man gets better. But look, Juan, whispered doña Gloria Gutiérrez Bayle de Alday into her cupped right hand, Toño hasn't even cried for you. Strange, don't you think? Maybe it's because you never really understood each other. You were always looking at each other from a distance. From the day he was born.

I don't say this because I love my two other children more, said the old hag again loud enough to be heard. Because as far as I'm concerned, Toño is my life, Juan. I've never treated him badly. I've never pushed him to the edge, as he must sometimes think. It's just that the others are older and, naturally, they know me better. They have other needs. You'll see how I'll treat him from now on, Juan. Just as if you were still here. I know I have to see him as a man now. But I've already learned to do that with my Ricardo. Don't you worry. I'm sure you're listening to me, even though when you were alive you didn't. You must have heard my pain when the doctors didn't want to tell me anything. You must have heard the prayers of my older children, your children too, Juan, even though you were always looking at them differently. Maybe that's why I paid more attention to them than to our Toñito. He had his father, Juan. But let me confess here and now that I love him the most. That's why I need to be closer to the others. You understand, Juan?

They should be here, of course, the old hag excused them. But they have their own needs. Their own responsibilities. You should've

54

seen how sad our Ricardo was when he found out he couldn't come with us today. All the poor boy could say was that he would've liked to drive the Chevy, even if it was only at your funeral. Because it's true, Juan, he resented you for you never letting him drive the car. He wanted you to trust him. And Carmencita, well, she has her job. She has to do everything they tell her, it being Monday and all. But I'm here. With Toñito.

Yeah, sure, thinks Antonio Alday Gutiérrez at 12:40 P.M., divining that long ago, but inside, she must have been thinking: Those fluffed-up suede shoes are only made for thieves. Why does he only come home to sleep? Why doesn't he ever listen to me? I am his mother! She was always saying that: I am your mother! As if that could fix everything.

She must have resented her son; the youngest, the one who was there, assailed by the smell of marigold, the desert, the crosses; the one who was pretending not to pay attention to what his mother was saying and doing, the one with his own heart filling up with hatred of life because it only leads to death.

Now that you're no longer here, it's my turn, Juan. I have to stop his errant ways. I don't want him to turn to evil, as so many others do. But Toñito has a soft heart, Juan. He's not like our Ricardo, who sees opportunity, business, everywhere. Maybe he too has been born to suffer, like me. Ay, Juan! What wouldn't those black people do to him! Although they seem to take care of him. Especially the old women. They take him everywhere. They buy him clothes. They might even give him spending money. I have to get closer to him. I have to get to know more about his life. I've always left him on his own. But I did it because I didn't want to spend my life fighting you. I didn't want to risk pushing him away. But now it's my turn. I will no longer tolerate his way of living, sleeping all day and staying awake all night. Wasting his time scribbling in that old notebook of his. I'll force him to go back to school. You'll see. The truth is, Juan, I know I have to clip his wings, before it's too late.

The Augustino sky was clear and there were unusual hints of pink in the blue to the east. Far below, Lima was still covered by her ashen blanket of pollution. At the cemetery, the bells of the white chapel tolled seven o'clock. The mound of discarded, dead flowers on its south side gave the landscape a particularly desolate air. A soft Andean breeze swept down the bare gray mountain. It followed its ancient paths down to the desert, which had once been alive with playful sand and shadows but now was being smothered by cement, crushed marigolds, corpses, sad people, and mud. The sun was sinking, round and red.

Doña Gloria Gutiérrez Bayle de Alday moved closer to her son to whisper that it was too bad she had not forgotten his father's last wish: When I die, please bury me on that beautiful mountain. It reminds me of Tarma. Ay, Toñito! What I had to do to bring him here! I begged everyone. You should know, Toñito, people from La Estrella shouldn't be buried here. They say we should go to rest in the awful cemetery in Vitarte. But here we are, Juan. You'll rest here!

As the sun painted strange pink figures on the pale blue northern sky, doña Gloria Gutiérrez Bayle de Alday threw her fistful of sandy dirt into the high, open crypt where don Juan's black casket lay. She blessed herself three times and moved away, covering her bowed head with her black mantilla. Caught in the aura of her sacred moment, obeying a call from beyond all resentment, Toño wished to emulate his mother in showing reverence. He stepped forward somberly and threw his own fistful of sandy dirt into the narrow opening of the nicho. Just then an Andean breeze whirled upwards and playfully whisked away the sand. Toño heard the hard sound of pebbles hitting his father's casket. Too bad, he thought. Too bad.

At 12:50 P.M., Antonio Alday Gutiérrez remembers that many years later, chewing hard on his memories finally to bury his nostalgia, still enveloped in an unbending desire to exorcise the shadows of his past, at the Elmwood Avenue branch of the Providence Public Library, already Antonio Allday but not yet Mr. Anthony Allday, he wrote down, tight between the red lines of his brittle Peruvian Notebook No. 1, the lines he is now determined to read in full:

The boy has his light brown eyes idos, gone, as if he were someone else, as if he were onstage. He takes something out of his pocket,

56

something crumbled, moist, dirty, and he throws it hard into the nicho. The object hits the casket and, as if taken up by an invisible hand, it opens slowly: Entrada. Teatro Municipal. 7 de Noviembre 1973. Matiné—a theater ticket. At that very moment, doña Gloria Gutiérrez Bayle de Alday turns her eyes quizzically towards her youngest son. She sees he is crying. But she finds he is not sobbing or sighing, as she herself would. Toñito is letting his tears roll down his face as if they were not his own. Taken aback, sensing something unnatural unfolding before her eyes, doña Gloria Gutiérrez Bayle de Alday approaches her son, wipes his tears with the back of her right hand, and tells him to be brave, that it is God's will that his poor father is finally at rest. Toñito looks at her through new tears and tells her it is not for the old man that he is crying: It's for myself, Mamá. I'm crying because from now on, I have no one else to blame. I'm alone. With a pale shadow in her heart, the old hag tells him he shouldn't be talking like that, he still has her, things will look different in a couple of days. But Toño escapes her embrace, her smell of dry marigolds, her black eyes glistening under that red sun. He turns away from her, looks in at the casket for the last time, and walks to the old Chevy, to wait there for the funeral act to end. By the time doña Gloria Gutiérrez Bayle de Alday joins him there, Toño has changed. But not even he knows how or why. And then, as through a glass darkly, he hears his mother scolding him for having left her behind, among the dead. Too bad, he thinks. Too bad.

One O'clock

August 8, 1990
Canto Grande

Mr. Antonio Alday Gutiérrez
209 Rogers Lane
Lima
Delaware County
Pennsylvania, 19037
USA

Dear Cousin Antonio:

Just a short note to say that I am very glad to know you are doing so well in your new sitio. Everything over there seems to be just great. How I would love to be over there with you, Cousin! As I wrote to you in my prior letter, there are several outfits here that guarantee to make all the necessary arrangements for travel to the USA. They take care of everything. It's not like it was when you left, Cousin. The only thing is that it is very expensive. They say that this is because they have to contact lots of people and make lots of deals. They say that sometimes people have to go through Bolivia, Mexico, or Canada. But they also say that sometimes people can go directly to Philadelphia. Can you imagine that! I am saving my money, Cousin. It might not be this year or next, but I know I am going to make it over there. Things here are going from bad to worse. There are no jobs. There is nothing. People worry all the time. I would like to help the family. I do not want to bother you, Cousin, but we don't have resources. If you could help, just enough for the fees they charge, I promise I would return the money. I could work in one of your companies. I could sell things. I am willing to do anything, Cousin. Please let me know if you have received this letter. As soon I hear from you, I will do what I have to on this end. Meanwhile, I can tell you, dear Cousin, that no matter what, I am not going to give up. I know God will help me. It would be so beautiful for me to arrive in Layma, as you say people pronounce Lima over there, to knock on your door. It would be like a miracle. I hope that this little letter reaches you, Cousin. I hope also that I hear from you soon.

Your cousin who remembers you,
Genaro

1

Not everything is perfect, of course, thought Anthony Allday as he glanced at a decorated Benetton store, breathing in the dry, recycled air of the Springfield Mall. Of course not. He felt his left big toe beginning to swell, as it always did near the end of his first round. He consulted his wristwatch: 10:55. Almost time for the mall to close.

Of course not. There were many things he detested in his new sitio. Mostly odd things, nothing of fundamental importance. Like the fat people, for example. He detested the noises they made when they gasped for air, the shine on their sweaty faces, even in winter, their dogged determination to stuff their faces. There is something obscene about a fat American, he had said to Hannah once. Since we have the money, there is no limit to our gluttony. And, tell me, Hannah, how do you think they manage to make love? It's disgusting.

And she, lifting her chin, as she always did when ready for a fight: Would you rather we had nothing to eat, like the rest of the world? Besides, we are not as unique as you think. Food, like everything else in our lives, is related to politics. And Anthony Allday thought that, to Hannah, everything was related to politics.

He hated the mallrat hordes. They acted as if they owned the place. He hated their poses, their torn pants, their dyed hair, the way they looked at him: with defiance, with pity even. And Anthony Allday considered himself lucky for not having any children. It would have been such a waste of his time and money. Yeah, of course, he recognized there was a time when he had not yet discarded the possibility of a family. But that was a long time ago. So long ago, in fact, that he hardly remembered how he must have really felt about it. He did remember letting Alex Sosa go on assuming that he too could see himself as an honest family man, a man who would come home at night and spend the weekends barbecuing in the backyard, growing old and fat. Besides, for an immigrant like him, the idea of having a family in America only meant falling prey to the power of nostalgia. How many poor souls had sacrificed their lives to bring their relatives to America, to have a family? A real waste.

Granted, Alex Sosa's plans were slightly different. He wanted to marry in New England and have a real American family. He had already dated several American women in New Bedford. And he had followed Cheryl, an Irish American girl, to Providence, Rhode Island. She might have been the reason Alex Sosa decided to stay behind when Antonio Allday asked him to come with him to Philadelphia, back in 1984. All Alex Sosa wanted was to become a regular Joe. Anthony Allday, on the other hand, wanted to be free from all the routines that scarred the body and the soul. He had to avoid developing attachments to people and things.

After this reconstruction, Antonio Alday Gutiérrez thinks at 1:00 P.M., resting his tired body against the vinyl couch, how could I ever share my life the way Alex Sosa did, with genuine sincerity? The fact of the matter is that before too long, it was too late. The hard shell he had built for himself very quickly made it impossible even to think about genuine love. Hannah would be the American woman closest to his heart, but she too had come too late.

Antonio Alday Gutiérrez tries to shake off any feeling of regret by focusing again on the possible reasons for what had happened. And yet he cannot help but wonder whether his determined claim to freedom from routine and nostalgia came at too high a cost. Was he callously unfeeling toward Genaro, a man he hardly knew, because of his fear of attachment to routines, people, and things? Did he resent his cousin because in his fear-filled eyes he embodied the power of nostalgia? Was that why he became a murderer? Did his desire for freedom from routine and nostalgia mean an embrace of freedom from shame and morality? Was it wrong to have become other after all?

No, Antonio Alday Gutiérrez protests. He leans toward the soft light of the winter sun entering obliquely through the large window of his ugly apartment in Lima, Delaware County, Pennsylvania. No. He did nothing wrong in inventing a past for himself. After all, the life of Antonio Alday Gutiérrez, the illegal Peruvian—full of suffering, hatred, and shame—no longer adequately represents who he became, who he now is. He ceased being Peruvian, a boy from Tacora, the moment he crossed the Río Bravo. Mr. Anthony Allday became the natural bridge between a past that no longer exists and a future, however dismal under the circumstances, that was yet to come. There was nothing wrong with that.

That is why they trust me, Anthony Allday thought that cursed night at 10:55 P.M., as the mall was closing. Because I am totally free from that past. Otherwise, would I have been able to carry this gun? Would I have been trusted with the millions and millions of dollars that surround me? Not a chance, carajo! Nostalgia would have cut me down at the knees. Antonio Alday Gutiérrez, the illegal, had done too many things on the run, scared, ashamed. That man had been smothered, imprisoned by the crust of Tacora. Of course, it was not Toñito's fault that he was born into poverty, with a crazy father who died convinced he had been cursed, with an enigmatic mother always looking at him through a veil of tears, reading and weighing the effects of her pain on him. I am Anthony Allday, carajo! To hell with the rest.

He reached the mall's east entrance. Tom was there. How goes it, Tom? What do you think, is it going to snow? It's freaking cold out.

And Anthony Allday thinks to himself that Thomas Parker is a fucked up man, a man who truly does not know who or what to be. He shows up every night with two gold earrings, but he takes them off before putting on the uniform. He keeps them wrapped in a pink cotton cloth, inside a miniature cedar chest, in the bottom drawer of his desk. Damn! People do the weirdest things. Becoming a homosexual goes against all sense. Why choose to become something that makes your life miserable? No doubt about it: Tom has chosen badly. Now he can only be what he wants to be in secret. And Anthony Allday smiled, almost imperceptibly, remembering the night he discovered Tom's secret, in West Philadelphia, back in 1986. There he was, cavorting with his friends: tight leather pants, padding on his butt, pink rouge on his cheeks. What a sight! But at work, Mr. Thomas Parker, carajo! A serious man. The boss. Yeah, Anthony Allday thought, people do the weirdest things.

2

Anthony Allday preferred not to travel on trains and buses because he disliked meeting poor blacks and Latinos. He was offended by their barrio smell, by their cheap and ill-fitting clothes, by their empty stares that suggested they were looking, in vain, to explain some calamity that had befallen them. That was why he had purchased the red '77 Corvette, on the Golden Mile, Springfield Township. He had to have an automobile befitting the scion of a wealthy Peruvian family, carajo. By the summer of 1986 he was already Mr. Anthony Allday and had to act the part.

On that hot August day in 1986, however, Anthony Allday had taken the train to Philadelphia. He had decided to take the train partly because Tom had encouraged him to do so. You don't have to pay to park, Tony, Tom had said. You can even read the paper on your way there. Why make trouble for yourself, buddy? But, even more, he had taken the train because he was afraid someone might steal his Corvette. The City of Brotherly Love was no place for beautiful cars. At least not that August, when it was so hot and humid that people flooded the streets by opening the fire hydrants with their bare hands.

But then, thinks Antonio Alday Gutiérrez at 1:10 after the murder, keeping his eyes shut, letting himself be taken away by his most recent memories, perhaps everything that happened that day was *una obra del imperdonable Azar,* the work of unforgiving Chance. Because, he ventures in his feverish fatigue, there are things in life one can never foresee or control but that can change our destiny in the blink of an eye. There is always a chance that worse things could happen but, at the same time, there is always hope of a turn for the better. There has to be.

3

Peruvian Notebook No. 4
January 2, 1987

At last! Dr. Krinsky came through. Money well spent. A green card
will give me added invisibility. I will apply for American citizenship in a few years. What to do while I wait? It might be good just
to rest. Enjoy life a little. As for the future, who knows? There is
plenty of time to think about that. I have a bottle of Almaden. I'd
like to celebrate. I wish Alex were here. Or Betti. Or even snooty
Ana María. ¡Puta madre! Hannah has not called.

4

The warm air was thick at the Elwyn train station, near Lima, Pennsylvania. There was not the slightest breeze on the boarding platform. Commuters dressed casually. The men wore shorts and the women light tops and short skirts. America, Anthony Allday thought disdainfully—the land of comfort. He walked to the southern end of the boarding platform to wait for the 10:15 train. He was dressed as usual: white cotton shirt, long cream linen jacket, cuffed khakis. As his only concession to the dog days of August, he wore his brown sailing shoes without socks. He carried a neatly folded *Philadelphia Inquirer* under his right arm. He wished to give the impression of a man with few worries.

The train arrived on time. As he had expected, the suburban travelers climbed into the cars in an orderly fashion. Each passenger took his or her place in a line governed by the invisible rules of consideration and good manners. Anthony Allday was glad not to be traveling on the buses and trains of Peru. He could still remember summer trips to La Herradura beach, in January and February. He made the two-hour trip hanging from rusted overhead bars, enduring shoves and insults, wary of pickpockets, assaulted by bad breath and the sweat of the people squeezing by. No doubt about it, Anthony Allday thought as he climbed onto the train under the watchful eyes of the conductor, the American sense of comfort had its good side. Since the Elwyn train station was near the beginning of the suburban route, he was able to make his way to the very last car and find an empty seat by the rear windows.

Looking out to the back and to his right, Anthony Allday could enjoy a view of the little towns along the road to Philadelphia: Swarthmore, Morton, Secane, Yeadon. . . . They all looked clean and well kept, even though the train passed through their less affluent zones. The little towns reminded him of New England. Morton looked much like the sections of New Bedford bordering La Calle de Saudades, the street where he had met his old friend Alex Sosa. Anthony Allday missed Alex Sosa. He missed the man's strange sense of adventure. He truly believed he would never get bored exploring only within the boundaries of New England, his new sitio.

66

All I need to be happy, Antonio, is my old eight-cylinder hearse! The world is as big as one makes it, man.

There are people like that, thought Anthony Allday, in places like New England. But there are neither people nor places like that in Peru. There, the towns and the trains are full of cholos, highlanders. This is another world, carajo.

Anthony Allday arrived at the Thirtieth Street Station by midmorning. The train stopped inside a massive gray station encircled by black iron lampposts and parking lots. The central hall, high and at that hour filled with dissonant echoes, gave Anthony Allday the feeling of being in a cathedral nave. The tall windows let in streams of summer light. The hall was flanked by two rows of underground stairways, through which people emerged into and disappeared from the hall, pensive and hurried. A small balcony jutted out over the eastern end of the hall, near exit doors guarded by an oversized bronze angel holding a wounded man. Anthony Allday followed the flood of travelers towards that exit. From there, he could see the outline of Center City. He paused before a wide bridge that spanned the Schuylkill River. The Philadelphia skyline seemed suspended in the haze of a summer's morning. The newest buildings, glass and metal, clustered and spiked into an open sky. Below, the river flowed southeastward, accompanied by swift gulls. The Atlantic Ocean was nearby. Anthony Allday breathed in the already thick morning air. Who would have thought it? He had traveled centuries on his way from Tacora to Philadelphia.

Anthony Allday crossed the bridge thinking that he was living through a new beginning. He felt the subtle breeze on his face as a welcoming sign. Filled with enthusiasm, he hurried his steps and promised to make Philadelphia his own. He would get to know the City of Brotherly Love better than he had known any other city, including Lima, Peru. . . . But then, all at once, Anthony Allday slowed down, overtaken by the flash of a crucial insight: in truth, he did not really want to make Philadelphia his own. What he really wanted was to make his own Philadelphia.

Why not? He continued at a slower pace now. Why could he not treat cities, rivers, mountains, people, just as he treated his own past? Neither people nor cities nor rivers are known to us as they truly are. They are all our creations and re-creations. That is what humans do.

Every one of us. So, instead of simply allowing our mundane concerns and inattention to fashion our cities and our rivers, why not actively choose what to include in our images of them? Anthony Allday knew he had no interest in the barrios of Philadelphia, for example. They would only spoil his image of Philadelphia, just as they had already ruined his Houston and San Antonio. He could no longer think of those cities without at the same time thinking of the garbage, the drunkards, the prostitutes of the barrios. No question about it: his Philadelphia would be spared all that. And so Anthony Allday visited Independence Hall and City Hall, the John Wanamaker and Strawbridge & Clothier stores, Rittenhouse Square, Delancey Street, the Bellevue Hotel. As he collected images and memories for his Philadelphia, Anthony Allday thought himself among the luckiest of men. He had discovered one of the greatest secrets of life: anyone can construct anything as he wishes.

It was not in vain, Antonio Alday Gutiérrez mutters to himself, at 1:11 P.M., hands clasped together, eyes lost in the soft light of winter, trying to follow the treacherous threads of the web spun by El Azar. That insight helped him overcome the old deep-seated fear, his paralyzing envy, before the pitucos of Miraflores. The image of his Philadelphia, which he kept just under his breath in all his dealings with them, gave him strength. It gave footing to his inner certainty that he belonged somewhere special, a place they could never touch. He could then look down on those who had always minimized him. That inner certitude had made it possible for him to be Tony with Rosaura and Mr. Allday with snooty Ana María, the woman who had nearly undermined his American sense of well-being.

It had been a hot, humid, suffocating Monday in August. It had sapped his body and spirit. Perhaps it had also induced him to dream of impossibilities.

5

Peruvian Notebook No. 4
March 12, 1987

I have an interview this Friday. I am getting ready. Mr. Parker sounded like a nice guy on the phone. This is it. Am I reaching for the impossible? Should I wait for a better opportunity? Something more interesting, more challenging? Not if I want to write. I could spend nights working and days writing. A good solution. I have to give it a try. If I fail, I will go to college, as Mrs. Rosenberg suggested. But not for accounting. Journalism? I hate to clean up after people. Watchman would be fine for now.

6

That hot Monday in August, Anthony Allday walked around Philadelphia collecting sights, sounds, smells. He was collecting and constructing memories to give the final touches to what could well be his permanent sitio. Deep down, Anthony Allday was ready to stop roaming in America and settle down. He had arrived in Philadelphia on the wings of El Azar, but now he wanted to make it his hometown. He walked and walked. Down Chestnut Street. Up Walnut Street. Across Market and Broad . . . until the sun disappeared over the skyline and the sky over Center City was tinted rose. Soon the people disappeared from the sidewalks and the streetlights flooded the empty spaces, producing in him a feeling of desolation. By then the inner-city pigeons and sparrows had abandoned the benches, the garbage cans, and the few patches of green. Philadelphia seemed at rest before an approaching storm.

Antonio Alday Gutiérrez clearly remembers feeling out of sorts when night fell in Philadelphia. But even now, as the sun touches his still-trembling hands, he finds it hard to explain why. He had felt as if he had been caught perceiving something not meant for him, as if he had stepped into a forbidden realm. It might have been a premonition, a hint that something was about to change in his life. Of course, had Anthony Allday not stayed in Philadelphia that night, he might not have discovered Tom's secret, and without that slight shift everything in his life might have been different. In the throes of a feverish fatigue, hands clasped, eyes peering into the light of the winter sun, Antonio Alday Gutiérrez still wants to relive that Monday night—and gain some clarity for himself.

Anthony Allday decided to meander back to the Thirtieth Street train station. On his way, he passed the Academy of Music and the Philadelphia College of Art. He followed narrow streets flanked by nearly leafless trees. He passed gaunt red-brick row houses facing narrow sidewalks taken over by parked cars. There were old streetlamps painted black and neat shadows projected onto lace-trimmed window shades. He thought he recognized that side of Philadelphia from a book he had read at the Elmwood Avenue branch of the Providence Public Library a

70

few years before. He remembered he had been so impressed by it that, very soon after, he tried to convince Alex Sosa to join him on his trek down I-95. He wished he could linger in that place for a long time. It was as if, for the first time in his life, walking those streets made concrete the possibility of having at least one of his desires satisfied. But it was already late, and he hoped to catch the 9:00 train for Elwyn. He moved on, promising himself to keep that neighborhood as a major part of his Philadelphia. He was now in a particularly good mood. He had gathered much for the future.

But El Azar had tricked him again: turning a corner by a small parking lot, he came upon The Black Cat. The bar seemed out of place. It was poorly lit and its small sign, a stylized drawing of a black cat in pink slippers, was nearly hidden under the eaves of its A frame. The double doors were open. Soft music was playing and mingled voices rolled out onto the street. But there were no people loitering at the door, as might be expected in a city bar. In fact, like the music, the atmosphere was subdued. This encouraged Anthony Allday to consider ending his successful day in the city by having something to drink, perhaps a cold beer, before heading back. He approached with the necessary caution. It was already late and he did not wish to spoil his construction of Philadelphia by inadvertently stepping into a bar for black folk. He had never felt comfortable around them in America. And he certainly did not wish to find himself among Hispanics in a cantina.

Anthony Allday realized his mistake as soon as he stepped through the pink double doors of The Black Cat. In the penumbra of the bar, he saw several men sitting around the counter with their arms around each other's waists and shoulders. They were talking together in low voices. Other men clustered on the crowded floor, swaying to the music with drinks in their hands. There were men sitting at all the tables and in all the corners, talking, smiling, laughing. Some were making out. At the far end of the bar, its glow cutting through the thick smoke, there was a single jukebox decorated with a large black cat outlined against a deep red light. ¡Carajo! Anthony Allday was quite upset. The damn homosexuals had spoiled his Philadelphia. He now had to make room for them. There was no way to avoid it. Anthony Allday looked around the bar in disgust. The mellow faces of those close to him only darkened his mood. He began to turn away. But then, to his astonishment, he saw Tom.

71

Tom was coming to the front counter from the back of the bar. The black cat on the jukebox appeared and disappeared behind him. He was nearly unrecognizable in his flashy gold earrings, a tight black T-shirt, black leather pants with a padded seat, and a thin black belt with silvery decorations. He was following another man, also dressed in black, who led him daintily by the hand. Anthony Allday stood motionless at his spot by the door. He could not believe his eyes. He did not know how to react. Meanwhile, Tom came ever closer, speaking in a high-pitched voice and waving his free hand dramatically. Who would have believed it? After all, at that time Tom was still only Mr. Parker, the boss. Sensing danger, Anthony Allday wanted to turn around and leave. Yet he lingered long enough to be noticed by Tom's friend who, seeing him mesmerized and unable to take his eyes off the scene, whispered in Tom's ear and shook his head softly in the direction of the front door. Tom turned around. He smiled.

Not knowing what to do, Anthony Allday raised his right hand slightly, making a gesture between hello and goodbye. He was ready to escape the dragging hooks of the moment. In his gut, he felt an urge to leave Philadelphia altogether.

But he could not leave just then, because Tom was already on his way toward him. Hey! What're you doing here, buddy? This is Craig. Want a beer, Tony?

And Tony: No, thanks, I am really on my way back, I was just walking around, lost. You were right, Mr. Parker, it was easy to come to Center City by train, I'll see you tomorrow at work. I have to go now. . . . But Tom held him in place with his intrigued gaze. And Anthony Allday again: I'm so happy you're having such a great time, Mr. Parker, I'm not at all bothered by any of this, sincerely, but no . . . maybe some other time, Mr. Parker. But Tom was not worried. He was not asking for favors. He was not offering explanations. He was natural, comfortable. He offered to shake Anthony's hand, something he had done only once before, when he had offered Anthony Allday the job.

He offered me his hand because he thought I expected it, Antonio Alday Gutiérrez thinks back. It was his way of opening the doors of friendship. *¡Y tenía un apretón de mano fuerte!* He had a strong and frank handshake. He was sincere. And after that, it was as if nothing fundamental changed in our lives. But, of course, the encounter had to have made a difference. El Azar was surely at work that night. . . . Good God! People do the weirdest things.

They had a few drinks that night. They talked about the city, the hot summer, the trains, the taste of beer. It's cheaper than wine, Tom said. Besides, wine is for more refined palates, like yours, Tony. I'm a beer man.

And Tony admitted, I've drunk my share of beer, as a young man, while still in Peru, as I cut across the horizon in my father's sailboat, which was actually a sizeable yacht, Mr. Parker.

And Tom: Call me Tom, buddy. You should go to the Schuylkill and up the Delaware then, Tony. The kids from Penn row and sail there. Didn't you know?

And Tony: I am no longer a rower. He said he had foresworn all such things since he dropped out of college. And they shared their impressions of America, the land of opportunity, the only place in the world where anyone could become whatever he wanted, as long as he tried hard enough. And, boy, are we trying! celebrated Tom.

And Tony: I know what you mean. I know what you mean. . . .

The next day at work: Hey, Tony! And Tony: Hi, Tom! How goes it? Same old, same old. . . . Consummate actors. ¡Carajo! And then, after a few weeks of not talking about it, after sharing that pregnant silence, Anthony Allday began to sense a tenuous but real bond had begun to grow between them, a bond that from then on would keep them at once separate and united. Separate in their preferences but united in the knowledge that they were fashioning themselves as they pleased.

Yes, Antonio Alday Gutiérrez acknowledges at 1:15, after the murder, finding a small measure of relief from his anguish. Perhaps the bond of silence that Anthony Allday and Tom had fostered and then maintained was their way of accepting the need to forgive each other for what they could not or would not cease to be. Tom would never know Tony's past, his secrets, of course. He couldn't. But Antonio Alday Gutiérrez is now convinced that it doesn't really matter. Had he known, by some unforeseen circumstance, he would have understood. Surely. He would have understood because Tom was also reconstructing himself.

73

Feeling the warmth of the oblique rays of the winter afternoon sun on his guilty hands, trying to hold on for a little while to the oasis of inner calm he had found, Antonio Alday Gutiérrez cannot fend off the thought that perhaps, if he had confided in Tom, things might have turned out differently. Had he told Tom how he hated the prospect of Genaro's visit, how much resentment and hatred was nestled in his heart that cursed night, perhaps El Azar would have had to weave a different destiny for him. In his feverish fatigue, Antonio Alday Gutiérrez cannot fend off the thought that perhaps, if he had only had a few beers with Tom, in a different place, to find a little space to stand and compare fears, if they had come together to confess to each other, as people in Tacora do when the world seems about to overwhelm them, perhaps then everything would have happened differently. Tom might have understood him then. He might have said something helpful. But things did not happen that way. The crust of Tacora remained unbroken.

7

Peruvian Notebook No. 2
April 2, 1984

Here is an idea for a novel. It's my old man's story. It is supposed to have been true, although I take nothing he ever told me too seriously. The story is set at the end of the nineteenth century, just after the Pacific War of 1879. It needs some changes, to make it less pathetic. Still, it's a good beginning.

. . . . .

A long time ago, war came to Tarma. As the enemy advanced on the valley, the people fled to the outlying mountains. They stayed in hiding there for fifty-seven days and fifty-eight nights. When they came back, they found their town destroyed. Everything had to be rebuilt. Including the church, the central plaza, and the cemetery. The war had been worse than the plague. Father Cipriano said that because of the collective shock, the children of Tarma might be born bald, the fields might become less productive, and the nights might be longer for years to come.

But not everything had been lost. A few days after their return to Tarma, there appeared in the center of the plaza a lone soldier. His name was José Altamirano Huascar, the only man from Tarma ever to return alive from the southern front. The poor man was deaf, blind, and nearly dead, but he survived. The people of Tarma took the miracle of his return as a sign of better times ahead. They made him an honored citizen and showered him with benefits. José Altamirano Huascar took advantage of his good luck. In a few years, he made a lot of money. He then married Crisostola Mano Guamán, the most beautiful woman in town, and built the biggest house in Tarma. The pink house, with a wide balcony facing the plaza, has been there ever since. In due time, the couple had twins: Ada María and Carlos Alberto.

The children grew up very close. They laughed and cried at the same things. They could even communicate without words. And the people of Tarma say that when they were still very small, they swore never to be apart. As a sign of things to come, Carlos Alberto promised never to marry unless Ada María did first. As it turned out, Ada María grew up to be a shy and retiring woman. She hardly ever left the big house and was mostly seen on her balcony, looking down on the plaza. Carlos Alberto, on the other hand, grew up to be everyone's darling. They say he had beautiful lovers all around the valley. Then—such are the affairs of the heart—he fell in love with Remigia Robles, a frail young woman who lived at the edge of town with her two aunts.

Forgetting his childhood promise, Carlos Alberto proposed marriage. This must have been when the twins were about twenty-five. The lovers began to stroll daily around the plaza. They would walk arm in arm to profess their love in public. Needless to say, the people of Tarma were very happy. They made preparations. They painted the church. They assigned responsibilities for organizing the festivities. They were going to eat, drink, and dance for at least three weeks. The wedding was set for early September, at the beginning of the planting season.

Only Ada María was not happy about the planned wedding. In fact, she was determined to stop it at all costs. She did not want to lose the only man to whom she had ever been close. And the people of Tarma say she used Carlos Alberto's childhood promise to justify herself. And so there followed a series of events that would prevent Remigia and Carlos Alberto from ever marrying each other.

At the end of August, Ada María hanged herself from the balcony of their pink house. She was barely rescued by her servant, doña Pochita, who climbed onto the roof like a cat, despite her advancing years. The wedding had to be pushed back to March, at the end of the harvest. Just before that date, however, Father Cipriano was kidnapped and disappeared for several days. The wedding was postponed again. This time until June. But in May of that year, José Altamirano Huascar died of a heart attack. Given their love for the old man, the town mourned his passing for several years. At the end of that period, Carlos Alberto proclaimed his love for Remigia again and this time he set the wedding for January, in the middle of Tarma's

76

rainy season. He probably thought it would help, somehow. But just as the date approached, Ada María hanged herself again. This time she died. More years of mourning followed. And then, before anyone could even think about a wedding party, Crisostola Mano Guamán de Altamirano died in her sleep. After that, not many years later, the oldest of Remigia's aunts fell out of her bed and died instantly. And on and on.

As time went by, the people of Tarma began to resent the lovers' public displays, in part because it detracted from their enjoyment of all their other birthday parties, baptisms, and weddings. But there was something else: with each new obstacle the people of Tarma began to suspect there were hidden designs in the entire affair. They grew fearful. In time, with every new attempt to set a wedding date, Carlos Alberto came to be seen as a fool bent on doing what was clearly beyond human capacity: to escape the invisible web of El Azar. The people of Tarma did not want to be part of such a foolish endeavor and eventually withdrew their affection altogether. They even stopped saying hello when the lovers took their daily stroll around the plaza.

Carlos Alberto continued to tip his hat and Remigia to nod her head for years. But they must have understood the feelings of the people, for they stopped making wedding plans. They contented themselves with beginning and ending their daily stroll by the large pink house. As was inevitable, things changed around them. Father Cipriano died. A year later, on the anniversary of his death, a strong earthquake shook down his church again. The town took that opportunity to expand. The new church and a companion cemetery were built on a hill overlooking the plaza. The center of town grew crowded. Carlos Alberto's and Remigia's daily stroll became an invisible part of the routine life of the town.

Many years later, on the fiftieth anniversary of their wedding announcement, Carlos Alberto and Remigia linked arms and walked the plaza as usual. She donned a white shawl to protect herself from the cool air and a pink parasol to protect her aging eyes from the setting sun. As for Carlos Alberto, he wore his black suit and his black felt hat. His only concession to the passing of time was the use of a walking stick with a silver handle in the form of a bird. They moved around the plaza with tired steps, surrounded by ever more unfamiliar sounds and smells. Fifty years! he said, at the end of their walk, bending low to be heard. Fifty years! she said, looking up at him, smiling and squeezing his arm as a sign of her devotion.

. . . . .

As far as my old man was concerned, the lovers might still be wasting their lives on their daily routine—a futile gesture against the power of El Azar.

8

Anthony Allday had finished his first round and was back at the security office. It was midnight and time to take a load off his feet. He sat on the metal chair, took off his left shoe, and examined his big toe. It was not terribly swollen. He massaged it, trying to soothe away the pain that extended from the tip of his toe to his heel. Anthony Allday thought that he always found reminders of life's harshness in the smallest things. And yet, as he had written in his Peruvian notebooks years before, often such harshness provided the occasion for experiencing life's sparse gifts.

Anthony Allday thought that when Hannah used to rub his left big toe with her cotton-soft fingers, it seemed he had been born to be spoiled only by her. Hannah was the only woman who had known how to soothe him in that way. Was there a direct connection between identity and intimacy? Rosaura, for example, would never have done that. Not because of shyness or loathing. It simply would not have occurred to her. And Anthony Allday thought that there had been different connections between him and Rosaura. There had been slivers of darkness, of desire, shared between them; there had been a mutual peering into their souls.

What had happened to her? Where might she now be, with her peculiar thick shell, her special mask? Rosaura had invented herself to live a life of obstinate solitude masquerading as patience. What a life! She had convinced herself that her mask would protect her against the daily routine of a miserable existence that was making furrows in her soul. Poor Rosaura. And then, for an instant, riding on a fragment of memory he tried to dodge, Rosaura's face filled his mind. He still missed the woman he had known a lifetime ago.

Anthony Allday let the smell of detergent in the room envelop him. He had never been able to figure out where the smell came from. It seemed to rise from the ground and crawl everywhere. It was a way to make the place shareable, he thought. In America, sterility and comfort went hand-in-hand. Meanwhile, Tom was complaining loudly enough to be heard. He was saying he was tired of his way of life and that one of these days he would leave it all behind to start a new career as a gambler. Life does suck, Tom. But hold on, buddy; the night is almost over.

And Tom: I'm taking off early tonight. Got to get some shut-eye 'cause Gail wants to go Christmas shopping today.

Anthony Allday no longer paid much attention to Tom's complaints. He took his friend's daily protestations as part of a repertoire of histrionics buttressing his ill-chosen identity. He never expected to be taken seriously. At first, not long after their meeting at The Black Cat, Tom would look at Tony out of the corner of his eye, perhaps trying to judge the effects of his antics. But in reality, he just liked to hear himself complain. Watching Tom go through his routine that cursed night, Anthony Allday thought that what was truly tragic, what he was not sure Tom really knew, was that it was now much too late for him to choose to be otherwise. People have only so much energy to make or remake themselves. One has to be practical. Take his case, for example: stupid Genaro was coming *a joderlo todo,* to fuck up everything, as if Anthony could just remake himself on the spot, for him. Stupid Genaro was asking too much.

Antonio Alday Gutiérrez senses his body slumping against the hard vinyl couch and feels compelled to sit up straight. He thinks it ironic that even now, after the dismal deed, good manners are a fundamental aspect of his being. What he initially displayed only in public slowly came to saturate his inner self. A small price paid for becoming a pituco from Miraflores. But there are more important things to worry about now. Is there a direct link between his economical way of thinking—a mental ledger of re-creation efforts—and the events that followed? Is that why he hated the thought of Genaro's visit? Was it because Anthony Allday knew he was going to be asked to reconstruct himself yet again, and knew also that he no longer had the energy for it, that he became a murderer?

Antonio Alday Gutiérrez accepts that Anthony Allday believed it was too late for him to start all over again. In that, he was just like Tom. What el maricón had chosen—God only knew how, when, or why—was also going to determine his road for the rest of his life. And so, slumped in the vinyl couch, watching the light of the winter sun crawling over the wooden floor of his apartment strewn with old newspapers and catalogues, Antonio Alday Gutiérrez accepts that perhaps he became a murderer out of laziness.

Take Ana María. Once she had reconstructed herself as a pious woman she could never have renounced her choice. Not ever. *Se jodió,* she was screwed. She will spend the rest of her life fighting the whole world on behalf of abandoned children, ill-treated prisoners, oppressed grandmothers. . . . She, too, chose badly. And now that she must be past her prime, Antonio Alday Gutiérrez thinks with a strange nostalgia for a woman who had once soured his life, now that she must be an old maid in the stodgy social circles of her precious Lima, who is going to give her some attention, some tenderness? Her willful fight against the world—because it is always the entire world that is twisted and never just a part of it—must have cost her dearly.

Antonio Alday Gutiérrez remembers how, in the brief time they spent together in Barranco—how long ago was it?—he tried to help her, he tried to open her eyes. But he also remembers that in the end, upon his return to America, thinking about their encounter and writing it down in his Peruvian Notebook No. 4, Mr. Anthony Allday came to accept that Ana María must once have chosen, with utter determination, just as he himself had done, to be who she was. Mr. Anthony Allday then had to accept that, having chosen the pattern for her life that way, Ana María had no energy left to reinvent herself and turn her back on herself yet again. No matter how convincing all his arguments might have been, her past choices had already settled in her soul. . . . Tom. Ana María. Anthony Allday. Perhaps they are all the same.

9

Peruvian Notebook No. 4
September 2, 1987

It was nearing eight o'clock in the evening. The ficus and palm trees were ghostly apparitions in the dove-white garúa, the thin drizzle that enveloped Barranco. The old streetlamps bordering the small plaza were umbrellas of light. There was an eerie quiet in the air. The few people who crossed the plaza, in groups or pairs, seemed unusually circumspect. Meanwhile, Anthony Allday was pacing the perimeter of the plaza cloaked in his long London Fog trench coat. He was in Barranco on the advice of the helpful concierge at the Sheraton Hotel who had said Barranco was the Bohemian zone of Lima, a place where one could still enjoy jaranas de guitarra y cajón, the typical Peruvian coastal party scene.

Anthony Allday had never been there before. When he lived in Tacora the city of Barranco was a mythical place: es el Perú jacarandoso, don Luna never tired of repeating: a place blessed by Creole creativity. Its magnificent views of the Pacific, its inviting corner bars, its dark little theaters, its distance from the oppressive eyes and ears of Lima, have created a unique place, Toño. A place that has inspired the best Peruvian poets, playwrights, and composers. ¡Por mi madre! Felipe Pinglo and Chabuca Granda, the Great Ones, drank from its creative well, Toño. One day we'll perform there. One day we're going to be famous, too. ¿No? . . . No. The Antonio Allday Gutiérrez of Tacora never got there. He had neither the money nor the opportunity. Barranco was another Peruvian myth he had had to leave behind.

Anthony Allday decided to walk down an ancient cobblestone path on the southwest corner of the plaza. The path was wide and flanked by large uneven stones. It curved west until it became a set of stairs leading to a bridge set over a deep gorge. In the old days, according to song, the gorge had cradled a whispering brook and the bridge was known as El Puente de los Suspiros, the Bridge of Sighs.

But in the twilight of that day, suspended in midair, seemingly by the dove-white garúa, the gorge and its bridge were merely silent.

Don Luna once asked Toño to commit to memory the Creole waltzes celebrating the mythical river and its bridge. Some day we'll perform them there, Toño, he said. We'll dance on the bridge after our triumph. That's a promise.

And Betti: It's in my blood, Toño. Look at me! I'm the flor de la canela! I'm the woman who will walk down that path, enveloped in the light of dawn and dusk, for all of eternity. You are my chalán, my swain on horseback! Stand up straight, caballero! . . . That was so long ago, sighed Anthony Allday. The few words of the waltzes he could still remember had survived in him disjointed and dispirited. Echoes of a poor and naïve life.

Two streams of light flanked the bottom of the gorge. They dimmed in the distance as they neared the cliffs over the Pacific. Standing in the middle of the bridge, Anthony Allday could see the sinuous trunks of the ancient ficus trees clinging to the rocky sides of the gorge. Across the bridge and up a gentle slope perched a small white church. To its right, in the direction of the Andes, a row of restaurants was getting ready to open. Young women in white shirts and black pants lit torches, arranged chairs, and shook table linens into the darkness. Closer to the bridge, a few men had stopped to gaze at the moon rising over the Andes. It looked bright and round in its unexpectedly clear patch of sky.

Anthony Allday crossed the Bridge of Sighs and turned left, towards the ocean. He stepped down a set of cement stairs to a gravel path. The crunch under his feet lessened the forlorn quality of the place. He raised the collar of his trench coat. Every now and then along the path, lovers emerged from the garúa. They shared their warmth under cotton coats or alpaca ponchos. They seemed to float in the garúa and the silence of the gorge. Anthony Allday could almost hear their eager whispers promising eternal love. The path ended abruptly on a lookout protected by a low stone wall. On a clear day one could probably see the ocean from there, but now he could only hear the breaking of distant waves.

On that lookout, Anthony Allday let himself be swept away by a strange and fleeting desire: to ride the ceaseless rhythm of the waves and let his mind fold over itself as he retraced the steps of his life in Peru. If he could do that, he might relive some forgotten happy moment. It might be something to take with him to his welcome yet interminable exile. He rode the unremitting playfulness of the waves, wishing with all his heart to remember. But nothing remotely pleasant came to him. The sound of the ocean only made him feel ill at ease, and he realized then that whatever promise it offered of unlocking happy secrets of the past, it was something that he, Mr. Anthony Allday, an American tourist in Peru, could never receive.

Anthony Allday returned to the plaza with a heavy heart, feeling disconnected. But he did not wish to spoil his evening completely, so he decided to look for the Manos Morenas restaurant. Your best bet, Mr. Allday, the helpful concierge had said. One of the few places left where Creole and Afro-Peruvian jaranas are still being made a pie calato, con guitarra y cajón, barefoot, with guitar and cajón, sir. A place that'll bring you back to the good old days, when Lima was the envy of the Americas and people still traveled by carriage or tramway, not like the old, rusted, smoke-spewing buses in use today, a time when Lima wasn't yet inundated by the cholos who came down from the mountains like a waico, a mudslide, to spoil everything, sir, if you don't mind my saying so. Just take a taxi. Here, I can hail one for you, sir. Hey, you! Come on over here! In Barranco, ask someone for directions, sir. Can't miss it.

It was clear Manos Morenas catered mostly to tourists and their Peruvian hosts. It was furnished to resemble an establishment from the colonial past. The massive outer walls were made of adobe and painted in an earthy yellow with broad and well-defined white stripes on their middle and upper sections. A black iron gate led to a small but carefully manicured interior garden: a dwarf fig tree in each corner, sculptured red and purple bougainvilleas in its center, creeping grass bordering a path of large red ceramic tiles. Two large windows protected by arabesque ironwork and wisteria let some light into the interior of the main building. The front door, dark and set at the west corner of the garden, was made of thick planks of rough mahogany with rustic black iron hinges.

The interior itself, including the large foyer and reception room, had whitewashed adobe walls accented with dark wooden strips of old supporting beams. From the foyer he could see another room now illuminated only by the gray evening sky showing through a skylight.

On the far right, some distance from the foyer, old corner lamps sent subdued amber light into a large semicircular hall where several large tables and chairs of wood and leather surrounded a small proscenium. Old Peruvian horse saddles, wooden stirrups, pitchforks, and other farm tools hung from the wooden beams embedded in the whitewashed walls. Old porongos, large earthen pots, rested against the corners. Black-and-white drawings and prints of Tapadas, veiled women of the old Lima, fighting cocks, and black folk engaged in daily activities, were dispersed throughout. The hosts, waiters, and waitresses, were all Afro-Peruvian and dressed in colonial fashion: the men sported mid-calf-length white cotton pants secured at the waist with a red cotton scarf and unbuttoned cotton shirts. The women wore bulky skirts and colorful turbans. They were all barefoot.

10

I just had a dream about Betti. She was playing Cleopatra, in Houston. I was in the audience, with Alex Sosa. She stepped off the stage to whisper to him that I was a really bad actor and that he should not give me more work. She said I was a better bullfighter, then went back onstage. I wanted to call out to her, but I knew she would not hear me because the audience was giving her an ovation. I looked at Alex Sosa. He was crying.

I wonder how she must be doing.

It's 4:00 a.m.

It's cold.

11

It was 9:30 p.m. and the Afro-Peruvian dance revue was set to begin at eleven. The host informed him that, unfortunately, there was no seating for singles available that evening. She offered him a place reserved for guests who would be arriving for the performance. Not wanting to give up and leave, Anthony Allday accepted and was led to a large table next to the stage. He ordered a piqueo—hors d'oeuvres of deep-fried yucca, deep-fried pork, spicy chicken and beef, deep-fried plantains, black olives, salted corn nuts, and anticuchos, beef heart on a skewer bathed in a hot cilantro sauce. A waitress brought him a large complimentary pisco sour.

Anthony Allday enjoyed the time he spent savoring the piqueo and sipping his pisco sour. The night might be saved after all. He examined the ceiling with its tarred eucalyptus beams. He took a closer look at the large prints depicting life among the black folk during colonial times and La Tapada—by legend the black lover of the Spanish viceroy of Lima, in his time one of the most powerful men of the Americas. He felt at home in the culture that surrounded him but, at the same time, he experienced a palpable distance from it. He absorbed again the sights, smells, and tastes that had saturated his Peruvian past and yet did not feel choked and trapped, held back, by a life he had so desperately wished to leave behind.

Ana María arrived at about ten, earlier than anticipated. She was accompanied by four young women. Her friends were dressed noticeably better than she and carried themselves with desparpajo, a pertness typical of the pitucos from Miraflores. It was apparent they had dragged Ana María there to show her a good time. Even under the faint amber light of the hall, the woman had a very sullen look, as if she had been dogged by an unhappy experience for a long time. She did not smile as readily as her friends when they engaged her in light conversation and overall seemed uncomfortable at finding herself there. Her shoulders bowed down under a light lúcuma-colored alpaca shawl. Her delicate fingers curled into soft fists, which she kept on the table, showing from under her shawl like weapons. She kept her eyes straight ahead and at chest level. Despite all of that, Anthony Allday believed it a good thing that the host had offered him a seat at her table and that she and her friends had acquiesced.

As the night wore on, Anthony Allday came to appreciate Ana María more. She was in fact delicate but not fragile; she was courteous but not stiff; unlike her friends, who carried themselves like pitucas for whose pleasure Peru, the world, is never enough, to whom everything and everyone around them is always beneath concern, and for whom life is so hard they need to distract themselves with banal activities—¡ay! ¡si fuésemos pobres siquiera! if only we were poor! Ana Maria had a soft dimple in her left cheek that accentuated her timid smile. And yet—a sign of things to come—when she spoke, she did so with utter conviction. She gave the impression of being in possession of extraordinary forces which she might unleash at any moment.

Animated by the pisco sours the friends began talking freely, ignoring their unintended guest. They laughed at shared embarrassing stories, repeated personal conversations with abundant detail, and laughed conspiratorially at the tourists who surrounded them. They guessed their nationalities and tried listing the good and bad aspects of the French, Italians, Moroccans, or Americans as writers, lovers, or cooks. Anthony Allday felt uncomfortable. Not because he felt he was a part of their pituco game as the tourist he already was, but because it reminded him of a pastime he had abhorred even in his youth: judging others without knowing them. Not everyone in Tacora was a pimp or a prostitute, as most people in Lima thought. Not everyone there was resigned to live and die in its muddy callejones. There were others, like his old man, who worked hard to get ahead, against all odds. . . . Anthony Allday was about to excuse himself and leave. But just then, Ana Maria tossed him the bone of inclusion: What do you think, Mr. Allday? It's surely not all true, right? We are often much too quick to judge. And Ana María suffered the hiss of her friends. She seemed a sensitive person after all.

But her sensitivity did not last. Zigzagging through discussions of gourmet experiences, new poems, dress styles, love affairs, and unforgettable parties, the friends came around to the topic of Latin American politics. The young woman across from Mr. Allday, dressed in a tight black turtleneck and wearing a choker of diminutive pearls, started what she called an all-inclusive list of Latin American caudillos huachafos, low-class and uncultured dictators. She included Fidel Castro among them. At that moment, and for the first time that evening, Ana María seemed energized. She defended the bearded revolutionary vehemently, claiming that when all was said and done, the vexing problems of Peru would only be solved by the implementation of a socialist regime. Perhaps with regret at having conjured up Ana María's foolhardiness, her friends hissed, chuckled, and tried to change the topic. But Ana María would not budge. She went on to praise the socialist experiment as if she were in possession of self-evident truths. And then: What do you think, Mr. Allday? Even though a Yankee, you must surely have some common sense, right?

In the beginning, the disagreements between Mr. Allday and Ana María were offered with the expected courtesy. As the conversation went on, however, it became impossible for them to maintain the charade. With the Afro-Peruvian singers and dancers performing their typical repertoire surrounded by tables full of happy tourists and their guests, the conversation between Mr. Allday and Ana María turned more and more truculent. Each was now attempting to defeat an articulate and stubborn but utterly mistaken adversary. Ana María's delicate face had gained color under the faint amber lights. Her hazel eyes had opened wide. Her tireless lips curled and flapped and her nostrils quivered as the smoke from cigars and cigarettes filled the hall with an ashen hue. The woman was impossible.

Mr. Allday knew the woman was utterly mistaken, of course, in believing that Cuban socialism was the only answer to Peru's problems; that charity, when correctly understood, makes of every Christian a progressive militant; that to think about the poor means to think not only of workers out of work but of abandoned women, of old people living in squalor, of decaying buildings, of paperboys, of shoeshiners, of girl servants, of married women with abusive husbands. Rubbish. An absolute misunderstanding of things, since the capitalist system helps the most productive members of society to get ahead so that everyone, even the lazy and undeserving, can eventually be better off; since each one of us, even the weakest, is responsible for his acts; since there will always be the poor in the world and it is not always someone else's fault; since we can all reconstruct ourselves to live a new life!

Antonio Alday Gutiérrez pauses. He turns back the brittle page of the notebook and looks again at the date of the entry: September 2, 1987. He lets the notebook close and wonders whether he had truly managed to convince himself he was an American tourist and whether the anger in those pages was real. Was it pure fiction? He shakes his head, feeling the light streaming in, and murmurs: it's all the same. He still feels animosity. Even now. . . . He begins reading again.

A strange meeting, indeed. They both knew they were not going to convince each other, so both embraced their vehemence. They both knew they would never see each other again, so both set aside all courtesy to have the last word. It seemed that El Azar had brought them together so they could explain their truths to themselves, one more time, since those around them were either unable or unwilling to hear them. Mr. Allday felt the gaze, the words, the gestures of that woman injuring him. And he made the exchange personal: You will never be happy thinking that way, you will always find something or somebody to make you unhappy, and there will always be those around you who would say that you dream only so as not to see yourself as you truly are: a woman who seeks to spoil the little goodness there is in life in order to feel at home under your skin!

Mr. Allday had wanted to be cruel. Had she not been cruel to him first? Had she not thrown her truths in his face? An inauthentic life is worth little, Mr. Allday, she had hissed. Turning one's back on one's people by fleeing abroad, like los gusanos, the worms that fled to Miami; or by living in luxury behind barbed wire, like many of us here; is sheer cowardice, don't you think? No one could ever be happy without recognizing his origins and getting closer to those who are of value in his life. Those who triumph under capitalism sell their souls for un plato de lentejas, a plate of beans. In the end, such cowards end up utterly alone, without the love of disinterested people. They die without even forgiveness, because they do not know how to ask for it! . . . Of course, Mr. Allday knew Ana María Corvacho y Muñoz was not pointing her accusing finger at him. But what did that matter? The pituca's "truths" were meant to hurt. He had to defend himself.

When the performance ended and the public applauded with brio, Mr. Allday could only manage to pretend to clear the detritus on his side of the table. That woman had been the last straw in his awful night. And to top it off, she dared to tap his arm gently as a gesture of maternal piety and reconciliation. ¡Carajo! As if he had been a poor abandoned man in search of solace! As if he had been one of her charges! And her friends? Enjoying themselves. Pretending not to notice, of course; but enjoying the unfair exchange between Mr. Allday, a man who was trying to succeed in a foreign country, paying dearly for every little thing he could get, and their old bitchy friend who had finally found a patsy to put down in order to replenish the air of superiority about her, and all because she considered herself a woman with a good heart!

Anthony Allday returned to the Sheraton Hotel to spend his third night in Lima. When he looked at himself in the mirror with the gilded frame in his room on the tenth floor, he felt such disgust for everything Peruvian that he wished nothing more than to leave that country full of crazy and stupid people. Yes. Anthony Allday left the country three days before the end of the week he had planned for his stay in his old world. That was why he ended up with money left over and could afford to buy the huacos from Cosme Salvatierra, a young artist who did know the value of the freedom of expression promoted and protected by the ebb and flow of the free market. In a socialist society, thought Anthony Allday as he stood before the mirror with the gilded frame, in Fidel's utopia, it would be impossible for anyone to reconstruct himself as he pleased. The Socialist New Man is a man cut to size by people like Ana María.

Strange, thinks Antonio Alday Gutiérrez, at 1:20 P.M., feeling at once sad and annoyed by the memory of Ana María, strange that after all that time he still feels animosity towards her. God only knows where she might be now. Lost, perhaps. Alone. Like him. Who knows? Had he listened to her, had he let himself be influenced in a minimal way by her zeal, perhaps El Azar would have played a different trick on him and he might not have become a murderer. Who knows. Perhaps. Setting aside his notebook again, Antonio Alday Gutiérrez gazes at the dark lines on his hands for a long time. When he lifts his eyes he sees a patch of blue in the afternoon sky. He sighs and lets a feeling of regret cross his heart.

12

Anthony Allday checked the time on the metal wall clock: 2:00 A.M. Tom was stretched out in his chair, his shirt partially unbuttoned and his feet resting on a stack of fall catalogues. He was reading a Tom Clancy novel. Anthony Allday stood beside him and cleared his throat. It was time for him to begin his second round. This time he would go to the north end of the mall and check the cargo entrance. I'm on my way, Tom. Would you like me to bring you some coffee? Tom shook his head without looking up. Anthony Allday put on his cap, straightened his black tie, and went out.

The lights of the main walkways were low and cast no shadows. The gaiety of the earlier hours had been replaced by an eerie quiet. Suddenly enveloped in the artificial penumbra, Anthony Allday thought that the mall, a monument to the American sense of comfort, was now oddly filled with an air of desert, of muddy riverbanks, of a religious procession. He began walking, and his steps resonated as in an empty chamber. The narrow path of black-and-white floor tile disappearing in the bends of the long halls conveyed a sense of mystery. He heard the faint hum from invisible heating vents. Up above, in corners, video cameras moved from side to side, tirelessly.

She chose to be the same, Anthony Allday said to himself that cursed morning, thinking about his mother. No one said she had to put up with don Juan's temper. No one said she had to hide behind her youngest son whenever her husband came home drunk and foaming at the mouth. That had bothered him most about his mother: that she had hid behind him when she was afraid of the old man; a stupid old man who had spent his life thrashing about, lying or being lied to by everyone. He was no businessman! All he wanted was to have a few pennies in his pocket and to fuck any highlander girl who arrived in La Parada. Hiding behind her youngest son, his mother would swear that all she wanted was to be obedient, humble, constant, eternally Sra. Gloria Gutiérrez Bayle de Alday, wife and mother.

That was the reason Anthony Allday had not wanted to see her ever again. He had not even pitied her, carajo! On the contrary. He had always felt blind resentment because she had let herself be intimidated by the old man. Not like Anthony Allday, the night watchman at the Springfield Mall, who would not be cowed by anyone. Not even Tom. When he discovered Tom's secret, he set him straight: As for last night, Tom, I had a good time. It was good to see you there. And let me tell you something: I'm bothered by very few things. I believe that each one of us has the right to choose who and how to be. As for those who think otherwise, to hell with them! Right? A man does not only have to do what he has to do—he also has to be who he has to be. From then on, Anthony Allday convinced himself, feeling the Smith & Wesson .38 against his leg, they had been friends. They now regarded each other with a measure of respect. No, carajo, Mr. Anthony Allday was not going to tolerate superior looks from anyone, and especially not from Tom.

Not that he believed everyone could attain what he had. He well knew there were Peruvians, Italians, Mexicans, Salvadorans, Greeks, immigrants from all over who were incapable of even conceiving of the possibility of reinventing themselves in their new sitio. They clung tightly to the comfort of their races, their cultures, their names, their poor man's dreams. The Latin Americans got together in their barrios to get drunk and listen to *huaynos,* cuecas, tangos, salsas, *pasillos,* to cry like abandoned babies. And when they could return to their old cities and towns, they did so sighing. Ay! I have missed all this so much! If I could only stay here forever.

Anthony Allday didn't do any of that. No, sir. He stood firm. For years. Far away. He never allowed himself sighs of nostalgia. And when he returned to Peru, he did it as a new man, carajo! He returned knowing that Lima, Delaware Country, Pennsylvania, was his true sitio, with not even a hint of fear that he might wish to stay in the shit hole that was the other Lima. Yes, carajo! My new sitio, said Anthony Allday to himself, even if it's only this mall, with its odd smell of muddy riverbank, of religious procession. After all, what Peruvian wouldn't wish to work here and be surrounded by these beautiful things, in a cozy environment, without drastic changes in light or temperature to unsettle the body, the mind!

The sound of Anthony Allday's footsteps seemed to float in the empty halls. When he arrived at the very center of the mall, he looked up through the wide glass skylight. He could not see the stars. He somehow knew it was about to snow.

13

Peruvian Notebook No. 2
January 8, 1984

Toñito did not feel well the night before. He was afraid. The idea of going to the beach on a school outing alarmed him. Señorita Cristiana had reassured him that the beach was beautiful and peaceful. But he was afraid that the ocean, which up till then he had seen only in books and movies, would envelop him and take him away. That night Toñito dreamed of very high waves. They were rasped, transparent curtains hiding a million minuscule tentacles ready to grab him. When the waves tumbled and hit the sand of the beach, they dug up mud, worms, old books, and thousands upon thousands of glassy dead fish eyes.

Pucusana was not like that. Rather it was a very nice, clean summer resort. In fact, it was the cleanest place Toñito had ever seen. The sand was golden yellow, the low wind fresh, the sky open and blue. The beach was punctuated by red-and-white striped canvas changing tents. They could be rented for half a sol. Vendors walked on the beach with difficulty, their feet digging deep into the warm sand. There were kites of all colors tied to posts by the tents, their long tails fluttering in the breeze. When the children from Colegio Nacional No. 412 arrived in Pucusana in the plum-colored bus that Señorita Cristiana had borrowed from a friend, it seemed that the entire place was an open fair.

The other children went around laughing and chasing each other, but Toñito preferred to stand at the edge of the ocean and feel the sandy water tickling his toes. He was happy to notice that the air there was warm and soft, that it smelled and tasted different—pure. Toñito filled his lungs with delight, thinking about his mother. She would have liked that air, because she always said she only liked the night and morning air of Tacora. She said she didn't like the midday air there, because it tasted too much like mud and smoke. Standing at the very edge of the ocean, Toñito now saw a fat lady walking with difficulty on the sand. He pitied her, although he could see she was carrying a basketful of turrones on her head. She set the basket down and children came from everywhere to buy her sweets. Toñito now felt happy for her. Nearby, the seagulls played so close to him he could almost touch them. Not like in Tacora, where the sparrows stayed far away from everyone. He liked the ocean and everything there.

But not everything was well with Toñito that day. Even as he stood at the edge of the ocean, he was trying hard to ignore the waves of pain shooting through his body. The pains had actually started the night before. He had told his mother then that they would begin in his chest and cascade down to his stomach. It feels awful, Mamá. I don't think I should go tomorrow. I don't want to go! But his mother would not hear of it, not even that morning. She reassured him that it was only el vaso, that he had upset his stomach by running around after his sister on a full stomach. You'll have lots of fun in Pucusana, Toño; don't be a marica, a sissy. El vaso, thought Toñito, where would it be? Maybe right here, in the middle of the chest. As he stood at the edge of the ocean, he was feeling that with each new wave, the pains grew stronger. They came without fail, over and over again, like the waves of his dream. And now the golden yellow sand burned his face, the low wind made him nauseated, the sound of the birds made him dizzy. Toñito did not want to be a marica. He held on. He held on. Until lunchtime.

He went to sit down in the shade of the bus, because its doors were locked. Sitting there, looking out over the sandy beach, with his back against a huge tire, he began to miss home. He missed his mother, even though she had sent him off as if nothing had been wrong with him, earlier that morning, before he was even fully awake. He missed her, because she still let him climb into her bed. And she often said he was her favorite child. He missed Ricardo, too, thinking it was too bad he couldn't come to Pucusana because he was already too old. He would have held his hand and told him that things were going to pass. He had always done that when Toñito was sick with the flu, and even when he was scared after watching the movies at El Paraíso. He didn't want to miss Carmen, because she pulled on his ears whenever she wanted and called him mariconsito, little sissy. She was always mean to him. She even told him he was not her mother's son. That he had been found, lost, in La Parada.

That wasn't true, of course. He knew that. She was just mean. He missed his father more than anyone. As the waves of pain came and went, Toñito imagined don Juan Alday Alzamora tousling his hair, telling him that the pain was going to go away. He missed his dark hands that smelled of cigarette smoke. . . . And the pain that would not go away.

Alcázar, the son of the cop Quispe, came to sit with him. Maybe he came to give him courage, to keep him company, since he saw Toñito was totally alone. He sat in the shade with a bag full of muy-muys he had collected from the water's edge. The poor little critters were in a frenzy, moving their little antennae and rubbing their hard shells against the brown paper, trying to find a hole to escape through and run away, into the water. Alcázar—everyone called him that, even though it was really his mother's surname—told him he had brought him something to lift his spirits. He took one of the muy-muys from the brown bag and showed it to Toñito, smiling. He then used his right thumbnail to take the muy-muy's shell right off its body. The poor animal flayed its numerous tiny legs in all directions. He was trying to escape. But Alcázar had already killed it. A dark and slimy liquid ran down his hands. Alcázar was now laughing, looking at Toñito for approval. At that moment, Toñito felt the full fury of the waves breaking in his head: Blum! Whoosh! Blum! . . . He tried with all his will, but he couldn't hold on. He hurled against the bus tire. And with the pain and the exertion of vomiting, Toñito let his bowels loose and soiled his pants and shoes.

Alcázar ran out from under the bus to tell everyone what had just happened. At first he seemed concerned for Toñito. But then, as the other children approached to see what had happened, his attitude changed. He yelled out that Toñito had made number two in his pants because he had gotten scared by a little muy-muy. Look! Look! ¡Se ha hecho la caca! he said, pointing at Toñito's soiled pants. Se hace el dos por las puras. He's a sissy. And then all the children stood in a line on the sunny beach looking at Toñito curled up in the shade.

Toñito closed his eyes. He wanted to disappear from the world forever. Even if he would never see his mother again, even if he would never grow up to drive his father's car.

14

It's about to snow, thought Anthony Allday, continuing on his second round. The whole world will be white, clean, soft. The sky will be blue again. There are no skies like that in Tacora. There, the sky is always a dark gray. Everything is gray. Even in summer. Gray, the walls. Gray, the cement sidewalks. Gray, the faces of the people. One had to go far to see the clear blue coastal sky. As far away as Pucusana. But places like Pucusana were resort towns, and the people of Tacora never took vacations. That was why, in time, when the people of places like La Estrella couldn't turn around in their compounds without bumping into each other, they fled into the gray foothills of the Andes, into the surrounding desert, to face the westerly winds. That was how Canto Grande was born.

That must have been when and why those cojudos left not only La Estrella but Tacora itself, Anthony Allday said to himself, thinking about his brother and sister that cursed morning. Or, rather, that must have been how they justified their forbidden desire to continue to live together. Because they will never grow apart. They will never allow anyone to come between them. Tacora will never leave their souls.

Antonio Alday Gutiérrez tries to stop his recollection of Anthony Allday's thoughts that cursed morning. He knows they will only lead him to memories best left undisturbed. But it is too late now. In his feverish fatigue, his thoughts twist and turn until they lead directly to what he wrote down in his Peruvian Notebook No. 4, sitting on this same yellow couch, nine years ago. It was to be the first chapter of his first novel. Back then, in 1986, Anthony Allday still believed he could be an honest and therefore a good writer. And what could be more propitious to his writing success than the story of Ricardo and Carmencita, honestly told?

15

Peruvian Notebook No. 4
November 4, 1986

It was only kids' stuff, Ricardo tried to convince himself, looking over the family's new plot of land in the gray desert. Of course they were close, but with total innocence. Toño had no reason to think ill of them. No era para tanto. He certainly had no reason first to sulk about it and then to disappear into thin air. But, of course, Toño had always been kind of strange. Since he was a baby. Maybe he was just jealous.

It was true that between himself and Carmencita there had always existed a strong bond, a tie that had protected them against all the bad things that life threw their way. Like now, even: looking for a little plot of desert, with Mamá in tow—she, always looking inward, lamenting for herself, day and night, calling out for el cojudo who is God only knows where doing God only knows what. We're not even that far apart in age, thought Ricardo, his big black eyes panning the surrounding bare, gray hills—less than four years apart. ¡No, carajo! They had done nothing wrong. Toño was always too suspicious. He walked about as if the whole world were about to betray him. It was nothing.

Ricardo called Carmencita to his side.

La Carmen let her chestnut hair grow long. It fell down her back in natural curls. Her narrow waist seemed about to break every morning, as she smoothed her hair, standing before the mirror. She had full rosy lips. Her teeth were dainty, even, and very white. Her eyes, almond shaped and light brown, seemed always to be smiling. She moved her delicate hands in soft motions, just like her mother. Her voice was low and raspy and her words rolled out of her mouth at once distinct and enigmatic. La Carmen was always calm, never hurried. It seemed as though, at twenty-three, she had already found whatever it was that would make her happy for the rest of her life.

Even though she was four years older, she looked like Ricardo's twin. She now stood beside her brother and put her arm around his shoulders. And Ricardo thought she smelled of yerbabuena, orange mint. He thought her warm breath was as dry as the desert. She said she had been carting things about, getting ready to start building their new home.

We've got to end this, said Ricardo, freeing himself from her embrace. We've got to move on, Carmencita. La Carmen smiled. She tousled his hair tenderly and said that it was time to divide up the plot. And they felt so happy tracing the lines for their new bedrooms in that desert! It was so good to know they would finally be able to leave the callejón, La Estrella, behind. Isn't it so, Carmencita! Even if we're the only ones accompanying Mamá. The poor viejita, getting older by the minute, bent over by the weight of her pain over el cojudo Toño's disappearance. What a bastard! No?

The sun was rising over the squat, bare hills that surrounded the dry valley of Canto Grande. To the west, closer to the center of Lima, the reed-mat huts of earlier settlers looked flat against the horizon as the morning sun bathed them with golden light. The sound of desolate desert still lingered in the clear, crisp morning air. But the sky was already a pale blue.

La Carmen paused in her labor. She put both hands on her hips and told Ricardo that perhaps there was no need to make so much space for the future living room. Maybe we should plan for a bigger kitchen, Ricardo. What d'ya think?

No, Carmencita, answered Ricardo, looking into her smiling eyes. We need to leave a large enough spot for the living room, in case we decide to start a new store. Because, as you well know, Carmencita, the family has always been in business. Since before we arrived in Lima. Since before Toño left us high and dry by selling the Chevy and all the other things, then gotten himself lost. We've got to start again, Carmencita. We've got to do it for Mamá's sake. We can't expect the poor vieja to spend the rest of her days in the market, selling spoiled fruit to the newcomers from the highlands. We've got to do something about that, right?

Ricardo did not tell La Carmen how much he hated Toño for selling the Chevy and disappearing. He sure could have used that money right now! He hadn't told anyone about the hatred that continued chewing at his insides and keeping him awake at night. Not even

Carmencita. The idiot! Selling the Chevy to none other than the cop Quispe! How could I even threaten him to get the car back? Now the son of a bitch parades around Tacora as if he were a pituco from Miraflores. ¡Chucha! And the worst thing is that no one has the slightest idea where el cojudo has gone. Not even don Luna or the other blacks from the theater who were always singing his praises. Now even they walk about with tight lips. Why? It's as if everyone in Tacora is glad he's gone away. Maybe he robbed them too. It had to be. El cojudo pulled the wool over everyone's eyes. Everyone got suckered by his baby face, his meek demeanor, his maricón gestures! He sold even the mechanic's toolbox, which would have fetched some real money to buy the esteras, the reed mats, for the hut, until they could make bricks ¡carajo! in this fucking desert!

What the hell! Ricardo shook off the poisonous feelings. He's gone and there is nothing anyone can do about that. Besides, Mamá is already forgetting him, little by little. She even seems rejuvenated since we decided to join in the settling of this piece of desert. Here she can at least breathe clean air. Best of all, though, she'll no longer have to worry about the thieves, the pimps, the destitute, the sick, the crazy people of Tacora. Where in hell might he be? They say he might have gone to Los Estados, the States. Impossible! It's so far away. I hope he wasn't killed by the coyotes. And Ricardo again scanned the bare hills with his big black eyes: Where do you think Toño is, Carmen? Let's hope he's not screwed up somewhere. Suffering. No?

And La Carmen, looking at him with infinite love: I'm sure he's fine, my dear. Who knows, maybe he's making it big in Gringolandia. He'll be all right, Ricardo. He's too savvy not to. Really. You worry too much.

It's not true, thought Ricardo. People said those things to warm la vieja's heart. Like Betti, for example. She came over just the other night to tell the old lady that Toño had gone to Gringolandia through Mexico, that he had wanted to go there to find work as an actor. Because as you know, doña Gloria, everyone in Tacora, including don Luna, says he was the best actor of the barrio, ever. So, you see, I'm happy for him, doña Gloria. ¡Mentiras! All lies! If Toño tried going there it must have been because someone pulled the wool over his eyes. What with so many people dying on their way to Los Estados! . . . But, of course, it was better not to tell la vieja anything about that. It was better to let her think that her Toñito might be a hit among the gringos, that he would come back healthy and rich someday. Even though the gringos probably don't give a damn about his acting.

Do you think we ought to paint the border stones white, Carmencita?

And La Carmen: of course, Ricardo. One can never be too cautious. The cholos and the Indians may not steal as much as the blacks do, but still, one never knows. And Ricardo thought that, weighing everything, el cojudo was definitely not coming back. It was better that way. If he made it, they wouldn't have to suffer his strutting about like a peacock. And if he failed, he would not come back to tell everyone how he had fucked up.

We need to finish before it gets dark, Carmencita. And perhaps we should set aside a piece of the lot for Toño, in case he comes back. What do you think?

La Carmen looked at him sweetly: You're always thinking about him, Ricardo. Perhaps. . . . No, no. Better not. There isn't enough room. . . . Look, if Toño comes back, I'll give him my room and I'll stay in your room with you.

And Ricardo thought he had to do something to change his life. He did not want Canto Grande to be another Tacora.

16

At 1:30 P.M. Antonio Alday Gutiérrez remembers that the Elmwood Avenue branch of the Providence Public Library was near Roger Williams Park. In its heyday, Elmwood Avenue had been a main artery of the city. It had a trolley line that connected the western suburbs with downtown. Near the park, it was lined with tall elm trees and large Victorian mansions overlooking woods and a lake. But things began to change after the Great War. As jewelry factories and small businesses moved into the area, the old residents retreated to the exclusive shores of Newport, Jamestown, and Bonnet Shores. Irish and Italian immigrants moved in to take their place. Brownstone Catholic churches contributed to the drab, industrial look of the city. Things changed yet again in the mid-1970s. Pushed out of downtown by crime and poverty, large numbers of blacks, Puerto Ricans, and Dominicans moved west. Some of the big old houses along Baker and Rugby streets were subdivided into apartments. During that time Brown University expanded into the Portuguese neighborhood on Fox Point. Most of the poorest Portuguese families ended up in New Bedford, Massachusetts, but a few moved into the area around Roger Williams Park. Among them were friends of Alex Sosa's.

In the summer of 1975 Alex Sosa moved down from New Bedford to Providence. He rented an apartment on Baker Street on the advice of one of his old friends, who now worked as a floor manager in a jewelry factory. The narrow street, bordered by thick privets and shaded by tall sycamore trees, lay over a gentle hill that connected Broad Street on the west with Eddy Street on the east. His two-bedroom apartment was on the third floor of a large Victorian house that stood at the very crest of the hill. It had three wide dormers that overlooked the city in all directions. On a clear day, facing east, one could see Narraganset Bay. Alex Sosa also rented space in a parking lot five houses down, near Eddy Street. He would eventually keep his long black hearse there.

A year later, in the summer of 1976, Antonio Allday came to visit and Alex Sosa convinced him to stay a while. Since poor Antonio had little money, Alex Sosa let him use the smaller of the two bedrooms for free. Antonio lived there until he left New England for good, in 1984.

Those eight years would be crucial for the development of Mr. Anthony Allday.

Alex Sosa started his own housepainting business in 1979. He carried his ladders and all his other painting equipment in the long hearse. Antonio Allday, whom Alex Sosa had begun calling Tony, became his de facto associate. They would spend most days and many nights together, except for the occasions when Alex Sosa would drive his hearse to the permanent fair at Roger Williams Park, where Cheryl, his fiancée, worked as a cashier. During those times Antonio Allday would spend hours reading at the library.

The Elmwood Avenue branch of the Providence Public Library was housed in a converted Victorian mansion, the main entrance set far back from the avenue. From its layout, it was clear that in its glory days the house had been surrounded by ample gardens. It was now encircled by a parking lot. The building had three full floors and its roof was made of copper. In winter, when the sun set over Roger Williams Park and its rays filtered through the sparse evergreens, the roof took on a reddish glow.

The library's imposing wooden front door was framed by thick pillars and a lintel painted white. The door led to an ample foyer with two large mirrors on either side. The foyer had a smaller wooden door, which opened to a reception area next to the main hall. Every piece of furniture and all the wood decorations were made of chestnut or mahogany. The tall arched windows were protected by dark red drapes tied back with golden ropes. There were several long, wide tables with heavy wooden chairs. There were reading lamps on all the tables. The walls were covered with books. A large American flag and the white Rhode Island state flag stood in opposite corners. To the left of the main hall, close to the foyer, sat the elevated and rather small reception counter. From near the counter one could see a set of stairs with lustrous mahogany banisters, spiraling to the second floor. Overhead, a narrow balcony with small tables and chairs along its railing cut the view of the upper stacks in two. Beyond the balcony there were rows upon rows of books. Not the smallest space was wasted. Antonio Allday had never seen anything like it.

In January of 1977 there were several breaks in the friends' work routine. It was deep winter and jobs were scarce. Alex Sosa took advantage of the free days to sleep late and spend his afternoons with Cheryl.

Antonio would join them, but only for a while, because their love talk made him feel lonely. Since he had not developed a liking for outdoor activities, he ended up with a lot of free time on his hands. That was how it came to pass that Antonio Allday ended up at the Elmwood Avenue branch of the Providence Public Library.

It seems so long ago, thinks Antonio Alday Gutiérrez, letting his memories awaken the fading but still distinct smells of New England and its old library books. I wonder if all of it remains the same.

One day, Alex Sosa came to Tony's room to tell him he had found a small job at an old mansion that was now a library. They say they teach good English there, Tony. There are books like you can't imagine. And best of all, Tony, they don't tell La Migra anything. Cheryl says they even lend books out to anyone. That's another thing, though. Got to be careful, 'cause they'd have to take your picture. Got to be careful. But Antonio didn't get to see the inside of the library while they worked there. They had been asked to paint only the section by the service platform. And so on each of the four days that the job lasted, as Alex Sosa's hearse left the parking lot at the rear, Antonio would look at the front entrance with curiosity and trepidation. Were he to go in there, it would be his first time inside an official place in America not as a worker but as a patron. He was not yet used to the idea.

Days later, when they were once again out of work, Antonio mustered the courage to walk to the old mansion. He dressed in his best clothes—including a long black woolen coat he had purchased at the American Thrift Store on Eddy Street—closed his eyes to danger, and plunged into the unknown. He walked down Baker Street and up Elm Avenue with absolute determination. He somehow knew that that short trip was the requisite next step, if he truly wanted to find his sitio in America. The sting of the cold wind on his face and the empty feeling in the pit of his stomach were the price he paid to belong.

Besides, Antonio Alday Gutiérrez says to himself, now remembering that other winter day, he had nothing better to do. He had to take the chance. And that is how he met Mrs. Rosenberg.

17

Mrs. Rosenberg was a diminutive woman in her late seventies. She sat straight as could be on her perch near the entrance, overlooking her domain. She wore a blue sweater draped over narrow shoulders, and her hair, gathered into a bun at the back of her neck, was jet black, except for a few streaks of white near her temples. A thick, long black cord hung from her thin, wrinkled white neck. At the end of the cord was a pair of blue-framed reading glasses. She had deep black eyes. Her lips and cheeks were dry and leathery. Her fingers, adorned with several silver and gold rings, were long and knotted. She had a soft, motherly voice.

Good morning! she said, clasping her knotty hands together. What can we do for you today? Come in! Come in! First time here, yes? First time, yes. Antonio did not know what to say. He let his eyes survey the reading hall and marveled at the quantity of books.

And Mrs. Rosenberg: Well, then. You need to fill out this form, here. If you want, you can leave that for some other time. Are you interested in books or magazines? . . . Books? Follow me. Come. Antonio Allday followed the old lady to one of the small dark desks with a lit reading lamp.

Thank you, lady. Thank you.

And she: I will bring you something. Sit, sit. A moment later, she came back with a large, heavy book about raptors. She placed the book softly on the desk in front of Antonio, smiled, and went back to her place by the door. But she kept an eye on Antonio, who didn't know what to do next. He had kept his winter coat on and was beginning to feel hot. He looked at the pictures. He smelled the paper. He turned the pages.

It wasn't long before Mrs. Rosenberg realized that Antonio didn't know how to read English. She saw the poor fellow just flipping the pages back and forth. Mrs. Rosenberg descended from her perch, walked up to Antonio and, without a hint of hesitation, told him he needed to learn how to read English. Startled by such directness, Antonio Allday looked into the old lady's black eyes—almost hidden in her wrinkled face in the penumbra of the library–and felt her eager and kind conviction as a command. You need to come by three evenings a week.

I have a room especially for this. What's your name? As he answered, Antonio Allday was seized by an odd certainty: The old lady's eagerness had dovetailed with his own desires.

He returned that very evening. As it turned out, he was Mrs. Rosenberg's only pupil. So it came to pass that while in Providence, Antonio Allday spoke English with a slight German accent. All the new words he learned at the Elmwood Avenue branch of the Providence Public Library had the flavor of Mrs. Rosenberg, a Jewish woman who had come to America from Germany to escape the Second World War. After a few weeks of regular lessons, Mrs. Rosenberg issued Antonio Allday his own library card: You can now take home all the books you want, Antonio. All the books you want.

And so by the summer of 1983, six years later, Antonio had been ensnared in the wonderful worlds of Poe and Hemingway, Stevenson and Melville. And it was also by 1983 that he finally mastered his imitations of Clark Gable and Robert Wagner.

Antonio read everything during those years—from the *Kenyon Review* to *Popular Mechanics*. But he was especially fond of novels. Since he had never seen so many novels in Spanish in one place, he decided to split his reading fifty-fifty. And all through those years, Mrs. Rosenberg kept an eye on him. They became friends. She used to chide him: It's good for you to read about the past, about dreamed-up worlds, too, she would advise him, but it is even better to read more about today and your future, Antonio. Look ahead. Look ahead. There was a stretch of years when she was adamant that Antonio read and learn about accounting as preparation for getting into Roger Williams Community College, to get his CPA certificate.

I like to paint all right, Mrs. Rosenberg. Really. Maybe someday I'll go to college. But for now, I like it this way. I like to read novels. They're really good! Antonio could always smile at Mrs. Rosenberg.

Poor Mrs. Rosenberg, thinks Antonio Alday Gutiérrez at 1:35 P.M., seeing how the glare of the winter light had moistened his eyes, feeling tired beyond belief. Poor Antonio. He had wanted to write novels and lose himself in his invented worlds. What happened to those dreams? Did his choice to become Mr. Anthony Allday preclude their realization? Is reconstruction incompatible with novel writing? . . . Peering into the light, Antonio Alday Gutiérrez accepts that perhaps it is true: a man has energy for only so much. Perhaps he could have become either Mr. Anthony Allday or a writer, but not both.

Back in Providence, Antonio Allday still wanted to write novels because he still believed himself capable of inventing worlds like those he read about and because he had always dreamed of being a writer. Even when he lived in Tacora. He had always believed don Luna when he would scratch his head and say that a man's life is like—or even better than—a novel, that all one needed to be a good writer was to tell one's story straight. But back then Toño was naïve and didn't have the courage to write about his life. In Tacora life smothers everything. He tossed away his first notebooks when he left that world behind. In Providence, however, in the company of Alex Sosa and Mrs. Rosenberg, Antonio began to believe that a man could invent stories just as easily as he could invent his own life. He began to believe that he could write novels with happy endings. He even wrote down some beginning chapters and a few plot outlines in his Peruvian notebooks. But in the end, he was never able to finish writing any of them. By the end of 1986, shortly after he arrived in Philadelphia and became Mr. Anthony Allday, he all but stopped writing.

18

Peruvian Notebook No. 4
November 4, 1986

That Carmencita had no boyfriends that he knew of, despite all her twenty-three years and such a beautiful body, did not bother him. Ricardo was more than happy to have her near him always. She supported all his ideas, all his dreams. She always took his side, even against their stepfather, who did not hide his preference for el cojudo Toño. As for Ricardo himself, he had had affairs, of course, since he was quite young. And Carmencita was always there to help him with that, too. And Ricardo thought that he was more than happy to confide in her.

Tell me everything, Ricardo, she would ask him after his dates. Despacito mi amor, very slowly, darling. And he would tell her everything. She would listen to him, lying down on her bed with her eyes transfixed on the dark ceiling, enveloped in the hum of Tacora. So, what else did she say to you? How exactly is she nice? Did you kiss her then? And Ricardo would talk and talk for hours, until she fell asleep.

She never talked about her own adventures. But she must have had plenty, thought Ricardo. All the men in Tacora desired her. Everyone teased him: Tell her that I'm dying for her, Ricardo! Of course. What with that bronzed body, with that long chestnut hair shadowing her face, with those full lips, with the way she walked on the muddy streets. ¡Chucha madre! And, sometimes, when Ricardo came back late from his forays, she would not sleep at all; sometimes, she would start teasing him, pulling him down on her bed, to wrestle the satisfied look off his face. Who do you think you are, Ricardo? ¿El jovencito de la película? The hero of the movie? I'll wipe that smirk off your face! I'll teach you to treat women like that, you devilish boy! Sometimes they played too long and went too far.

They went too far during the carnival days of 1969. That February was so hot people in Tacora walked on the narrow and muddy callejones quivering, as if crossing a desert. The mud was so dry it cracked into deep fissures, exposing the layer of black asphalt underneath. It was then that the people of La Estrella finally believed don Gustavo Paez's story that the streets of Tacora had once been paved, back in the thirties, by order of President Leguía, who had fallen madly in love with La Picotita, one of the legendary prostitutes of the barrio, and who, in a moment of sobs and pleading, promised her he would straighten the streets where she lived. But he only managed to pave them because the people of Tacora rose against the attempt to unbend their houses, and La Picotita, seeing that, forgave the president his unfulfilled promise and agreed to move into the back rooms of the presidential palace, where she was killed by a stray bullet from a revolutionary mob.

It was so hot people slept naked in front of their houses, covered by only a thin cotton sheet. It was so hot El Cholo Huanta rented his wicker chair, which held the body suspended without blocking the breaths of an always warm wind, for a nominal fee: one sol per hour. It was so hot people stopped dousing each other with water, as was the custom during the carnival month of February, and turned their buckets on themselves instead. It was so hot, Ricardo came back from the streets unexpectedly early, by mid-afternoon, sweating bullets. It was so hot, he took off his shirt, his socks, his pants, and lay down on his mattress. It was so hot, he laced his fingers behind his neck and sighed with tedium and fatigue. It was so hot, his breathing soon became shallow.

In those days all the Alday children slept in the same room. Toño had his lumpy mattress on the floor at the far end. It was some distance from the noise of the callejón and, strangely enough, cooler in summer and warmer in winter. Toño loved to take his siestas there, before going to the theater. And he seldom had trouble falling asleep. In fact, Toño was blessed with the uncanny ability to sleep on command. He could completely ignore his siblings' and parents' bad moods, even when he was the cause and target of their agitation. This particular night in February, however, he was unable to take his usual nap. He was kept awake by worries about his upcoming debut performance as Daniel, the old man in No hay isla feliz, a play by the Peruvian Sebastian Salazar Bondy. It's a rare honor, Toño, don Luna had said. To play Daniel is to prepare for anything that life might throw in your path as an artist. We're counting on you. Toño had accepted the part with some apprehension but with good humor. He had promised don Luna to be the best Daniel he could possibly be. But now he was awake. He was listening to the low hum of the heat waves rising and falling to the rhythm of Ricardo's shallow breathing.

La Carmen entered the room like a whirlwind, determined to do something. Toño could hear her heavy breathing like a whisper in the silent desert Tacora had become. He closed his eyes and pictured her standing next to the door. She had both her hands on her hips, as she always did when she was seized by an idea. Toño kept his eyes closed. He feared something, but did not know what. He could smell her inside the room now—the sweet smell of yerbabuena. She began to undress. Toño felt her dress land on the floor. He pictured her white underwear, like a sun in that darkness. He kept his eyes closed. She crawled onto her bed on the right side of the room. And Toño recalled the tiny red flowers on her sheets, the wide frilly fringes on her pillow, the indentation made by the shape of her body on her narrow blue mattress. He kept his eyes closed. And he heard La Carmen's voice, low and raspy: Ricardo! She whispered forcefully. Ricardo! Come scratch my back.

Ricardo did not answer. Toño kept his eyes closed. An eternity, carajo! Then he heard Ricardo moving, tossing his thin cotton sheet to one side. Toño could now feel the heat of Ricardo's body in the room. It was not the heat of summer, of February; it was a heat enhanced a thousand degrees by curiosity and undefined fear. Ricardo moved towards his Carmencita's place with practiced quiet. And Toño divined him sitting beside her, peering into the darkness, guessing, sensing the shape of her body. There was a long silence. And Toño could hear his own heartbeat—hurried, loud. An eternity. Until La Carmen whispered: A little lower, please. Yes. There, there. Ahh. A little lower, mi amor. And Ricardo never said a word in the passing eternity. And Toño divined La Carmen's long hair and bronze body, too. And the heat that grew and grew in the room. Until Toño could not bear it anymore. He lifted himself on his elbows, turned to his left, and opened his eyes.

Ricardo was kneeling, straddling La Carmen's body. He was pressing her long thin torso with both hands. He was arched, facing the ceiling with his eyes closed. She was facedown, her arms extended along the curve of her body. Her long legs were slightly apart. Her chestnut hair was spread on the wide-fringed pillow her mother had made for her. Toño knew the scene in that penumbra was awful. Forbidden. But he could not stop himself from looking. And she now began to whimper. And Ricardo continued to caress her torso, facing the ceiling. And then, as his hands found La Carmen's white underwear, she arched and whimpered even more. And Ricardo slid the panties down her legs with one movement.

And La Carmen: Don't stop, Ricardo. Don't stop, please. It hurts so much! And Toño could feel the heat rising in the darkness of that room. No pares, mi amor. No pares. Don't stop, my love. Don't stop. And then she ceased whimpering and began breathing heavily, in waves. The smell of yerbabuena filled the room. Ricardo was now rubbing her thighs. Toño wanted to close his eyes. But he couldn't. And still facing the ceiling, still with his eyes closed, Ricardo touched his Carmencita between the legs. And then La Carmen turned to face her Ricardo. She was biting her lips. And she caressed his legs, up and down. And she drew up her right leg, long and smooth in the penumbra. And Toño wanted to close his eyes. But he couldn't. And Ricardo pinched her nipples. A long time. And then La Carmen raised her right hand and pressed down on Ricardo's shoulder. And Ricardo obeyed by lowering his head. And she played with his hair. And they touched their lips together, eyes closed, in the heat. La Carmen started to whimper again. She let out her forbidden noises softly, rhythmically. They rolled out from her full lips smelling of yerbabuena. She seemed about to burst. And Ricardo swaying. Toño felt the smell of many strange flowers fill the room. He felt the warm air of the room swaying, back and forth, like ocean waves. And La Carmen undulated in the penumbra. Toño felt the forbidden waves in his body. He felt a fear he had not felt since his trip to Pucusana. The waves began in his chest and traveled down to his stomach. Burning waves. Icy waves. And the heat grew and grew in the shadows. And Ricardo was riding the waves. And La Carmen had joined him. They were lacing their waves of heat, of pain, in rhythmic motion. And La Carmen now held Ricardo's face between her legs.

Sí, sí, Ricardo. Sí. And Ricardo obeying, in silence. And the smell of strange flowers grew in the room. Ohh, Ricardo, mi amor. . . . Until Toño could not stand it anymore.

Toño tossed his own sheet of thin cotton aside and ran out of the house. He ran out to the end of the callejón, to the limits of La Estrella. He stopped by the hot red brick wall of the last apartment, to swear and curse into the heat of the day. He stopped to cry in the empty street. Toño was ashamed, though at that moment he did not know of what. Was he ashamed of their act or of his? Was he not old enough to close his eyes, his mind, his heart to what he could not change? Toño didn't know the answers to those questions. All he could do at that moment was throw up on a garbage heap. And when he had emptied his stomach, he sat against the hot wall, trying also to empty his mind.

Up until today, Antonio Alday Gutiérrez thinks twenty-six years later, feeling the soft light of the winter sun in Lima, Delaware County, Pennsylvania, that hot day in February was the worst day of my life. It colored all the other days to come in Tacora, and perhaps after. But time has a way of dulling the hardest edges, and now that tragedy seems quite mild. In time we all learn to catalogue such events as part of our bundle of regrets and disappointments. We call that personal growth. Of course, accepts Antonio Alday Gutiérrez lifting his eyes up to the light, I didn't know that then when I sat with my back against that hot wall.

Personal growth. Antonio Alday Gutiérrez lets the soft light of winter blur his vision. He imagines himself back in Tacora. He can almost feel the heat and the aroma of his old sitio. Yes, he says low, as if to dismiss old doubts: There is truth in these pages. He sighs. He wishes to rest. But at that very moment, he suddenly realizes he had written down another truth. Picturing himself back on Baker Street now, overlooking Narraganset Bay, he remembers writing down that the night after that hot day in February had also been the best night of his life. That night Toño shared his pain without shame. He grew in the company of another. Antonio Alday Gutiérrez returns his gaze to his brittle notebook and murmurs under his breath, with a hint of regret: I know it is possible.

After their debut performance at the theater, in the mezzanine of
El Paraíso, watching Gone with the Wind dubbed in Spanish, Toño
mustered the courage to confess his shame and fear to Betti. . . .
She listened with averted eyes, her skinny neck stretching out into
the dark of the movie theater. When Toño had finished, she took his
hands in hers and, gazing far into her own distances, she said with
deep resignation that life was shit. That was all. La vida es una
mierda. . . . But in that fleeting moment, Toño knew she fully understood his inner turmoil. For the first time in his life, he knew
it was truly possible to share one's despair and grow through it. He
knew it was possible for him not to be so utterly alone.

19

The only other person who understood some of my fears, acknowledges Antonio Alday Gutiérrez with a sense of loss, was Alex Sosa. He knew full well the risks involved in any attempt at reconstruction because he too could have become whomever he had pleased. He said so, many times. But he chose to remain the same. He loved Cheryl and New England too much.

I guess I should be glad for that. Alex Sosa was a good friend, a good man. He never judged anyone for their choices. On the contrary, Alex Sosa was more than willing to help Antonio carry his load. *Cada uno con su cada uno,* he would say in a weird mixture of Portuguese and Spanish accents: to each his own. As long as one gets to be better off. Right, Tony? What the hell, life's too short for anything less. Go for it, Mr. Allday! While he remained the same.

Would Antonio Allday have become the person he eventually became had Alex Sosa joined him in Philadelphia? Was it better that he stayed behind? Antonio Alday Gutiérrez cannot say. The only thing he knows is that when Antonio Allday left Alex Sosa's side—when was it?—he felt oddly grateful for it.

And now more than ever before, at 1:55 after the sinful deed, Antonio Alday Gutiérrez misses their time together. He misses walking down La Calle de Saudades, in New Bedford, Massachusetts, eating *toicinho do céu,* a custard pie, talking about movies, dreaming of making it big in America. He misses the good times they spent together jumping into the cold waters off Matunuck Beach in late summer, fishing for flats in the bay at Bristol, driving the hearse around Goddard Park.

What is Alex Sosa doing now?

20

Peruvian Notebook No. 4
November 4, 1986

Carmencita is going to get married one of these days, thought Ricardo at the end of their first day in Canto Grande, setting down the last stones marking the boundary of their future home. Even though she says she's too busy with her work to think about such things, what with all the jobs the nasty nurses ask her to do at the hospital. She wants to get a degree. She hates being treated like a maid. And Ricardo looked far into the bare surrounding hills, now bathed in the rosy glow of the setting sun. And his mind wandered off into the past, into the years they had spent together, just the two of them, in the callejones of Tacora. And Ricardo convinced himself they were finally ready to leave all that behind. He convinced himself that in the pampas of Canto Grande they were beginning a new life. They would each have their own bedroom. And in the mornings: Hola, Ricardo! Hola, Carmen! Nothing more. Each would have to make his own way in life, dancing to his own tune. And Ricardo promised to accept losing Carmencita, just as he had come to accept losing Toño.

To brush away such heavy thoughts, Ricardo reminded himself that it was good that Uncle Aniceto, who had come down from the highlands just before Toño left, had also been fortunate enough to get a plot in the desert. The man was a touch indolent, with much to learn about the ways of the big city, but he seemed eager to please. And good thing, too, that he had four small children. They would look after the huts when the adults had to go back to the city to find work. And Ricardo amused himself thinking that Genaro, the youngest child, was truly a sight! He was painfully shy and cursed with deep black lamb's eyes. He spoke in short bursts and seemed always in awe of the world around him. Still, he was a lucky boy. He did not have to grow up in the muddy callejones of places like La Estrella. The lucky lamb would have a totally different life and destiny.

When they had finished building the two-room hut, Ricardo approached his Carmencita to tell her he was requetecansado, tired as could be. And looking into her almond eyes, he said theirs would be a happy place, right? Too bad Father didn't live long enough to see it. Fortunately, Mother's still with us. And she's even getting better. Yes, Carmencita. Things are going to be better, right?

And his Carmencita: Of course, my darling. But listen, we cannot stop yet. We still have to put away everything, before the long shadows take over the pampas. Go, Ricardo! Go! When we're all finished, if you ask me nicely, I'll give you your reward. I promise, mi amor. And Ricardo, picking up nails and string from the sandy desert, told himself that all that had to end, that in their new home things would have to be different, that they were no longer children.

Two O'clock

November 27, 1995

Mr. Antonio Alday Gutiérrez
In the United States of America

My Most Esteemed Nephew:

I hope that the present letter finds you enjoying good health in union with your good friends in the United States. We are all well here, thank God. This past winter has been a little harsh, but we have all fared well.

After greeting you, I go on to give you some good news: God willing, your cousin Genaro is going to visit you! It is a blessing for all the family. At last one of us will be able to visit you where you are. After much effort and deprivation, we are making it possible. All of us here beg you to look after him when he arrives. He is going on American Airlines, flight 912. He will be arriving in Philadelphia on December 10, in the morning. Everything has been arranged. We are all praying to the High Almighty that he will have a safe trip. He is taking with him the address you gave me: Rogers Lane number 209, Lima, Delaware County, Pennsylvania. We know that the United States is a very big country, but we have faith that he will find you. As you recall, he is a humble but determined young man. We also hope that our dearest Gloria, your dear mother who is in heaven, will watch over him and protect him during his trip. Please meet him at the airport in Philadelphia. He will be looking for you.

Hoping with all our hearts that God will help us with Genaro, I say goodbye with a warm embrace. All the rest of the family send their greetings.

Your uncle who misses you,
Aniceto Gutiérrez Bayle

1

The snow of the night before has melted away and the sidewalks glimmer under the light of the winter sun. What a miracle! thinks Antonio Alday Gutiérrez, his hands warmer and calmer. In his new sitio even nature helps one's reconstruction. Everything changes with the seasons. And it occurs to him that perhaps it is because the seasons never change in Tacora that people there cannot imagine new worlds, new identities. It is harder to be reborn in Peru.

Antonio Alday Gutiérrez drifts into a lazy melancholy. His eyes follow the brown privet rows in the clear afternoon light and trace the dark lines of the knotty branches of a nearby sycamore tree against the sky. It seems the warmth of his hands signals an inner calmness—a serenity that borders on resignation. Antonio Alday Gutiérrez lets himself be drawn into a dense stupor by the soft white light of the winter sun. He escapes the weight of the dismal day by looking into his inner labyrinths and seeing himself young, naïve, blameless. A good place to be. And he wishes to follow the lead of his exhausted body to the very end, into oblivion. He is tired of digging into the past. So tired. All he wants now is for his body to go limp and fall asleep. Forever.

But sleep does not come. Just as he is about to doze off, Antonio Alday Gutiérrez catches himself and makes himself sit up straight on the hard vinyl couch. He rubs his face with both hands. He stamps his feet on the bare wood floor. He feels the diffuse pain of his left big toe. And he returns to his memories. He still wants to make sure there really is nothing in his turbulent past that could somehow justify what he has done. He knows he has little time left. It is 2:00 P.M. What else did Anthony Allday think this cursed morning? How did he feel?

2

Anthony Allday thought it weird that his uncle Aniceto did not believe in progress. Shampoo takes away the good oils from our scalp, Toño. That's why all the gringos are bald. Don't wash your hair so often. And don't put on that Glostora cream. It'll ruin your face, your eyes, everything. It's a gringo invention. Look at you! Are you trying to be a pituco or something?

And Toño: No, Uncle Aniceto. It's the style, like Elvis Presley. The stupid man never bathed because he didn't want to lose his oils. And that's how he raised all his children. Including Genaro. God only knows if el cojudo has changed. If he hasn't, he'll smell like Tacora, even if he now lives in Canto Grande.

Thinking about his cousin Genaro and how little he knew about him, Anthony Allday felt a twinge of regret: Perhaps it would have been better to maintain some contact with those people. He would then at least know what to expect now. But it was not possible. A part of him wished he could have belonged to both worlds, of course; won one without losing the other. As time went by, however, the wish diluted. It sank deep into the labyrinths of his mind. Until it became recognizable only as one among many discarded possibilities, as one less *bulto,* dead weight, in his journey towards rebirth.

A bulto like his very name: Alday. Where in hell did the old man come up with that? It probably wasn't even Spanish. Vergara, Guzmán, Sánchez, Espinoza, at least those were recognizable, but Alday? It only messed him up. At school the other boys taunted and threw kisses at him saying it was a marica's surname. That was the reason he didn't give a damn about changing it. In his own heart, he had welcomed the change, good riddance!

It had happened on a cold autumn morning, in New Bedford, Massachusetts, back in 1977, when he and Alex Sosa were painting a stadium.

By God, there's a lot of work in Massachusetts! they had told him in Houston, where he had spent almost a year, shining the tile floors of a huge green glass building. They pay well, too, Antonio. Everyone there speaks Portuguese. Like Spanish. It's just that no one wants to go

122

there because it's too cold. They say people walk around like robots in their winter clothes! But maybe that's why the pay is good there. Better yet, Antonio, they say they don't hate Hispanos over there. They even say that some end up getting married. They buy houses and everything, despite the snow and the Canadian winds. *Anda,* Antonio! Go and see for yourself. . . . That was why he had come to New Bedford. He had bought a one-way ticket for the Greyhound bus that made its way north through Chicago, and to hell with Houston. He did not stop until he arrived at the bus depot in New Bedford. That must have been some-time in June of 1974.

And it was true! recalled Anthony Allday, pulled down by the weight of the Smith & Wesson .38. People did speak Portuguese, which is very similar to Spanish. And with a little effort, cocking his head to hear bet-ter, he could actually understand everybody. He got a job as a painter's helper as soon as he stepped off the bus. Next thing, he found a little room on the far end of Pleasant Street. The newly arrived Portuguese called Pleasant Street La Calle de Saudades, because they could buy there *vihno verde, bacalao,* and toicinho do céu. Because, to tell the truth, Anthony Allday thought with disdain, many Portuguese there wanted to continue to live as if they were in Lisbon or the Azores. ¡Cojudeces! That damn nostalgia, Anthony Allday thought with pity. It plagues ev-eryone.

Everything was going just fine. Antonio Alday Gutiérrez, the illegal Peruvian, kept to himself. He saved his pennies. He dreamed of buying a little used car. He dreamed of buying his clothes at a regular store, like K-Mart or Sears, instead of at the Salvation Army thrift store. It was not only because the thrift store smelled of foul detergent. Robert Lopes, a giant black Portuguese man who sold earrings and other trinkets at the market had told him he should be careful buying clothes there because the CIA put something in them to keep the poor quiet. That smell goes to your brain. It keeps you very quiet. You don't say anything about anything then. Why do you think there are no strikes and rebellions like back home? It's not because life here is so great, you know. . . . An-tonio did not quite believe Robert Lopes' story. Not least because the giant made a living selling the same trinkets one could find in that thrift store. But still the clothes had a very strange smell. And it was kind of creepy that all the clothes in all the thrift stores of New Bedford had the

123

same smell. . . . But, yes, recalled Anthony Allday, when Antonio Alday Gutiérrez arrived in New Bedford he had even had dreams of finding an American girlfriend.

But one day, as they were painting a small stadium near the center of town, people began to protest, God only knows why. La Calle de Saudades filled with an angry mob, Robert Lopes among them. They took over the main intersections, stopping traffic. Perhaps they were demanding an end to the military-industrial complex, as some of their placards said, or perhaps Robert Lopes had convinced them all that the CIA was waging war against them. Antonio Alday Gutiérrez didn't know much about such things then. The fact was that the police arrived in large dark green buses and dressed in battle gear. Some brought German shepherds. In a matter of minutes, they arrested dozens who had come to New Bedford with their green canvas backpacks, flowers painted on their faces, and dreamy ways. In the blink of an eye, everything went upside down. Just like in Peru. ¡Carajo! Tear gas. Sticks. Barking. ¡Puta madre! . . . Then once the crowd had dispersed, the police closed off La Calle de Saudades and several adjacent streets. The eerie sound of police sirens was everywhere.

There were rumors the police had received orders not to let anyone leave New Bedford. Mr. Pearson, the big boss, told the gang of painters to stay put and be quiet. And so the workers grabbed their gear and made a place for themselves under the bleachers. Yes, Anthony Allday remembered as he noticed how the checkerboard path before him curved away in the distance, that was how Antonio Alday Gutiérrez spent his very last night. Because it now appeared that it was under the bleachers of that stadium, in early autumn, in New Bedford, that his rebirth had truly begun.

All of a sudden, at 2:10 P.M., Antonio Alday Gutiérrez senses he has come upon a previously hidden connection: perhaps El Azar, which brought him all the way from Tacora to Lima, Delaware County, Pennsylvania, to commit the murder, began spinning its threads in earnest from the moment Mr. Pearson told him to stay put. But all at once he finds himself without the energy to decipher the full meaning of that event. Still, he has the sensation that on that night El Azar took his side. In fact, he realizes now, El Azar has been on his side all along in

America, until this last, dismal day when everything has come to a bad end. What did he do to deserve such a change of fortune? What did he leave undone? Fatigued and unable to answer such questions, Antonio Alday Gutiérrez returns to his memories.

Feeling the Smith & Wesson .38 hitting his right leg as he made his last round at the Springfield Mall, Anthony Allday remembered vividly that he had been very scared. Who wouldn't have been? After all, the cops were asking everyone for papers. The eyes and ears of La Migra were all around. That was the reason Mr. Pearson had told them to stay put and be quiet. The old man knew most of his crew were illegal workers. Who else would be willing to climb the forty-foot ladders and take on the cold Canadian winds for only $1.50 an hour? He knew. And so what was the newly arrived Antonio Alday Gutiérrez to do but keep quiet, low, covering himself with the drop cloths, the buckets, the brushes, the rollers, the putty knives, with only his ears in the open, following the sound of the sirens, shaking, clasping his hands hard to keep away not only the cold but also the fear, fear of being sent back to Tacora. ¡Carajo! I should've stayed in Houston, damn it, at least there it wasn't so cold!

Are they coming, Alex? Are they coming?

And Alex Sosa: Stay low, Antonio. Stay low. Happens all the time. It's going to pass. Stay low.

He couldn't stay low forever. El Azar was always on the move. It sprang its trap at 4:00 A.M. when, because of the fear and the cold, he had to go out from his hiding place to take a leak. ¡Mierda! He was already coming back. He was almost in his *guarida,* his hole, carajo, when he heard the harsh voice of the policeman: You there, stop! Antonio Alday Gutiérrez was paralyzed. It was as if at that moment, in America on that cold autumn morning, he regurgitated and brought back to life the blind Peruvian fear of all power, a fear that had survived in him despite all his attempts to exorcise it. He didn't know what to do. He wanted to run, to escape, but his legs, his hair, his skin held him in place, already a prisoner. He sensed the cop coming ever closer as he sank deeper and deeper into despair. He was lost. Lost. . . .

Just then, through the veil of his terror, Antonio Alday Gutiérrez heard the clear and respectful voice of Alex Sosa: Mr. Allday! Mr. Allday! He was addressing him, in his perfect English: We're all waiting for you, Mr. Allday. Please, sir. This way. Mr. Pearson sent me to find you. This way. . . .

Antonio Alday Gutiérrez didn't get Alex Sosa's ploy right away. Alex had addressed him with such conviction and yet so oddly that he was confused. Fortunately, it seemed El Azar was still on his side. Just before Antonio Alday Gutiérrez turned around to give himself up, he saw Alex Sosa's knowing face, clear as could be, under the autumn morning sky. He understood. He smoothed his painter's overalls, took off the Glidden painting cap, and walked towards his friend without hurrying and without turning toward the cop who was approaching. When he was close enough, Alex Sosa placed a hand on his shoulder and repeated, loud enough to be heard by the policeman, that Mr. Pearson was looking for him and that he should go quickly because there were some serious problems with the materials.

They walked a few paces. When they reached an iron gate that led from the stadium to La Calle de Saudades, Alex Sosa halted. He pointed Antonio Alday Gutiérrez toward the exit: You go on, Mr. Allday. I'll stay here to see that things don't get out of hand. Better hurry, though. Mr. Pearson is really upset. Imagine, at four in the morning! . . .

With the old fear chewing at his entrails Antonio Alday Gutiérrez made it through the iron gate. He heard the steps of the policeman, still approaching. He feared another order to halt. And yet he walked away, straight, calmly, for the first time in America. He put on the best performance of his life. Once on La Calle de Saudades, empty and silvery in the autumn morning, Antonio Alday Gutiérrez strained to hear his friend Alex Sosa explaining to the policeman that it had been such a miracle to find Mr. Allday there and at that hour: As they say, someone's always in trouble. You know that. Must be tough to be responsible for people, be it a crowd or a crew, right, Captain? Take Mr. Allday: He's going to get hell from the boss. It seems the protesters have stolen more than thirty cans of paint. Imagine that! Even when you guys are out there in force! Damn!

At that moment, standing alone on La Calle de Saudades, cold and still disoriented, Antonio Alday Gutiérrez realized that he had suddenly changed into Antonio Allday. One additional letter, a simple shift in accent, had made all the difference in the world. And he wanted the change to be permanent.

126

3

We laughed heartily after everything passed and things in New Bedford calmed down. After that, now and again, Alex Sosa would tease me by calling me Mr. Allday. I only pretended to feel uncomfortable, and we both knew that, in truth, I felt otherwise. We both knew that perhaps more than anything else in my life, I wanted this change to be permanent.

And Alex Sosa said: So what if you have to add a letter, Antonio? You saw what happened. It'll spare you a great deal of grief. In America, you can be whoever you wish to be. No one here can stop you.

I told Alex Sosa that maybe things are not always so easy.

And Alex Sosa: Yes they are. Con tal que no te joda la vida, so long as it doesn't fuck up your life.

It has been seven years since then. Now I can hardly remember Antonio Allday.

4

Peruvian Notebook No. 3
June 7, 1984

Alex Sosa bought himself a black hearse from the Irish Catholic funeral home in Cranston, Rhode Island, in 1978. Since the O'Shea Funeral Home had lost most of its business to Cianci and Patriarca, he was able to purchase that boat of a car for a song.

Ever since then, he has gone all around New England with me as his copilot. The painters whistle and applaud when they see us coming. To disguise the origins of the eight-cylinder dinosaur, we have painted red stripes on its sides and adorned its antenna with Sporting Lisboa banderines. Sporting Lisboa is Alex Sosa's favorite soccer team.

In 1980 he installed a brand-new tape deck we got from Crazy Vito Cusato at Guido's, in Federal Hill. He likes to open the windows of his boat and let the music flow. Yesterday, he bought yet another copy of Simon and Garfunkel's Greatest Hits. He likes the track "Cecilia." He says it reminds him of the songs he used to hear as a child. I have told him I never liked "El condor pasa."

5

At 2:20, after the murder, Antonio Alday Gutiérrez feels he has gained an undeniable insight: Mr. Anthony Allday was constructed not only by Alex Sosa, but even more so by circumstance. In truth, Mr. Allday was a chance attribution. In this regard at least, his memory of an initial premeditated choice was an invention. His choice amounted to no more than a willingness to go along with the designs of El Azar. But Antonio Alday Gutiérrez does not let that insight shake loose his growing stupor. After all, it seems connected only to the foggy labyrinths of long ago. What does it matter how it all started? What really matters is how he acted thereafter. And so, Antonio Alday Gutiérrez lets the insight slink away.

He thinks of something else: What is Alex Sosa doing just now, two weeks before Christmas? Is he still in Providence, driving around in that hearse? Did he marry Cheryl, as he had planned? Or is he, at this exact moment, resting his back against a hard wall somewhere, under other bleachers, with pain curving his back, tired of so much sun and so much moonlight?

Antonio Alday Gutiérrez remembers Alex Sosa's answer to his invitation to come with him to Philly, to seek a life in a warmer climate: *el pintor pinta tal como el torero torea*—the painter paints as the bullfighter fights. Antonio Allday never understood what Alex Sosa meant. He wanted to ask Alex Sosa to explain, but he didn't dare ask. He was too embarrassed to admit he had failed to understand something so profound. Even years later, however, when he had become Mr. Anthony Allday, he did not quite get its meaning. Now, at 2:20 P.M., it seems plausible to Antonio Alday Gutiérrez that Alex Sosa meant to say that each one of us must do what are meant to do and be who we are meant to be; that there is no point in trying to unbraid the webs spun by El Azar. Perhaps Antonio Alday Gutiérrez is meant to end in this way, prostrate on precisely this yellow vinyl couch, feeling the soft light of this winter sun on his face, in Lima, Delaware County, Pennsylvania, waiting to be taken away.

Alex Sosa did not want to leave New England, and he made it clear that he did not wish to hear another invitation. And so they had to say goodbye. On a clear day in the fall of 1984, they had breakfast at Guido's, on Federal Hill. They talked about too many things to remember now. Cheryl. His business. Mrs. Rosenberg. The new movies showing at the Seekonk Drive-In. Afterwards, they drove in the hearse to visit the beaches of Matunuck, Jerusalem, and Galilee. It was truly beautiful there. The surrounding fields, bordered by rhododendrons, desert pines, and shore oak trees, gave the empty beaches a character of seclusion and solitude. They had lunch at George's, by the pier. They walked the sandy beaches from Matunuck to Jerusalem and back. They smoked Salems. They skipped stones over turbulent eddies. They laughed. Until the sun sinking on the horizon painted the sky red and the flight of the gulls signaled the coming night breezes.

They returned to Providence in silence, the rush of air from the open windows of the hearse drowning all thought of warnings or well wishes. They got off I-95 at the Elmwood Avenue exit, wound their way through Roger Williams Park, took Broad Street towards downtown, and stopped at the newly refurbished and renamed John F. Kennedy Plaza. The train station was not far. They got out of the hearse and embraced long and hard, knowing they would never see each other again. Tony never turned back to wave goodbye.

And now, Antonio Alday Gutiérrez says to himself under his breath, it is too late for any kind of turning back.

6

¡La gente hace cojudeces! people do the weirdest things, Antonio Alday Gutiérrez remembers Anthony Allday thinking on the cursed morning. We shouldn't play the impotent victim too often. The truth is we choose *nuestra mortaja y nuestro traje de luces*—our own shroud and our own bullfighter's dress. Circumstances may help or hinder, but they never determine our acts. The power of El Azar does not explain everything. That is why I am not too impressed when people say that they had no choice, that they got screwed, that there are things beyond our control. ¡La gente hace cojudeces! That is why I have never pitied Hannah, for example. She chose her life just as much as I chose mine. That we have ended as we have—together at times and yet strangers to each other—is because of a decision taken with premeditation. It is not like the pain in this toe, carajo. I have no control over it. It comes from within and yet it is beyond me. If only one could change things like that!

7

I never liked cats, Tony. From the beginning, even the idea of having cats made me feel separated from the world, layered with loneliness. Do you know what I mean? Perhaps it is because when I was a child I was terribly impressed by Mrs. Krugovoy—a small woman, fragile and half crazy, who lived in an old house on the corner. She had seven cats. Can you imagine? Seven! She talked to them as if they were people. The neighbors said that was why she stopped speaking English altogether and returned in her mind to the steppes of Russia, where she was born.

Hannah was afraid of the old lady.

But it wasn't a physical fear, Tony. It wasn't like fearing a dog. It was more like a spiritual fear. You know what I mean? A fear that, somehow, I was going to end up like her. I would hide from her, Tony. From her eyes. From the air around her. And the fear stayed after the old woman died and the neighbors had to throw her ashes into the Schuylkill River because there was no one to claim and keep the jar, and my mother refused to let the funeral home dispose of it. It was such a downer, Tony. We stood on the riverbank, heads bowed, not saying anything, pious. Afterwards, my mother invited everyone over for tea and cookies. She is always doing things like that for perfect strangers. Although, to be fair, they had talked to each other before. In Russian. But, standing on the bank of the river I felt glad inside, Tony. I felt free. I wished so much for my fear to dissolve like Mrs. Krugovoy's ashes in the water.

But the fear did not leave her. Not for a long time. On the contrary, with the passing years it mixed with something ineffable and perverse: a sense of doom. Hannah felt it like an attraction, like an itch in her conscience, whispering to her that it was only a matter of time before she became as old, as lonely, and as crazy as Mrs. Krugovoy.

It was a fear that circulated like ice in my veins, Tony, I swear.

When she was a sophomore at Penn, as if the old lady had cast a spell upon her from the bottom of the Schuylkill River, Hannah bought a cat.

If someone had asked me why I did it, I would not have been able to say, Tony. I didn't know. It was a day like any other, I swear. I was walking down Locust Walk, near the McNeil Building, when I saw the cat in a cage, for sale.

And so, as if Mrs. Krugovoy had whispered in her ear, Hannah took the cat home. That was that. And not even years later, not even after she had gotten used to living with her four cats in her various apartments around the city, not even after she had celebrated, alone with her cats, her thirty-fifth birthday, not even then could Hannah explain why she was becoming very much like Mrs. Krugovoy, and why she was getting used to the idea that she would never marry and have a family.

Hannah insisted she had tried to fight against her attraction to loneliness.

I've tried to find suitable companionship, Tony. With blah men, with good men, and with bad. They all turned sour eventually. No matter what I did, Tony, I always felt trapped in my own skin. Can you explain that? The closer I got to them, the more trapped I felt.

And so, in the end, Hannah convinced herself that her obsession was as inescapable as it was inexplicable. Perhaps it was something she wished neither to escape nor explain, Tony thought upon hearing her story, when they talked openly for the first time, sitting on a bench by the medical school under a cluster of locust trees in summer.

She seemed so vulnerable, Antonio Alday Gutiérrez thinks now. She seemed so lost that he almost ran away. He had his own burdens, thank you. And yet he stayed. Inevitably and inexplicably, too?

Perhaps he stayed because he was ready to share something meaningful with someone. Ready to toss away his own growing solitude. After the sinful deed, Antonio Alday Gutiérrez wants to believe that. Desperately. He truly cared for Hannah then. And even now, despite how things stand between them. But he knows he stayed mostly because it was convenient. After all, he had been preparing for a while to try his new reconstruction on someone, to see how it went—posing before his mirror, listening to his own voice on the Sony tape recorder, watching the television without sound, to better see the gestures, the expression in the hands. He was eager to show sincerity. He might then be able to tweak and improve his self-presentation and find a new job. He was already tired of working as a busboy at Smokey Joe's.

And Tony confessed to Hannah, with all sincerity, that his own life was very similar, that he also had the sensation there were many moments in his life that seemed to obey decisions made a long time ago by someone else. That is why, Hannah, darling, I believe it's better to accept the portions of pain and happiness that destiny offers us. Why fight it? Right? I understand you. I do.

In the days and nights of intimacy that followed, walking hand in hand along Forbidden Drive, in Fairmount Park, Tony told Hannah that it had been precisely because of his sense of predestination, his sense of being the plaything of an uncharitable destiny, that he had finally stopped dreaming of returning home to Peru. A disagreeable country, Hannah, a land filled with resentful people who never think twice and exiled me for trying to improve things. And looking into her brown eyes, Tony whispered low: We are sometimes urged on by invisible forces, Hannah. We find the reasons for what we have done only later, if we are lucky. Most of our reasons are nothing but justifications or, at best, untimely insights. I never wanted to leave my country with the police at my heels. I desperately tried to avoid it. I even tried to become a secluded writer and to stop thinking about politics. But the outlines of my life in Peru had already been drawn. I could not stop fighting injustice. Corruption. Poverty . . . until I was kicked out.

It is my destiny to live as an outsider, Hannah, watching from here how my family profits from its cozy relationship with filthy powers. They tell me they have to cooperate with the government, for otherwise everything would truly get out of control, that if they do not profit, some other less honorable or patriotic families would and that, after all, my family are the human face of the tyranny. Justifications, Hannah. Do you see what I mean? I, too, have scars that do not heal. God only knows if and when I'll return to see the familiar things of my innocent childhood.

That was how Hannah found in Tony a kindred soul. That was how it came to pass that they both understood that everything they had done or would do with their lives had been decided before they were born. We must live as we are meant to, Tony repeated to Hannah later, on a summer afternoon in 1987, as he rowed their canoe on the Schuylkill River. We are meant to be lovers, Hannah. Nothing more. It is my destiny to wait in exile until, perhaps, I will return someday to my country, to my family. It will perhaps only be when my return can no longer disturb the family peace or the political landscape. You are meant to wait, with your heart in your hand, until a way appears to overcome your fascination with loneliness—which is also a desire to be free, Hannah, a desire for a life that demands nothing more permanent than, at most, these moments of happiness.

Hannah said later that sometimes she felt that her relationship with Tony left her empty. It drained her energy. In part this was because Tony was always seeking solace and consolation for an exile that seemingly would never end, in part because she felt that their relationship would stall and that it might be better to try to find another escape for her loneliness. But these feelings were fleeting, she would confess. She knew she had to ignore them; they were futile rebellions against her destiny, a rebellion that in the end would only make her more miserable. That was why Hannah allowed to grow—nurtured rather—a wall of cold understanding between them. That was why, whenever her mother and sisters asked her to demand more from that relationship, she resisted. They had no right to ask. They simply didn't understand.

In the beginning, Antonio Alday Gutiérrez thinks at 2:22 P.M., in her lonely afternoons, her four cats on her lap, Hannah must have thought about other possibilities. She must have asked herself whether there was something she could do to change their relationship into something more permanent while making sure she did not become a suffocating and needy woman. She said she detested that possibility. She said she loved to give but hated to need affection. . . . But she must have finally given up. Why? And when did she stop fighting? Was it two years ago, almost to the day, on the trip they made to the Poconos? Did he lose her there? Did they lose each other? Antonio Alday Gutiérrez misses Hannah as he has never missed her before.

8

The cleaners arrived. They entered the mall in small groups. In the hush of the morning their footsteps, the clearing of their throats, even the clicking of their tools, gave the impression of cultivated furtiveness. The women wore baggy sweatpants and oversized shirts. Some began dusting the corridor's light posts and windowsills with long, multicolored plumes. Others vacuumed the carpet, the long black cords of their machines twisting behind them. The men had bulky scarves around their necks and large yellow work shoes. Some pushed their quietly humming waxing machines, following the meandering checkerboard paths. Others removed overflowing plastic bags from the garbage receptacles and stacked them in piles. Each person worked in total self-absorption. And yet, precisely because of this lack of communication, their actions gave the impression of having been choreographed. These poor souls emanate a most deceptive sense of freedom, thought Anthony Allday watching them out of the corner of his eye. In truth, each in his own way forms part of a herd. He felt deeply thankful not to have to do that for a living anymore.

How exactly had he left all that behind? How had he overcome the smell of toilets, floor wax, paint, poverty? Dreaming. Dreaming. Imitating Robert Wagner's thief Mundy in *It Takes a Thief;* mimicking Clark Gable's sardonic voice and smile: *I'll say one thing: The war makes the most peculiar widows.* . . . Dreaming. Moving south. Saying goodbye to family and friends. Until Tom gave him the job.

What would have happened if he had known then, when he came for the interview at the mall that Friday at 8:00 P.M., all alone, that Tom was gay? He probably never would have even entered the security room for the interview. He was too Peruvian still. Too afraid. For sure. He had changed so much since then. Even when it came to that. His old repulsion for homosexuals was disappearing, just as surely as his fear of the cops. And Anthony Allday remembered that Tom had behaved properly. He had not had the slightest hint that Mr. Parker was gay.

Anthony Allday rehearsed for the part as never before: relaxed facial expression, comfortable clothes for his refined gestures, selective vocabulary for his soft accent. He had read and reread the books on police

136

officers and their work that he had picked up, by chance, from a basket of free books laid out in front of House of Our Own, a used book store in West Philadelphia. Dreaming. Believing he could be a damn good policeman but would settle for a job as a security guard, given his circumstances. He had to be a realist. Remembering Clark Gable: *Why? Maybe it's because I've always had a weakness for lost causes, once they are really lost. Or maybe, maybe I'm ashamed of myself. Who knows?*

There! Antonio Alday Gutiérrez remembers Anthony Allday remembering the cursed morning at the Springfield Mall. It was there, in the security office, that I, Mr. Anthony Allday, was truly born. And Antonio Alday Gutiérrez also remembers that Anthony Allday had thought the reconstruction had been entirely his choice. Granted, finding the books on the sidewalk might have been the work of El Azar; he was no longer interested in denying that. At the same time, it was none other than Anthony Allday who had decided to answer the ad in the *Philadelphia Inquirer*. It was none but Anthony Allday who had decided how to dress for the interview. Yes. It was he and he alone. And now for the first time since becoming Mr. Anthony Allday, Antonio Alday Gutiérrez realizes that it was no one else but Tom who first saw Anthony Allday come alive. Incredible! He had performed for a performer.

Glad to meet you. Please, have a seat. So, you're interested in the job. Good. Where are you from?

I am from Peru.

Peru! Really?

Yeah.

I mean, where do you live? What have you been doing up to now? Do you have experience in security work?

And Anthony Allday remembered that Tom's soft blue eyes, his honest smile, had put him at ease. With his stomach in knots, with his heart in his throat, he took the decisive step: His family had sent him to Penn, to study business at Wharton, but he, tired of always doing what they told him to do, had decided to stay in America, to make it on his own. And Mr. Parker need not worry, he had his working papers in order. And he was not about to leave his post all of a sudden. . . . He paused to assess the effect of his performance. Tom's soft blue eyes encouraged him. He went on: Yeah, to hell with his family and their yachts that cut the Pacific horizon, to hell with his grandparents and their commercial houses in Lima and Buenos Aires, to hell with his uncles and their factories of Eternit in Canto Grande, to hell with his great-aunts with their determination to maintain their English accents. To hell with everyone. I am an individual, Mr. Parker. I want to be proud of what I can achieve on my own. This job would be my new beginning, as an American.

Tom leaned back in his black vinyl swivel chair. He laced his thick fingers across his broad chest. He cleared his throat. Squinted. He seemed mesmerized by Mr. Anthony Allday's arabesque hand gestures, gestures of a *niño bien,* of a pituco, of a privileged scion from a proper family. The work is kind of boring. Maybe this isn't something you'd be interested in. Perhaps you should think about it. Call your parents. You see, Mr. Allday, we're about to open the very first mall in Delaware County. I need people I can trust. Particularly for the night shift. Know what I mean? I need people who won't disappear on me. It's a position, a responsibility. I mean, I want at least one person I can trust. Depend on. The security company will hire the rest. I'm not concerned about that. I don't know if you understand me. . . .

Mr. Anthony Allday straightened up like Clark Gable, approached Mr. Parker with hand extended, and told him with utter sincerity: I will take a day to think about it, as you suggest. But I assure you, this job fits perfectly well with my plans. It will permit me to have two weekdays free to spend on my two favorite pastimes: rowing and the opera. I will have to make minor adjustments, of course. I would have to notify the university, for example. But believe me, by tomorrow all these details will have been resolved. Can I count on your help for this? Could you wait until my call tomorrow before you make a decision? Please. I promise I will not let you down. You can count on me.

Mr. Parker looked with curiosity at Mr. Anthony Allday standing before him. He seemed of two minds, drumming his chest with his fingers. He squinted again. Finally, he smiled. He stood up from his chair, shook Mr. Anthony Allday's outstretched hand, and told him he would expect him back the following night. If he had managed to take care of the preparations for the job by then, he could complete the paperwork. I'll also need to show you around. Nothing you can't handle, I'm sure. Still, there are procedures. A medical exam, for example. By the way, can

138

you walk long distances? That's required, more than anything, really. And smiling again, you've never had a problem with the law, right? This won't get me into trouble, right?

As easy as that. With one masterful performance Mr. Anthony Allday had become the night watchman of one of the most important commercial centers in Delaware County, Pennsylvania. And his life changed dramatically. His biweekly paycheck was more than he had ever earned. Given his frugal lifestyle, he could now save enough to go back to Peru, if he wanted. He could live like a pituco, if he wanted.

9

Shortly after three o'clock in the morning, Anthony Allday mused that he had eventually earned enough money to buy what he had always wanted: a red Corvette. All in all, becoming Mr. Anthony Allday had not been a bad deal. Even his occasional loneliness was from then on measured differently. It was now a loneliness without deprivation, a loneliness that showed itself in the silence and not in the cold, in a crowd and not in hiding places. He could now buy a television set and walk the streets of Philadelphia without fear of being stopped by the police or La Migra. Eventually, he even managed to live like a regular American and rent an entire apartment in the Lima of Delaware County, Pennsylvania. And Anthony Allday had thought that El Azar was also ironic: it had brought him, tumbling, full circle from Lima to Lima. Who would have known?

10

Peruvian Notebook No. 3
July 4, 1984

The Seekonk Drive-In was built in the middle of a small pine desert in southern Massachusetts. It was accessible from the main highway by a narrow, winding road. When the westerly winds blew low and hard, especially in early April and early November, the road was nearly covered over by a fine desert sand. Antonio Allday had never seen anything like it: a movie in the open air. He noticed it for the first time at dusk. The enormous white screen of the Seekonk Drive-In towered over the pine trees and desert shrubs like a menacing ghost. The surrounding field was shaped like an amphitheater. Low mounds of packed dirt and gravel were set in semicircles, which the patrons would mount with their cars' front tires, facing the screen. At the crest of each mound was a metal post with a sound box attached to it. In the summer, the patrons would set the volume on high and sit on the hoods of their long-nosed cars to watch movies and feel the occasional breeze that crawled all the way from Narraganset Bay. In late autumn, when the cold ocean winds swept over the pine desert with howling fury, the customers were provided electric heaters to put inside their cars. When it snowed unexpectedly, the moving pictures shone through a speckled veil of white.

The movies at the Seekonk Drive-In rotated with the seasons. The new releases came mostly in late spring and in summer. In early spring, when the snow had not completely disappeared from the winding road, there were reruns of old comedies, like the Three Stooges or Buster Keaton, or Walt Disney cartoons. All at half price. In late autumn they would show old black-and-white movies, also at half price.

People from all over southern Massachusetts and northern Rhode Island went to the Seekonk Drive-In. Young people went there to park and make out. Regular folk went there mainly because the theater charged by the carload and poorer families could afford the admission fee. They would come with their children, their grandparents, their dogs. They would bring jugs of Kool-Aid and brown bags of homemade popcorn. Some even brought dinner. On any given Sunday during the summer months, the Seekonk Drive-In had the feel of an open fair. As for Antonio Allday, he liked going there because he didn't have to change into clothes he didn't have. But most of all, he went there because it was far from the nets of La Migra.

Autumn was Antonio Allday's favorite movie season. He had always liked the old black-and-white movies, and when he still lived in Tacora, Toñito would go see them at El Paraíso, a flea-ridden and urine-soaked movie house in La Parada. He was whisked off to Paradise by the women on the screen: tall, thin, with perfectly sculpted platinum hair, silky voices, dreamy eyes, forever courted by rich men in evening jackets and bow ties smoking Lucky Strikes. They lived in paradise cities called New York, Chicago, London, Paris. But most of all, they lived in Hollywood, a world located at the bottom of a large mountain full of roaring lions.

Yes, remembers Antonio Alday Gutiérrez at 2:22 P.M., leaning back against the winter-hardened yellow vinyl couch. As a child he was transfixed by that world. He liked to go to El Paraíso even after taking in don Luna's acid commentaries about the capitalist corruption of the artist's soul. He felt at home in that make-believe world, even when there was suffering to be seen. And Antonio Alday Gutiérrez remembers that, in Toñito's eyes, the people of Hollywood suffered differently from those of Tacora. Their tender sensitivity caused them pain at the slightest misfortune in life. Toñito would often feel bad for the lack of viveza, street smarts and strength, in heroes and heroines that left them so vulnerable. On the other hand, the happiness in the people on the screen seemed somehow familiar to him—even if hard to explain. And Antonio Alday Gutiérrez thinks that perhaps their happiness was familiar to Toñito because it connected with his own naïve wishes and dreams. Life had already taught him that it was easier to hold on to wishes and dreams when they did not have to be protected from the surrounding reality. In Tacora, Antonio Alday Gutiérrez says to himself, dreaming was always preferable to living.

When Alex Sosa took him to the Seekonk Drive-In for the first time, Antonio Allday was quite nervous. He still felt in his bones the admonitions of his comrades who had crossed the Río Bravo with him: It's never a good idea to go to the movies, Antonio. La Migra is always waiting there. They don't go to the fancy theaters. They're always raking mojados from the cinemas de los barrios. They close all the doors and catch them in bunches. Forget the movies. A cantina is better. People there know. They can warn you. At the movies, forget it! . . . But Alex Sosa had told him, I've never seen La Migra there, Tony. You'd probably be the only ilegal watching Clark Gable! Besides, it's just too fucking cold. La Migra knows ilegales don't like the cold. . . . Since Antonio Allday was already on his way to becoming Mr. Anthony Allday, he decided to go with Alex Sosa.

Good thing, too. In the Seekonk Drive-In Antonio Allday came to know a different Clark Gable. This Clark Gable was somehow more real and more accessible. The Clark Gable he had known in Peru was mythical. His craft was unattainable. Now, however, he could see the actor's skill at work. Sitting enthralled before the giant screen, Antonio Allday thought he had caught glimpses of the arduous preparation needed to project Rhett Butler's unconcern: I'll say one thing: The war makes the most peculiar widows. . . . Rhett Butler sounded so different in English. His old sincerity—guessed in the eyes of a fuzzy Clark Gable, deciphered from a strange Spanish—seemed now much more genuine and believable. Antonio Allday began to see that, much like himself, Rhett Butler was a man unwilling to suffer the fools around him. In his case, the fools were those who remained attached to their old customs, to their old dreams for a South that was dying all around them: the cause. The cause of living in the past is dying right in front of us. Rhett Butler lived according to his own values. He constructed himself as he pleased: I believe in Rhett Butler. He is the only cause I know. The rest doesn't mean much to me. . . . Rhett Butler was an American hero through and through. He knew that every man is alone in the world and must learn to protect himself from uncertain love and certain death.

Antonio Allday and Alex Sosa returned to the Seekonk Drive-In many times. Like the poor families who came by the carload, they would sometimes bring their own Kool-Aid and popcorn. In late autumn, they would wrap themselves up in wool blankets and stay in that desert for hours at a time. But they did not go to the movies in early spring. Antonio Allday had never really liked comedies. At 2:22, slumping into the hard vinyl couch, Antonio Alday Gutiérrez remembers that this had been the case even when he was a child. It is sad that Toñito never really felt like laughing. He came to know early on that laughter was dangerous. It took people off guard. Pimps and thieves lost their lives that way. No question about it, in Tacora laughter was something one had to control.

11

Passing by the deserted coffee shop at 3:15 A.M., Anthony Allday was absolutely certain Tom had not given him the job with ulterior motives. Tom decided to become gay only after they met, a few years back. It had to be. When Tom offered him the job, in the mid-eighties, he was someone else. Definitely. A family man. A churchgoing man. A man with two young sons at Cardinal O'Hara in Springfield, Delaware County. A man with two tiny Yorkshire terriers. ¡Carajo! Tom was someone else even in 1986, the year he invited Anthony to his home for Thanksgiving.

Tom had a house in a housing development in Havertown. Like all the other houses there, the split-level was made of red bricks and white clapboard, encircled by a well-kept lawn. There were flowerbeds marked off from the Bermuda grass by black rubber edging. The driveway was lined with neat rows of small arbor vitae and two dwarf weeping cherry trees guarded the eastern and western sides of the house. A small American flag hung from a short pole in the center of the narrow white porch. The house was bright under the blue autumn sky. The air in Havertown was clean.

Gail, Tom's wife, came out to meet them. She was in her mid-forties and looked like someone who took good care of herself. She gave the impression of being somewhat shy, but kind. She shook Anthony Allday's hand as she invited him to come into her home. Tom's parents were there: Mr. and Mrs. Parker, the typical American older couple. Plainly dressed and amiable. Salt of the earth, as Alex Sosa would say. Chris and Tommy, six and eight, ran in and out of the house, playing with their dogs. In the air was a smell of what home should be. The whole atmosphere made Anthony Allday feel welcome and relaxed. And he realized that this was the first time he had actually set foot in the typical American home, as *Reader's Digest* portrayed it. Within a few minutes, he felt he could trust the Parkers with anything. Including his life story, of course. Yes, Mr. Parker, my parents miss me, I am sure, but I'm determined to remain here in America. They think I will go back to take over the family business. Perhaps. And with deep sadness from the uncertainty in his life: Who knows? If that were to happen, this part of my life would have been no more than a short vacation. Maybe things will turn out that way.

Mr. Parker was particularly impressed by his story. And he wished to share that, in his own time, he had been a man of action. I fought in Korea. Yes, sir. I did my bit in that forgotten war. We were young. We didn't know in what direction the world was going. What kept me going, despite everything, was the knowledge that in our small way we were contributing to a better world. We fought so that families like yours could have the opportunity to live as they wished, keeping their hard-won possessions, and not be turned into a mindless mass of the destitute, which is what communism did when it took power all over the world. . . . Seeing how Mr. Parker's tired eyes looked into the past, Anthony Allday thought that the old man was not bragging. He truly believed his story. He was being honest with himself. Nothing more. Nothing less. He had lost close friends in the war. He could still feel their absence.

And Anthony: Thank you. There is no better way for humans everywhere to live than our American way of life. And I do not say this because of my background, Mr. Parker. I believe that everyone, the poor and the well-to-do, have a better chance under our capitalist system.

Anthony Allday realized that his first Thanksgiving get-together in Pennsylvania was turning out to be magnificent. He seemed to have finally made it to the very core of the American dream. He was inebriated by the goodwill that surrounded him. And yet. And yet, there was something in the whole affair that made him ill at ease. It was nothing visible or obvious. It was more like a ripple in his consciousness, a bump of his hard shell against reality. The feeling came from the words—no, no, from the light in Mrs. Parker's eyes. I don't know, she said in a motherly tone, with an amazing tenderness, I'm sure your mother is praying for your return. When we are young, we are often more interested in our freedom than our responsibilities. Mothers always forgive their children. They always wish them the best. I know this. But they need to know what they're doing, and why. Anthony Allday had the sensation that the old lady had meant to touch the hidden creases of his murky past. She had looked at him intensely and yet kindly with her pale green eyes, almost lost in her powdery, wrinkled face. She had smiled, as if to let him know she knew more than was possible. And for the rest of the pleasant evening, Anthony Allday could not shake loose that feeling.

146

Exhausted and afraid, at 2:24 P.M., sensing the sunlight resting on his throbbing left toe, accosted by memories knocking at the door of his conscience and consciousness, Antonio Alday Gutiérrez has to acknowledge that that Thanksgiving Day might have been the last opportunity El Azar offered him to turn aside from his reconstruction. Or, at least, it might have been his last opportunity to reexamine his goal: Anthony Allday, el pituco.

Anthony Allday now saw a Hispanic woman turning a corner with a wide mop over her right shoulder. Who was she becoming? Who will she be ten, twenty years from now? Because she will be reborn. She has to be. To survive. Who cares about our past pains in our new sitio? To every new generation of Americans, the pasts of all their prior generations, every memory that could attach them to a different, older world is the same: anecdotes of a way of life now safely put behind. So why tell the truth? It means shit. In America, everyone is always moving around and away; everyone is an immigrant. Being reborn is a way of life here, Anthony Allday thought—an extension of our freedom. Those who refuse to change, like Hannah, never escape the grip of family, friends, acquaintances, strangers, pointed fingers, loose tongues, squinting eyes. They let themselves be defined, made, by others. They have no business complaining about their fate. No, señor. One has to decide on a path, embrace it, and as Alex Sosa might say, ¡a la mierda!

12

Engulfed in his chaotic memories, sensing his strength giving way to a growing feverish fatigue, at 2:25 P.M., Antonio Alday Gutiérrez is suddenly hit by the realization that he has denied the memory of his old friend for years. He has thought of Alex Sosa now and then, of course. But as the days went by and he settled in his new sitio, first in Philadelphia and now in Delaware County, he came to recall him only in passing. He let time blur the distinctive contours of his long face, the playful light in his dark eyes, the full black beard that covered his pockmarked cheeks. By now he has forgotten the story of his old friend's life.

With no energy to fend off his accusing memories, Antonio Alday Gutiérrez reaches again for his Peruvian notebooks. He leafs through the brittle pages of red lines and minuscule handwriting, looking for the entry where he had set down Alex Sosa's story. His eyes are now very weak and his hands are trembling uncontrollably again, but he peers at the pages with determination. He peers into his Peruvian notebooks desperately, hoping to recover the anticipation and adventure, the memory of moments of peace and true friendship he shared with Alex Sosa during his early years in America.

Before he can find and attempt to decipher those pages, however, Antonio Alday Gutiérrez is overwhelmed by a bitter realization: he has abandoned and betrayed Alex Sosa in more profound ways than by forgetting him. Wrapped in the soft light of the winter sun, seized by a sudden sadness magnified by fatigue, Antonio Alday Gutiérrez has to acknowledge that over the years, Anthony Allday transformed Alex Sosa into a Portuguese man who was always happy roaming about in New England. Anthony Allday reconstructed Alex Sosa to populate his own past with agreeable memories. In truth, Alex Sosa was not Portuguese, and he was not always happy.

13

Peruvian Notebook No. 2
April 20, 1984

Alex Sosa liked César Romero and Ricardo Montalbán. In fact, he liked all things Hispanic, even though he did not live in a barrio and hardly ever spoke Spanish. I don't speak it because I'm ashamed of my accent, man. You know, when I was a child I used to read everything in Spanish: El Gato Felix, Superman, Linterna Verde, everything. I grew up knowing all that. We lived in Ensenada, a little town on the Mexican Pacific coast, and my father liked to come up north now and again to make some money. Until one day he disappeared. Just like that, man. People said he had died crossing the frontier. Which was probably true. Except that my mother didn't believe it. She refused to believe her Alejo had died like a stray dog in some God-forsaken desert. And so—I only tell you this 'cause I want you to know that I no longer feel cheated by life, man, that I've gone way past it—she took me and my two sisters across the border. She came up to look for him. Can you believe that? We walked and rode and traveled and slept and traveled for God only knows how long. Until we ended up picking melons somewhere in California, or maybe Texas. It must have been around those parts, because there were lots of Chicanos. That's how I ended up in school. Well, I wasn't invited, you know? I was forced to go. One day, some people came and told my mother we three had to go to school. I went because I didn't want my mother to get in trouble. That's when they changed my name from Alejo to Alex.

Alex Sosa paused. He took a swig from the jug of Almaden wine, the only wine we used to buy because, since he had picked grapes at some point in a vineyard called by that name and since we all know wine takes time to mature, he said, perhaps the grapes he had picked with his own hands were now coming back to warm his belly, which would be only fair. Two years, Tony, he said, adjusting himself on a tuft of grass atop the rock promontory overlooking the Atlantic Ocean in Bristol, Rhode Island, by the construction site for the new campus of Roger Williams College, where we had gone to paint. Imagine that! That's how I learned English. I hated it, man. They wouldn't let us speak Spanish. My sisters and I would sneak off and speak it during recess. I think those were the only times when I actually spoke in school. For months, man. People must have thought I was a retard.

I learned all about El Alamo, where Davy Crockett died and we Mexicans were the bad guys. I used to sing songs about the American heroes. You know about El Alamo, right? In any case, I left school less than two years later because my mother decided to take us back home. She told me she had dreamed that my father was in our old house, looking for us. She was convinced it was true because, she said, she had dreamed it just about midnight, which is when the soul opens wide. So we left, and after some weeks I think, we got back to Ensenada. Man! When I got back there, everything was different, Tony. Not only the people, man. I'm talking about the trees, the houses, the sky even. Everything. I didn't like it. I know I should've. But I didn't. Right then and there, I began pestering my mother to come up north. I guess I kind of liked it here. Although if you were to ask me why, I wouldn't know what to tell you. Not then. Not now.

But wait, wait; it gets better. We didn't come back up for another two years. And we came back up north only because one of my mother's cousins told her she had seen my father in San Antonio, in that place where El Alamo is. She said don Alejo Sosa was on his way up to Massachusetts, a place beyond the pampas of Oklahoma, that he had even waved to her from the bus. She swore it was true because she had seen him with her own two eyes.

Another trip. My mother sold everything she had to buy the bus tickets. She didn't like trains. She said her stomach could never settle down. We didn't even have winter clothes. Man! When we got to Boston we were so cold we thought we were going to die. And it was only October. We didn't know what to do or where to go. Can you believe that? My mother just said we had to get to Massachusetts. Of course, we were never going to find my father. He probably died years before. Perhaps crossing the frontier, as they said, on his way back. Because in those days it was more difficult to get back down than to come up here. The coyotes would wait for you at all the crossing places to take your money. My father was probably killed because he refused to give them his money. At least that's what I like to think, man; that he died defending his money.

We ended up in New Bedford because my mother made friends with a fruit vendor at the bus station. After we spent two days there, not knowing what the hell to do or where to go, the lady, who I think was Italian, told her to go to New Bedford because, according to her, there were lots of jobs there. It wasn't true, man. There was nothing there either. Only thing was, we could understand the people there 'cause they spoke Portuguese. Alex Sosa took another swig from the Almaden jug, looked into the blue waters around us, and proceeded to retie his white-and-blue canvas painting shoes. In any case, my mother started working as a domestic in the house of a fireman and my sisters got jobs at a restaurant on La Calle de Saudades. As for myself, I was sent back to school! You see, the fireman gave that to my mother as a condition: You work for me but you send your boy to school. Why did he do that? I have no idea. I guess he wanted what was best for all of us. That's what everybody said to me then: it's best for everyone. And so I was back in school. By this time, I already knew how to speak English. I was quite good at learning, really. I guess that kind of stuff comes easy to me. Thing is, I spent two years in high school. There too, I kinda liked it. Maybe 'cause those kids weren't as mean as the ones in Texas. But, like I said, I didn't graduate from high school either.

See, my mother got sick. Not really sick, like with her liver or anything, only that she missed her family back home. She was losing weight and couldn't sleep at night. She got to wearing only black, like all the old ladies in New Bedford. She looked awful. And so my two sisters—the oldest one, Patricia, was almost twenty years old—decided to take her back home. So they settled the accounts, bought their bus tickets, and took off. I didn't go with them, of course. I liked it here. It wasn't because I hated Mexico or Ensenada. That's what Mr. Rose, the fireman, said: You stayed here because you hated to go back there, Alex. You made the right choice, son. Not at all, man. I just liked it here. What was it that I liked most? I don't know. I guess I mostly liked the idea of finding myself a job and spending my own money. I had already had little jobs here and there, mostly in the summer. I already knew what it meant to earn something. But the deal with Mr. Rose had prevented me from really working. Now that my mother was going back, I thought I would stay, earn some money, and go back to find her whenever I wanted.

Since it was still summer, it was easy to get a job as a painter. I began as a helper. Just like you. Later, I became really good. As I said, things kinda come easy to me. I learned to cut the job, you know? Plass! Plass! Like that! I learned to square the job with the brush. Found a way to make it so that painting was not boring but more like an art. Know what I mean, right? You've got to find that, too. Otherwise, painting is worse than picking melons, man. And Alex Sosa turned around, looking up against the vertical rays of the midday sun. Antonio Allday saw the twinkle in his eyes: I'm an artist, Tony; didn't you know that! I've been painting ever since. It's been my life. Became a foreman only a couple of years ago. Man! I have painted everywhere. I know New England, from Maine to Connecticut, like the back of my hand. I've always liked moving around. Hated to be confined. But now, I don't know. I'm thinking of settling down here, in Providence. It's a good place, Providence. Got lots of friends here. People who had to move out of Fox Point. And Cheryl is here, too. And now so are you.

I just don't want to do anything else, Tony. I like being a painter. Who knows, maybe someday, maybe even soon, I'll have my own little business. Have to, if I'm gonna marry Cheryl and have a family, right? But not for a while. Her family would strangle me now. Especially her brother Bobby. I've got to take care of him. A business would do that. Man! For now, give me another swig. And looking into Antonio Allday's eyes: I like it here, Tony. I like to paint in the full breeze and sun. Don't want to be locked up in some factory somewhere. What the hell. Things will turn out all right. Cheryl will wait. . . . Want to be a painter? I mean, what the hell do you want to be? Don't work in a factory or in the fields, man. That kind of work is only for people who don't really want to stay in America, for people who want to go back. Maybe a mechanic or something. What did you do in Peru?

Antonio Allday told Alex Sosa that he had been an actor, that he had lived in a place called Tacora, in Lima, that he had a brother and a sister and a mother still alive. He told him that he still missed them, now and then, but he was getting used to missing them. Soon it would all be gone. Had to be. It wasn't good to miss people.

14

It is strange, Antonio Alday Gutiérrez thinks at 2:30 P.M., Antonio All-day never lied to Alex Sosa. He never told him tall stories. Perhaps it was because Alex Sosa was a man at peace with himself and Antonio Allday wanted to be like him. On the other hand, he never told Alex Sosa all that much about himself, either. He kept his secrets secret. And Alex Sosa never probed. He never expected Antonio to talk about such things. Not even when they had a jug of Almaden and danced to salsa music. Alex Sosa was too American already. He was happy just to have a friend like Antonio with whom to share his food, his drink, his house, his memories. He was not one for hearing confessions. And Antonio Alday Gutiérrez wonders what would have happened if he had shared everything with Alex Sosa. Things might have been different, perhaps. But Alex Sosa never probed.

Alex Sosa must have known Tony was hiding something that gnawed at the blind knots of his being. He knew his friend that well. On Christmas Day 1982, Alex Sosa gave him a set of four notebooks as a present. Maybe you're really a writer, Tony, he said, since you keep bugging Mrs. Rosenberg to lend you all them novels. I think you're wasting your time reading that stuff. Should get a girlfriend or something. But, hey, who knows, man. Sometimes it's good to get things out from the gut. If one's a writer, I mean. So, here. Found them at the five-and-dime on La Calle de Saudades, back in September. I've been saving them for you, man. I bought the whole bunch, though. So make 'em count. It says on the back they were made in Peru. So all the better, right? But if you ask me, they were made in China. Do you remember these kinds of books when you were a kid?

How could he not? The blurry red lines and the smell of dry lemon peels were unmistakable. Everyone used them in school, back in Tacora. Everyone. Including Betti. Only hers were always neat and clean whereas Toño's were dog-eared and covered with blotches of Pelícano black ink. Hers were wrapped in blue kite paper and smelled like Mr. Sato's red roses, and Toño's were doodled all over—except for the ones he first carried in his back pocket and then stashed under his mattress.

15

When they were living in Providence, out of the blue Alex Sosa came up with the idea that César Romero was the best Latin lover in the whole world. The man was so fantastic, he said, he was a hundred times better than Clark Gable and even Robert Wagner. If you don't believe me, let's go see *Weekend in Havana*. They say he's great in it, man. Antonio Allday resisted the idea because the movie was supposed to be a comedy, and he had never liked comedies. But Alex Sosa harassed him all week long, until he agreed to go with him to Seekonk. They planned to stop at Guido's, in Federal Hill, and take calzones with them. As Sunday evening approached, Antonio let his guard down and began to expect a good show.

The outing ended in disappointment. César Romero turned out to be a real weakling. He played a character who was always nervous, as if afraid of being caught by La Migra. ¡Carajo! He had a stupid thin mustache, ropy legs, and a shameful accent. Shameful. He was no *galán* at all. Not like Clark Gable. That evening, sitting on the long hood of the hearse with Alex Sosa, feeling the soft breeze blowing from Narraganset Bay, Antonio Allday realized that a man could only be a galán if he was not an outsider. If Antonio were ever to be a proper American, galán or not, he would have to belong. Just as a gringo galán would never fit in Peru because he would be too naïve, too cojudo, a Peruvian galán would never fit in America because he would be too *saltón,* too jumpy. At most he would be like César Romero: an embarrassment. And that evening Antonio Allday decided to become a gringo.

He did not let Alex Sosa know about his decision right away. He let him go on talking about César Romero's virtues instead. He knew Alex Sosa admired Latin actors. Like Ricardo Montalbán, for example, who in those days was starring in *Fantasy Island* as Mr. Roarke. He's so great, Tony. Didn't you see him in *The Conquest* and *Escape from the Planet of the Apes?* Didn't you, man? . . . Alex Sosa was not alone in regarding Ricardo Montalbán as a galán, of course. Everyone in New Bedford, including the old ladies who dressed in black and walked along La Calle de Saudades wearing mantillas, considered Ricardo Montalbán sexy. But to Antonio Allday, the gimpy man was just another disappointment. He used his horrid accent as a little flag: here! here! I am Hispanic. ¡Carajo! All that was good for was that people could say: He's not bad, despite being Mexican. The only thing Antonio Allday conceded to Ricardo Montalbán was that he knew how to dress well. *Algo es algo,* he would admit, at least it's something.

The best way to become a gringo, thought Antonio Allday in 1977, was by imitating gringo actors. There were so many to choose from, of course. But he preferred Robert Wagner. He liked his worldly ways and his ironic smile, especially when he played Mundy in *The Magnificent Thief: I guess there's nothing better than good friends, good books, and good food. What else can a man ask for?* He liked how he dressed: fine black or white jackets, thin black or white ties, long white scarves. He liked the way he put his hands in his pockets, the way he ran, like a feather in the wind, the way he paused to drink his whiskey. But even Robert Wagner could not compare with Clark Gable, especially as Rhett Butler in *Gone with the Wind.* If Antonio Allday wished to learn from Robert Wagner how to project an air of mischievous mystery, he wished to learned from Clark Gable how to be sincere.

I'm not asking you to forgive me. I'll never understand or forgive myself.

Antonio Allday simply had to have that sincerity. And beginning in that summer of 1977, in the little room that Alex Sosa let him have for free in his apartment on Baker Street, Providence, Rhode Island, Antonio Allday spent hours repeating from memory entire scenes from *Gone with the Wind* and practicing Clark Gable poses before the mirror: *If you had it all to do over again, you'd do no differently. You're like the thief who isn't the least bit sorry he stole, but he's terribly, terribly sorry he's going to jail. . . .*

In the cold days of autumn, Antonio Allday spent his weekends walking along the beaches of Matunuck, Jerusalem, and Galilee with his face against the wind, reciting lines from memory and learning to control his blinking. That was something he had not been willing to do in Tacora, despite don Luna's constant harping. A good actor conveys more with his eyes and with his body than with his words, Toño. Don't ever forget that. Even when people can't see your eyes, you must control them. It's the rudder of acting, Toño.

Antonio Allday spent months developing the internal conviction that was to serve as the foundation of his new life. He did not let Alex

Sosa see him practicing. He did not want to court his disapproval. Until one day, slowly but as naturally as the waves fell on the sandy beaches of Rhode Island, he began to feel in his innermost self that he could be sincere. By midsummer 1983, he was certain he had finally conquered not only the betraying accent but, more important, the previously constant sense of being an impostor.

It seems we've been at cross-purposes, doesn't it? But it is no use now. . . .

One Friday night, Antonio Allday walked out of his little room feeling like a new man. As he had expected, Alex Sosa was quick to notice the change. The next morning, as they came back from a job, Alex Sosa smiled widely, patted the large steering wheel without taking his eyes off the road, and spoke as if releasing something he had kept in check for a long time: from now on, you're only Tony to me, man! I guess things come as easy to you as they did to me, huh? I know so many who just can't get rid of the accent, Tony. I mean, they can't get rid of the past. Period. 'Cause it's like a curse. You know? My sisters, for example; they never really lost it. They held on to it. Know what I mean? They were afraid of becoming somebody else. I guess you and I have become somebody else. In my heart, though, Tony, I'll always be Alejo and a Mexican. It's in my blood. My children will grow up knowing about El Alamo from *my* lips. Know what I mean? But what the hell, a man has to do what a man has to do. And you and I want to stay here.

I overcame all those obstacles, Antonio Alday Gutiérrez defends himself at 2:35 P.M. Completely. I accomplished what most people only dream of doing. Even Alex Sosa. Because, in the end, he was also attached to his past. He could have gone much further in reconstructing himself. He lost heart. Yo sí. Despite the obstacles. The suffering. I became what I wanted to be. Too bad things turned out the way they did. And, just then, the memory of Rhett Butler's words fluttered in his ugly apartment: *You think that by saying I'm sorry all the past can be corrected. . . .* Of course not, Antonio Alday Gutiérrez says. Rhett Butler was right. Nothing changes by being sorry.

16

They were rowing against the current on the Schuylkill, heading north, where the river curved east and disappeared behind a row of weeping willows, still green even in early autumn. A gentle morning sun bathed the valley and a soft breeze was blowing over the water. Behind them the outline of the City of Brotherly Love was set against a typical mid-Atlantic blue sky. There was a crisp smell in the air. Mallards searched for food on the grassy patches along the dark banks, their bright green and blue hues sparkling. Self-absorbed runners appeared and disappeared from view along paths hugging the riverbanks.

Hannah was exuberant that morning, accompanied by a playful shadow dancing under her abundant black hair. She was saying that to enjoy the cool morning wind against one's face and then to have lunch on the banks of the Schuylkill River was not to ask too much from life; it was good to appreciate the small things. Anthony Allday agreed. There was nothing like the open air on such a clear day like that Sunday. Thank God he had learned to appreciate such things when he still lived in Miraflores, where he had attended a high school founded on uncommon values and ideals. An education quite unique in Peru, Hannah. A relic of the past, really. Remnants of a time when the educated classes governed the poor country with measured sense; by example, not force.

Hannah looked at him with perplexity in her shadowed eyes. She pushed aside strands of hair from her face. She smiled and offered that she was impressed that Tony always remembered his country with a mixture of nostalgia and resentment. That's exactly how my father remembered Poland, Tony. And Hannah said, with sadness, lost in the labyrinths of her own memories, that Eviatar Brodsky, her father, remembered the ghetto of Warsaw as if it were a paradise to which he would have loved to return, if only it had been possible. But of course everyone knew the ghetto was no paradise. Perhaps he remembered it that way because he resented leaving it because he had to, not because he wanted to. And once here in America, he was anchored by something stronger than his desire to return—the inertia of a tired life. Until he died.

Are you doing the same, Tony? I mean, are you, too, wishing for the impossible: to return to a place that now exists only in your mind? Don't you think that with each passing day your return becomes more and more a mere dream? Anthony Allday looked into Hannah's eyes and knew she cared. He felt drenched in her growing love. Then, looking far into the bend of the river, I have no illusions. I know I will never return to the world of my youth. I know that when they exiled me they took a precious piece out of my heart, out of my life, forever. And Hannah noticed Tony's eyes had turned cloudy. It was always the same: whenever Tony talked about his country, his family, so far away, he became depressed. And Hannah knew she would need to nurture him back into the moment, so they could continue to enjoy the day. She smiled. Tony, let's go to the other shore. We came here last time. Let's go there and get a soda.

Bathed by the soft light of the winter sun coming through his window in Lima, Delaware County, Pennsylvania, Antonio Alday Gutiérrez thinks it was surely to rescue him from such despair that Hannah must have promised herself to help Tony with his burden. It had to be. That must have been why she offered him what she had never thought of offering anyone else: Why don't you stay here, Tony? I mean, why don't we look ahead? We can build a space where love and new memories can grow.

Anthony Allday stopped rowing. He moved gently towards her, balancing on his knees. He fixed loose strands of her undulating hair. He caressed her soft cheeks with the back of his warm fingers. He took both her hands in his. And he spoke with all the sincerity in the world: I love you very much, Hannah. And I know you love me too. But it would be totally unfair for me to take advantage of your love to cover up the loneliness I know will never go away. I am destined to live like this, Hannah, in exile. An exile that stopped being forced a long time ago, an exile now based only on a new way of seeing. I would like to give you more of what I am. I would like to promise you more. I swear. But I am not capable. At least not now. Maybe when the dark clouds in my life lift away. . . . I don't want to ask you to be patient. I have no right. Maybe someday I will be able to give you more—without strings to attach you to me, without asking you to share in the darkness that prevents me from seeing beyond my utter loneliness.

After that confession, Tony sensed Hannah loved him even more, if that were possible. She loved him because of his sincerity, because of his disinterested love, and because of his vulnerability. And at 2:35 after the deed Antonio Alday Gutiérrez remembers that Hannah leaned over and kissed Tony tenderly and intensely. He was now certain. She pulled back and under the morning sun the light in her eyes told him that she had understood; that she would stay with him as long as he wished because, such as it was, his company was infinitely better than the purring of her cats and the timbre of Barbra Streisand's voice in the darkness. He knew then that Hannah was prepared to love him unconditionally and without expectations. He had been successfully sincere.

On that Sunday on the Schuylkill River, Antonio Alday Gutiérrez insists, fighting against a feeling of regret at the edge of his consciousness, that he made Hannah happy. She was happy because, without really looking for it, she had found a man who would love her without smothering her. Happy because she knew she would never accept a man who would try to possess her, a man who would take away her loneliness which, after all, had become a part of who she now was. Happy because it was far better than for Tony to have asked her to live only for him, to please him, as Eviatar Brodsky had demanded of her mother.

17

Peruvian Notebook No. 4
October 20, 1984

This place on 69th Street is cheap. I don't like the job at Smokey Joe's very much. The university students remind me of the pitucos of Lima, although they leave me alone.

I need to move on. Soon. For now: save some money. Stay low. I would have been a good student. Perhaps Mrs. Rosenberg was right.

Need to find time to write. Have nothing else to do. In a few weeks, maybe.

Stay low. This basement is already cold.

Philadelphia looks great from here.

18

The poor woman had followed her husband everywhere. From their ghetto in Warsaw to San Telmo, in Buenos Aires, where they lived in a little blue house that flooded every year with the coming of the rains in the pampas, where they had to earn a living by selling print fabrics, door to door, to the poor, who never paid; back to Siena, where they had gone on the promise that he would work as a mason, refurbishing the old city, but where he had had to settle for work repairing the sewers; to God knows where from there, Tony, I swear, before arriving in Coney Island, where the old man found work as an ambulant photographer, begging and accosting people, wearing old shoes, an old coat, in the heat, in the cold; until we ended up in Paterson, New Jersey, where, after only two years—two years!—as an assistant clerk in a brewer's outlet, he died. And that was how Ruth Brodsky ended up old, tired, and sad.

She was finally free, Tony. And she was determined. After her husband died, she took matters into her own hands. Thanks to her tenacity, her wisdom, her love, Tony, Hannah and her two sisters had gone to college—can you imagine that!—each to find her own destiny. And not to any college, Tony. Rachel, the oldest, ended up at Princeton and then Columbia, to become a hotshot lawyer married to another lawyer. They've been successful in New York. Although I don't think she's happy, Tony; I can see it in the way she sighs when she thinks no one is looking. They have a child. My mother adores him. Libby, the youngest of the three, went to Vassar. She became a freelance writer. She writes on everything, from the fate of the homeless of New York to the wildfires of Canberra. She has traveled all over the world. But she came back home a few years ago. She lives with my mother. As for me, I might never finish my degree. Although, who knows, maybe I will. It's been twelve years! I don't really mind being a paralegal. I don't have to put up with the pressure. I know I'm my mother's disappointment. I sometimes think she sees my father in me. Even though we didn't speak much before he died, everyone remembers he always said he loved me best. When he was at the hospital, dying of liver cancer, he would call my name. I saw him die, Tony. . . . She must see my father in me. But don't get me wrong: even now, my mother continues to love that man,

162

her husband, my father. She reveres his memory. She still celebrates his birthday. On the twentieth of March she dresses as she did when he was alive, the same dress, the same hat, and goes to temple. Sometimes she comes back happy and sometimes sad, but always she says how much she misses him. . . . She cries for days after that. Her shoulders droop. Her hair and face turn ashen. She rereads the letters he sent her, asking her to join him here and there. She has never seen another man. Wouldn't even think of it. Not even after she finished putting us through school. It was for us, she said. It was for him, maybe. But never for her. . . . That's no life, Tony. I would never let that happen to me.

Absolutely, Antonio Alday Gutiérrez repeats to himself, I made her happy that Sunday.

19

Dawn. The woman with the wide dust mop on her shoulder followed the path of checkered tiles around a bend, the sound of her footsteps trailing behind her. In the penumbra of the mall lights, she bounced gently away, as if in a dream. With the weight of the Smith & Wesson .38 pulling him down, with his left big toe throbbing, fatigued from lack of sleep, Anthony Allday let himself be drawn by the trailing echoes into a familiar long ago, and he remembered his own youthful steps. His had been furtive steps too. Barely touching the ground. On tiptoes. The footsteps of a young man from Tacora. ¡Puta madre! He would slide on the muddy streets at all hours of the night on his way to see her. She would wait for him wearing her blue cotton dress, her slender neck and arms barely visible in that penumbra. She would take him by the hand and lead him through the labyrinths of bends and shadows, until dawn. She was never afraid. She was never cold. She was always there. . . . Anthony Allday admitted that he had tried to forget his own youthful footsteps and their trailing echoes. He had nearly succeeded, too. He had not thought of Betti for years. But now, perhaps because he had not slept for four days, or perhaps because El Azar had toyed with him yet again by pointing to one last exit on his seemingly inevitable path to murder, he paused.

20

Peruvian Notebook No. 3
May 15, 1984

They met at the theater, when she already looked like a grown woman and he still like a little boy. She frightened him. Not because
she was tall and black but because she looked at him in a way that
pierced his soul. Toñito was afraid to get close to her. He would
look at her from a safe distance, pretending disinterest. For weeks.
Toñito was not only afraid; he was also ashamed of his fear. For her
part, Betti enjoyed teasing him: Toñito burrito, Toñito chinito,
Toñito chiquito, Toñito papito, she would sing to him with a smile
on her face and a twinkle in her eyes. Toñito would hide among the
props and drop curtains, less to escape her teasing than to silence
his unfamiliar feelings.

Toñito was barely twelve and in love. For weeks he was at once
repulsed by and drawn to a sensation of drowning in a milky sea.
He managed to avoid direct confrontation with what he could not
understand by watching Betti from a distance. Except for three
times a week, when they had to attend the classes that don Luna
had declared indispensable if they wished to become really good
actors. With fewer than three lessons a week you'll only become
imitators, the worst kind of impostor there is. Does any one of you
want to be a mere imitator? You? You? The old man leaned against
the low desk on center stage, aiming his dry, curved index finger
at them, his thick woolen scarf dangling from his neck like a limp
tail, his bulky sweater puffing in and out from his heavy breathing, his curly black hair cropped short under his brown felt hat,
his bushy eyebrows turned upwards at the ends, his round yellow-
rimmed glasses dangling from his neck on a dirty cord, his eyes red
and swollen from studying and teaching. Well, then, three times a
week, at six o'clock. I'll be waiting. Everybody went silent whenever don Luna leaned on that black table to lecture. Betti would
then sit nicely, quietly, on the tall yellow table at the edge of the
room, her skinny legs swinging in the air, her little pigeon neck

stretched out, listening. She would not even look at Toñito then. He wanted to venture out from his shell and see her within the safety net provided by don Luna's eagle eyes, but she would not even turn around.

Things changed over time, as they grew up together, leaving behind their juvenile ways. Her teasing and his fear turned into an unexpected but deep friendship. They made their own safety net over which to share their fears and their laughter. Yes, Antonio Allday would remember years later in his little room on the third floor of the red-and-yellow house on Baker Street, Toñito used to laugh then. He had a loud, shameless, disgraceful laughter. He would laugh so hard he had to hold his stomach with both hands, to lessen the pain. He would laugh so hard he would fall on the floor and stop breathing, flailing his legs in the air. Betti said she loved to hear him laugh. She would tickle him just to see him fall apart. And she would join his merriment with her own pristine laughter, shoulders trembling, face smiling, eyes twinkling.

She was also serious and maternal. She kept at him to stay in school for at least two years. Even if it's a half-day, Toño. Someday, you'll have to walk alone. You'll miss then what you're throwing away now. Why do you think I keep going, even though I have other things to do? I'll see you at recess, if they let us out at the same time. I promise. And she never failed to look for him then, never failed to greet him with her eyes, from a distance. She always kept her promises. Toño trusted her. He could talk about everything. She could, too. She could trust him, then. They shared.

It was to please her that Toño kept going to the Colegio Nacional No. 412, even though he would always get there late and leave early. It was to please her that he would read the girlish novels of Corin Tellado by the handful. It was to please her and to be with her that he continued taking don Luna's classes. Because, truth be told, he hated auditions. He felt cheated by don Luna. Toño swore the old man had it in for him because he always gave him the most difficult parts: bitter old men, distraught lovers, repentant gamblers, washed-out actors, thwarted magicians, even murderers. You can do it, my boy. You can do it! he would say with that half smile of his. Toño was the tallest, since grown men did not act in Tacora,

166

but don Luna could have picked Pedro Pita or Gabriel Espinoza, who were a little older. Toño tried to mess up in the auditions, just to avoid having to play the Big Ones, as don Luna would call the principal parts. But the old man always picked him. The more he tried to mess up, the worse it got. Dorotea! he would shout to the makeup artist, clapping his hands like a child, do your thing! The man is ready! And it was to please her that he never talked back to his mother. She's your mother, Toño. What are you going to do? Besides, you're probably just misunderstanding things. All mothers love their children. That's a fact! She does love you, Toño. Ya, déjate de llorar. Stop your crying.

Many years later, at 2:40 after the murder, Antonio Alday Gutiérrez acknowledges with sadness that Betti had been Toño's truest friend. Was it a pure, innocent friendship, he asks himself with a murmur, caressing his Peruvian Notebook No. 3, or was it something else? And he has to admit that it was much more than that. He has to accept that they kissed, for real and for the first time, backstage by the artificial plants hanging from the ceiling on black ropes, after the premiere of *No hay isla feliz*. It was their first kiss. They chuckled timidly, looking into each other's eyes, surprised at their daring. And Betti promised to punch Toño silly if he let out his stupid laughter. Shush, Toño. Shush. If don Luna finds us, we're dead. You know how he is. Shush. And Toño tucked his laughter away, just to please her. They had a lot of fun together in those years. They drank warm Coca-Colas at night, under the bleachers. They shared *pepinos* on the hot nights of summer. They walked the muddy streets of Tacora in the dark. She always wore her blue cotton dress.

Years after their separation, when he was in Providence first attempting to exorcise the stubborn ghosts of his past, Antonio Allday wrote that, despite everything, there had never really been anything between them. In truth, he scratched in the Peruvian Notebook No. 3, looking at the nature of the matter with dispassionate eyes, the relationship between Toño and Betti was no more than a game. It was simply not possible that they loved each other. They were too young and too naïve. Their promise never to forget each other, to return for the other if one of them

167

ever made it out of Tacora, to always remember their sweet and forbidden moments in the dark, all of that was simply a game. A shadow.

But now, in Lima, Delaware County, Pennsylvania, remembering again the promises they made to each other, Antonio Alday Gutiérrez protests under his breath that he did not return to Tacora because it was impossible, not because he did not want to return. Not at all. His decision to become someone else did not preclude a return. Not really. Things happened. El Azar played its capricious hand. It was not his fault.

As soon as he mumbles his protest, however, seeing the soft light of the winter sun beginning to weaken, feeling himself vulnerable and at the end of his rope, Antonio Alday Gutiérrez recognizes that it is useless to deny it: he killed Betti by erasing her from his memory, because she was no longer convenient. He killed her the moment he decided never to look back. He killed her just as much as he had killed his mother, Ricardo, Carmen, Alex. And all the others. Antonio Alday Gutiérrez nods his guilt to himself. He has killed before. Were those deeds of memory premonitions of worse things to come? Were such killings a sign of what Antonio Allday was prepared to do so that he would never have to go back to Tacora?

Betti is surely happy, Antonio Alday Gutiérrez tries to reassure himself at 2:45 P.M.—wherever she is. And surely as pretty as ever. Maybe she is even married, with children. Unlike himself, who could never have started a family. Not even now. Definitely not now. It would be a luxury in view of his careful reconstruction. An exiled member of an old and traditional Peruvian family, a niño bien, does not get married just like that. Far too many questions. Far too many things to say, to justify, to fix. Better to hold on to the forever-postponed return. Better to protect the invented past, that ocean of shadows. And, of course, better for Betti to remain there, in Tacora, forever. She has to inhabit the ruins of what he once was.

What he once was. Exactly when did Toño and Betti really end it, for good? Did things just change over time, as part of their growing apart? Were they really finished? Antonio Alday Gutiérrez has to admit that for years after his departure from the Jorge Chávez airport, in that other Lima, Toño felt Betti's absence. He missed her warm hands on the coldest nights in New Bedford. He remembered her words, sweetly or harshly spoken, for years, as he traversed America. You have what it takes, Toño. You'll succeed. Can't have second thoughts. America or Tacora. There's no choice. Right? Look at me. Right? Words that filled his heart with courage in his most desperate moments: crossing the Río Bravo, hiding in San Antonio, practicing sincerity before a mirror. Yes. Her longed-for smile soothed the loneliness of his afternoons. The memory of their laughter together compensated for his silence in America. Toño carried Betti with him, in his wallet, in that fading sepia photograph taken by a roaming photographer in the central plaza of Lima, the one she gave him, with a kiss, when they said goodbye: *no me pierdas,* Toño; don't lose me.

Exhausted and overwhelmed by a formless loss and regret, Antonio Alday Gutiérrez confesses to himself that he still believes her; that Betti will never completely fade from his memory; that she will always be present in him, even now—especially now. In his confusion, and before he can follow the implications of that confession and come to a full reflection on Betti's divined, anticipated, expected assessment of his current situation—before he can guess her indictment of what he has done—Antonio Alday Gutiérrez seizes upon the conviction that, as Antonio Allday wrote in the Peruvian Notebook No. 3 on Baker Street, Betti is surely safe and happy somewhere; she is surely grateful for their time together in Tacora; she will be remembering Toño's ungracious laughter; she will be pitying him for having gotten lost in the strange world that is America.

Straying farther from the unwelcome reflection—from wondering what she would say now, in view of what he has done—Antonio Alday Gutiérrez recalls having heard that she was in Paris, the City of Lights, where she had always wanted to be. And he desperately wishes to convince himself that Betti has ended up in Paris because, unlike himself, she knows how to embrace her fate; that she has become the proverbial reed under the whims of El Azar. With his head aching and spinning from the strain, Antonio Alday Gutiérrez reflects: Wasn't that what Genaro said—that she is in Paris? And in this instant, Antonio Alday Gutiérrez regrets not having asked Genaro for more details, at the airport, before he killed him. And he regrets not having asked his uncle

Aniceto about Betti in one of his letters or when he returned to Peru and met him for the first and only time, in Miraflores, back in 1986. The old man must have known something about her. People in Tacora know everything. God. Too bad. Too bad. But, Antonio Alday Gutiérrez tells himself, she is all right. I can feel it in my heart.

21

Hannah is different, thinks Antonio Alday Gutiérrez at 2:50 P.M., feeling completely alone and without even the desire for company. Whereas Betti was always frank and often harsh, Hannah never asked too much of him, happy to leave him alone with his brooding and his past. She never second-guessed his silences, his inconsistencies, his daily reconstruction of a past she probably glimpsed only now and then. That was expected, of course. It was the price she was willing to pay for attaching herself to someone like him.

Hannah never asked him to consider living together. He had thought about the possibility himself, of course. And there were times when he would picture himself a married man, with Hannah and a child. Hannah was the only American woman he had ever even thought about making the effort to spend the rest of his life with. He loved her that much at least. All his other relationships in America were of expedience, and hence utterly forgettable. He hardly remembers the faces or the names of all the other women he has met over the last twenty-two years. When it came to intimacy, only Hannah made him feel adequate as a lover. She showed him the mature pleasures of the body. She helped him overcome his distaste for the purely sexual act. Because Anthony Allday feared sex just as much as he feared dreams or laughter. He disliked losing control. Hannah made him feel safe. She soothed his feelings. And yet, in the end, Anthony Allday decided to forego the soft intimacy people say comes from a committed life; a life where the daily interaction, the waking up together, the sharing of feelings with minimal gestures, the conspiracy of two lovers against the world, smoothes the hard edges of experience. No, thinks Antonio Alday Gutiérrez, Hannah preferred not to get too close to his past. It was as if she feared sinking into it, losing herself in someone else's shadows.

But she could not possibly have ignored his past so completely, thinks Antonio Alday Gutiérrez, somewhat calmer now, recovering his balance. When Tony looked overwhelmed by shadows surfacing from deep within his past, she must surely have wondered; she must surely have had a thousand questions. In fact, Antonio Alday Gutiérrez realizes clearly now, Tony could often see and feel her worry, even her despair.

At those times he felt bad for her, of course. He loved her that much at least. But Tony always opted for leaving her to imagine things, as long as she would leave him alone. It was better that way. He had to suffer his past alone. He was doing her a favor. But such deception could not last for long. Eventually, as a matter of self-protection, Hannah had to face the consequences of her choices.

22

In the winter of 1990, Tony and Hannah went to the Poconos. They had always dreamed about spending a few days up in the mountains, in a log cabin with a fireplace, surrounded by snow. It would be like in the movies! said Tony with the enthusiasm of a man in love. And this time, in the winter of 1990, Hannah came through: It's done, then. We're going! Perhaps El Azar had already begun to spin its web. Who knows? But Hannah was happy. Alive. And as they got ready for that trip, Tony enjoyed the ease with which Hannah organized.

They left Lima on a Friday under blue skies. By noon they had reached Jim Thorpe, the little town set on the skirt of a mountain with deep gorges. It had once been rich from coal mining but now survived as a tourist destination. The rustic stone and brick buildings, the touristy train station, the single traffic light, the people coming and going dressed in fluffy parkas and winter hats, they were all perfectly defined against the sky and the surrounding blanket of winter whiteness. The air felt pure and crisp; it gave off an aura of natural health and well-being that can only be found in the secluded mountains. Everything seemed just wonderful. Hannah had called ahead to confirm the reservation for the cabin. She had plotted the best road to take in case of a snowstorm. She had bought the necessities for the weekend. Everything seemed perfect. Only Tony was not feeling altogether well. He had turned quiet, listless.

Are you all right, Tony? You look down. Is anything the matter? Hannah touched his arm as she always did to show her concern. I'm fine, Hannah. Really. Don't worry. It's all this snow. I'm fine. But, of course, he was not.

That dreadful Friday afternoon, remembers Antonio Alday Gutiérrez, feeling the traces of an old shivering, he fell deathly ill with a high fever and piercing chills up and down his aching body. In the beginning, neither he nor Hannah were concerned. It was only the flu. It would pass. But, looking back, they should have been alarmed. Not for him; for her. Because, at 2:51 after the sinful deed, Antonio Alday Gutiérrez is quite certain that on account of that flu Hannah suffered a great disillusionment. That dreadful afternoon, with the high fever pressing on his temples, Tony became someone else. Hannah had never seen him like that before. He stole into a corner of the bedroom, clutching a blanket. He crawled into himself, eyes shut tight, possessed by desperation.

And Hannah: Everything's all right, Tony. There's nothing to be afraid of. Do you want me to call the hospital, darling?

Poor Hannah did not know that Tony was not afraid of the pain, the chills, or the fever. She did not know that what Tony was truly afraid of was being betrayed from within: that the Antonio Alday Gutiérrez of Tacora would come out from under his skin to claim his body, his mind, his soul. And poor Hannah did not know that Tony was afraid of what he was now seeing with the clear eyes of a feverish mind: his mother standing in the corner, beckoning him back to her arms, back to Tacora. Doña Gloria Gutiérrez Bayle de Alday looked just as her Toño had seen her last: long black dress, graying hair gathered behind her neck with a brown barrette, absent eyes, a permanent sad smile on her face. Poor Hannah did not know that Tony was afraid of following his mother and sinking into that ocean of shadows.

And El Azar was not yet done. It began to snow heavily. The mountains and gorges surrounding the town of Jim Thorpe became shrouded by a dense and silent whiteness. The mountain sounds seemed to be retreating in a faraway field.

And Hannah: I'm going to call the hospital, Tony. You'll be all right, darling. I'm calling the hospital. Tony heard Hannah's voice through the filter of his inner turmoil. She was saying they were coming for him. They would soon be knocking at his door. Tony opened his eyes wide, hoping to fend off the feelings that made him nauseated. He was terrified.

In a flash of feverish lucidity Tony recognized that his inner demons were overwhelming him. He needed to do something, before it was too late and he lost his mind. He tossed away the blanket and called Hannah to his side. He held her hand. Hannah, dear, I've something to tell you. He looked deep into her brown eyes. There is something you need to know about me.

And Hannah: Don't talk now, darling. Save your strength. She touched his arm.

And Tony: No, Hannah, I need you to know. It's been too heavy, too long. I'm not the man you think I am. I never went to college. My father died at a hospital, years ago.

And Hannah: You should rest, Tony. Rest now. Please. You can tell me tomorrow. Don't talk now. She patted his shoulder.

But Tony, searching the depths of Hannah's eyes for compassion, still felt the need to confess. It was such a relief to set the weight down. He sensed his weakness was giving him the courage to let go. Let me start from the beginning, Hannah, from the beginning: I was born in Tacora. . . .

Hannah got up and walked away, arms crossed, to wait by the window. She remained there, silent, looking far into the distances of the Pocono Mountains. She seemed to be listening. Meanwhile, feeling the cold light of winter on his face, Tony continued, his voice rising and falling with his heavy breathing, his lips as dry as desert, his fever-hot gaze lost in the shadows of his past.

Poor Hannah must have felt horrible, Antonio Alday Gutiérrez acknowledges, still feeling the traces of the almost forgotten shivering. She must have been afraid. And she must have thought it was no good to share her life with a man who had kept so many secrets from her. Poor Hannah must have cried inside.

23

Peruvian Notebook No. 2
January 7, 1984

I wonder if dreams can be read, like a book. Mrs. Rosenberg says they can be. She also says we are truly ourselves only when we dream— which is silly. To live an honest life we would have to spend all our waking hours deciphering our dreams. Our nights would take over our days. But people believe these things, apparently. There must be something more to this. Mrs. Rosenberg speaks in riddles sometimes.

24

They returned from the hospital late the next day. Tony felt better. The doctor had said viral flus were often violent and always dangerous, but that the worst was over. All Tony needed now was rest and lots of fluids. To ease Hannah's mind, she prescribed antibiotics and counseled her that there was no medical reason for them to return to Lima right away, provided they took it easy and were prudent. But Hannah must have realized their stay in the Pocono Mountains had been spoiled, and as soon as they were alone she suggested they go home. Since Tony was still feeling dizzy and weak, he did not object.

They returned to Lima shrouded in a silence that made the three-hour trip interminable. Tony kept his arms folded across his chest and his eyes half-closed. Hannah had both hands on the wheel and looked straight at the dark asphalt winding down the mountain. The snow had blanketed the hills and fields for miles, and the crows perching on low trees or slinking around small rocky mounds were like black dots on an empty page.

I'm sorry I spoiled the trip, Tony said at some point, regretting the awkwardness of the situation and wishing to reconnect with Hannah.

Don't worry about that, Hannah said without taking her eyes off the road. The important thing is that you're feeling better. She did not seem at all interested in clearing the air. In the distance, an open horizon signaled a respite from the storm.

When they arrived in Lima, Delaware County, Pennsylvania, Hannah helped him up the stairs to his apartment, tucked him into bed, and kissed him on the left cheek, as usual. I hope you feel better, Tony. Don't forget to take your medicine. It's important. Her voice betrayed nothing. Not even disappointment. But Tony sensed she was different, even though he did not know in what way. Whatever had existed between them just a few days before was snuffed out on that trip, and Tony feared that from then on, Hannah's love would cease to grow, that she would stop braiding her life with his.

Hannah walked to the door. She paused for a moment at the threshold. The playful shadow under her abundant hair stood still. She smiled at Tony, turned around, and closed the door behind her. Lying obediently on his bed, his head slightly raised on the pillow, Tony wished there were something he could do or say to prevent her leaving. But in his heart he knew he was incapable of that. He heard Hannah's slow and deliberate steps going down the stairs. They descended rhythmically, predictably. Until they were no more.

When Hannah reached her home in Devon, Antonio Alday Gutiérrez guesses at 2:52 P.M. of the cursed day, she deposited her keys in the blue pot on the dresser by the door, dropped her pocketbook on her long sofa, and called her four cats to her side. Their purring soothed her soul. When night came, Hannah undressed without hurry and went to bed in the dark. The timbre of Barbra Streisand's voice flooded her room. Outside, the wind kept swirling and the snow kept falling.

Good God Almighty! Antonio Alday Gutiérrez exclaims with regret. We continue to see each other. We still take long walks on the banks of the Schuylkill River. We make love some afternoons. But, little by little, things have changed. Every time I sleep by Hannah's side, she sees me ever more as a stranger—until the wall we have built between us will become too high. Tony noticed the growing wall. It was palpable in Hannah's reluctance to make plans that involved more than a few hours together. It was evident in Hannah's growing modesty. She stopped breaking the frequent silences with her natural eagerness to start something new. And she stopped caressing his feet after they made love.

This is why, Antonio Alday Gutiérrez accepts at 2:52 on the dismal afternoon, now that his life is unraveling, he does not have the heart to call her. He does not want to see in Hannah's eyes the gift of pity.

178

25

Despite their falling out, Anthony Allday was thinking at 5:00 A.M. on the cursed dawn, Hannah was still very much a part of his life. They shared something, if only an occasional intimate afternoon. She was bound to meet Genaro. He had to tell her something before then. Not out of obligation. They had managed to prevent that kind of relationship. Only to explain the inevitable changes that Genaro would bring to his life. But what could he tell her? He didn't even know what Genaro would look like. Was he light or dark? Skinny or fat? Happy or morose? He had seen him only a few times, long ago, and had not really paid any attention. Besides, people grow up and change. ¡Puta madre! After all his hard work, the idiot was coming to ruin everything. On top of it all, he would now have to share his ugly apartment! ¡Carajo! Genaro would have to sleep on the couch; he wasn't going to spend money on a new bed.

Anthony Allday thought he was lucky to have been born white, like his mother. Otherwise, he might still be sweeping floors. He had *presencia,* whiteness and good looks. He could imitate Robert Wagner, Clark Gable, or any other true American. Even so, things had never come easily. He had paid a high price. Hours before the mirror, carajo. Hours trying not to blink, with the wind drying his eyes. Hours squeezing his head between his hands, trying to imagine how Robert Wagner and Clark Gable might have looked at his age. Hiding from everyone, even from Alex Sosa, in the little room on Baker Street. How could he explain all that to Genaro? Look, man, you have to become more white and less cholo, more American and less Peruvian. No way. That kind of stuff had to be chosen freely, with premeditation and irrevocably. It was easier if one was spurred on by necessity, as he had been. He had jumped into the river of his own free will. He was escaping a fucked-up world: a world where cops screwed people over, asking for money, anytime, anywhere; a world where thieves and pimps stole even old shoes, especially before carnival; a world where everyone was always looking to screw somebody else; a world where people never stopped measuring themselves, weighing themselves, classifying themselves: by race, origin, size, emotions. Yeah, Anthony Allday thought, he was lucky to have his mother's looks and to have chosen to leave Tacora behind.

Hannah would not understand any of it. She would see his wish—his need—to become someone else as an affront to her liberal gringa sensibilities. She might even fall in love with Genaro! Because of his frailty! Damn it all! If she only truly understood what Tony had to suffer, what he had to do. But she would never want to talk about that. It might be better to hide el cojudo in his apartment, at least until he could talk to him openly. And the first thing he would have to get straight: Don't you dare fool around with my woman, carajo. I'll beat the shit out of you! Yeah, because in Peru men are used to going after anything in a skirt. Nothing is sacred to them. No . . . Hannah would not understand any of it.

The steel blue Smith & Wesson .38 pulled him down. The throbbing in his left big toe became ever more insistent. Anthony Allday tried ignoring such annoyances. He had more important things on his mind. Why not tell Hannah everything again from the beginning, this time including his misgivings about Genaro? After all, she knew him better than anyone now. If he could not trust her, who could he trust? Perhaps this time she would have some advice to give him, some encouraging words. She might share. Perhaps don Luna was wrong when he had said in Tacora long ago, In truth, Toño, good advice is only an intuition we already have ourselves but would like to hear from someone else's lips. Maybe all he needed was someone to help him reveal his fears. Better yet, someone with whom he could rehearse his possible futures. Because don Luna had also said, Never give up on the performance, Toño. Every misstep on the stage has a correction. All you need to do is find the balance. Improvise. On the stage nothing is ever truly lost, Toño. Not until the final curtain comes down. While the performance is going on, we're here for you, Toño. You've got to trust us. We are your safety net. But now, whom to trust, besides Hannah? And she is so distant. . . .

Anthony Allday stopped by a side exit door. He opened it. The cold air of the morning dug into his bones. A light powdery snow had fallen and covered the ground with new whiteness. The sky was now placid and clear. There was a hint of a rising sun on the horizon. Anthony Allday noticed he had little time left. He had to come up with something. For now, he continued his routine: he walked to both ends of the loading bay, checking to see everything was normal; he punched the security clock in the corner by the trash bin; he came back and stood by the exit door, exercising his toes; he watched how the steam from his breath dissipated in the winter air; he shifted the Smith & Wesson .38 that was getting cold against his leg; he cleared his throat; and he returned to the silence of the mall.

26

Peruvian Notebook No. 3
October 19, 1984

Today I went to Southwick's Wild Animal Farm, in Mendon, Massachusetts, with Alex Sosa. Cheryl and Yvonne came along. Weather was perfect. There were lions and zebras, monkeys and swans. All kinds of animals. Lots of people, too. In fact, zoos are mostly for people. They go there to be entertained. The animals seem a little sad. Particularly the turtles. As if they are waiting for something terrible to happen. While they wait, they cry. The elephants are also crying. Only people are happy at the zoo. Some animals seem shocked by what they see around them, by the new things they have to experience. Perhaps I could write a story about the zoo, from their perspective. A turtle, for example. Or an ostrich. Now there is a strange bird. They look at the world in bewilderment—as if they cannot believe their eyes.

It's getting kind of chilly already. They say this winter is going to be long and hard.

Yvonne was nice.

27

I became a night watchman by choice, thinks Antonio Alday Gutiérrez at 2:35 P.M., exhausted and confused, trying to slow down his overflowing memories and feelings, reading snippets from his Peruvian notebooks. I could have become someone else. I could have been a writer. I really wanted to. I planned it that way. What happened? When?

It was no small accomplishment, becoming a night watchman. He has nothing for which to apologize. Of course, even that had not been easy. Throughout the ordeal, his ardent desire to be reborn was often insufficient. Tacora followed him for years, like a shadow in plain sunlight. He would be walking, shopping, working, eating, when someone would call out, hey, José! and he felt compelled to turn around, full of apprehension. Bitterness filled his mouth, his soul. He hated himself for letting the gringos diminish him like that. He hated himself for allowing them to send him back to Tacora, where he was always saltón, looking over his shoulder, embracing his fear in order to survive.

Fear of the gringos. Even when they were neither men nor American. Like Mrs. Rosenberg. The old lady meant well, Antonio Alday Gutiérrez always knew that. But Antonio Allday had felt diminished by her kindness, when she looked down at him from her perch, her black glasses dangling from their blue cord: Stop reading those novels, Tony! You should read something that will help you. Here! This is a book for you. *Popular Mechanics.* So you can learn something useful. A trade. Here! *Reader's Digest.* So you can learn proper English. English! You understand? Stop reading in Spanish. Lord, some people have no sense of what's good for them. Here! Take this! *How to Build Anything.* And don't forget to give them back to me. Give them back to me. Antonio Allday resented her oppressive kindness. But he had no recourse. He had to put up with it. For years. Until, by the early eighties, Anthony Allday stopped turning around for anyone. Thank God! He then sensed his final escape from Tacora was at hand. All Anthony Allday needed to do from then on was to persevere. He held fast. He persevered. Until he became a night watchman. Until he was trusted with the Smith & Wesson .38. He had finally conquered his fear. Thank God for that.

How ironic, Antonio Alday Gutiérrez thinks, peering into the soft warm light of the sinking winter sun, feeling guilty and forlorn, wringing his hands, listening to the hum of his mind. How ironic, Tacora defeated him precisely when he believed himself safe from its power. That was it: Anthony Allday became overconfident and let his guard down. Tacora sneaked back stealthily on the wings of El Azar and finally won. All his sacrifices have been useless. How ironic that his life has come full circle, from Lima to Lima.

Three O'clock

September 3, 1986

Mr. Antonio Alday Gutiérrez
In the United States of America

My Dearest Son Antonio,

    Your uncle tells me you have been around. Why didn't you come to see your mother? Even if just for a little while? So I would stop crying for you. I knew you were alive. I told that to the whole world. They didn't believe me. You'll see, I told them, you'll see how my son is going to come back. And now that they know you are all right, they will no longer call me crazy to keep on waiting for you. I want you to come. I don't want to die without seeing you. The pain of old age is with me constantly now. I feel the cold at night. The sun takes away my breath. Although here, in Canto Grande, is much better than in La Estrella. You'll see when you come. We have a separate room for you in our new house. Ricardo and Carmen cannot wait to see you again. I am raising ducks in the corral so we can celebrate when you come. Oh, dearest son, you will come. My heart tells me that. You will come. Be very careful. Write often. Call me at the community center. Give me a date. Tell me what I can do to help.

Your dear mother who misses you,
Gloria Gutiérrez Bayle de Alday

1

Anthony Allday was letting his mind wander in that cursed dawn before the deed: Maybe if I were to see Cosme again, he might lend me an ear. I could just talk and Cosme would just listen. Unlike Tom or Hannah, Cosme would then go back to Peru to do his own thing. Unlike Betti, Cosme would not feel compelled to straighten me out. After all, Mr. Anthony Allday would not be looking for advice. He would just want to talk to someone. To clear his head. Before Genaro arrived to screw things up. They had talked in the past, just after he had been vilified by snooty Ana María. They could do it again. . . .

But Anthony Allday knew Cosme was not around. God only knew where he was now. Lima? Houston? Miami? Besides, he might have his own problems. No one escapes the designs of El Azar. Still, without a rudder for his wondering, having conjured up Cosme Salvatierra, Anthony Allday felt a vague desire, like an itch, to retrace his steps back to Miraflores, to the Peruvian winter of 1986. And on his last round in the Springfield Mall, hindered by the throbbing in his left toe, Anthony Allday went on to remember the thin and beardless face, the dark and sunken eyes, the plump hands and the coarse black hair of Cosme Salvatierra, the artist.

2

Their encounter had been surreal. Pushed by his desire to distance himself from Ana María and her world, Anthony Allday had gotten carried away and overplayed the gringo card. Many years later, at 5:10 A.M. on the cursed day, Anthony Allday felt a twinge of embarrassment about it. But he swiftly dismissed the feeling as part of the price he was willing to pay for being Mr. Anthony Allday, the tourist.

Anthony Allday had presented himself as the quintessential American male in Cosme's naïve eyes: herringbone jacket, Rockport shoes, a gold-colored Timex, and a slight gringo accent. He had not planned the act, of course. He had no apparent reason for it. But even nine years later, on the morning of December 10, 1995, there was something in the encounter that Anthony Allday did not quite understand. He remembered clearly Cosme's words, his mannerisms, his almost tragic figure cut against Lima's winter gray, but he could not figure out exactly what the man had tried to tell him during his unrehearsed confession.

At 3:05 P.M., searching for clues to explain his sinful act, Antonio Alday Gutiérrez wills himself to recall the exhibition in the Banco de Crédito, on Avenida Larco, in Miraflores.

Mr. Anthony Allday had been attracted by something odd in the huaco, the Peruvian pottery, at the periphery of the display. Its form—serene yet alluring—had touched something deep within him, something that enticed him to lose himself in endless inner labyrinths. Deeply moved, he sought out the artist to ask him, with his slight American accent: Do you have others like this one? You know, real huacos. He then struck his improvised pose of a successful businessman visiting Peru and said that he appreciated the artist's skill, but even more his ambition and temerity; unlike the others around them, who apparently had eyes only for dead or decorative objects, he said he could feel the alluring power of the clay: I believe you've captured something very special, my friend.

Cosme Salvatierra hesitated. His black eyes betrayed a cautious diffidence. But not for long. He would soon confess shyly to Mr. Anthony that he had been taken aback by such praise, unexpected from a gringo like him. Many had praised his *gorditos*—ceramics depicting fat and happy people—but no one until then had noticed that, in the huaco at the edge, the one with the human-bird head pushing up from the black clay, Cosme had thrown something from the inside out, like a spark of fire in broad daylight, Mr. Anthony, to see what would happen. A toss into the hands of El Azar. Because, in truth, he was not crazy about the gorditos. They suck up my tuétano, the marrow of my soul, because they don't express who I really am, have always been, and will always be, until the day I die: *un huaquero sin sitio,* a rootless huaco seeker.

Responding to these confidences and wishing to spend a few hours of peace in Peru, Anthony Allday invited Cosme Salvatierra for a drink at El Vivaldi, a bar-restaurant not far from Avenida Larco: My treat, friend—to celebrate my untimely departure.

And Cosme: With much pleasure, Mr. Anthony. And they walked along Avenida Larco half the time in silence, making small talk, waiting to see how things would turn out between them.

And once there, Mr. Anthony Allday ordered two Chivas on the rocks. My favorite drink in Peru, Cosme, even though your pisco sour is superb, of course. And at 5:12 on the cursed morning of December 10, Anthony Allday smiled, remembering that Cosme had also hesitated to drink the Chivas, saying he had never had whiskey before. But, of course, Anthony Allday knew that a few sips later el cojudo would confess himself a fan. He would then swirl the ice cubes with the thin red plastic stick and speak freely about himself and his art.

I'm interested in making huacos, Mr. Anthony, he said. I mean huacos that speak through silence: without figures, without colors, without lines. . . . How to explain it? . . . It's like, you'd see a huaco and, bam! you'd feel it touching your soul. . . . I've got this piece—maybe I'll show it to you someday—that I found near the mud walls of Chan Chan, up north, near Trujillo. It's a dark man. Or woman. Hard to tell. It's black. Pure black. And yet there is light in it. It's a light that fills and soothes the insides, the heart; a light that shines from the past. Inexhaustible. That's a real huaco. . . . Its light will be there until someone comes along who can understand its language, its message. Understand? . . . My father says that such light holds the key to many secrets. Perhaps even to the secrets of El Azar.

Before coming to Lima I used to work with my father up north, in Chulucanas. He has a little pottery shop there. What can I say? I think I was on the verge of understanding my huaco's secret. God's truth. I shared that feeling with my old man. He told me that perhaps destiny had touched me to unlock some secrets. That's why I have to go, I said. Perhaps in the big city, learning new things, it will be easier for me to find my way to knowing. I'll never get lost, Papá, I said. I'll come back. I promise. And when I make a real huaco, I'll bring it to our desert. I'll bury it there, so it will keep company with the older ones, for a thousand years. Understand? . . . When I boarded the bus to come here, I looked with these eyes at all those who had come to say goodbye. I saved their smiles, their love, their longings, right here, in my heart. They are my *fiambre,* my soul food, in this godforsaken place.

Strange how life is Mr. Anthony, Cosme Salvatierra said as he took a sip from his second whiskey, shaking his head in wonder, as if his mind were filled with intractable questions: I left home for the big city when I was about to discover the secrets of silence. I had big plans. Dreams. But now that I am here, it seems all the windows of my mind, all the tendrils of my soul, instead of opening up and expanding, are closing, shrinking. . . . Thing is, the gorditos have taken me by the throat and are choking me. . . . You might be wondering why I have not stopped making gorditos, if I resent them so much. Right? Why don't I return to Chulucanas. Right? Cosme Salvatierra examined the stout glass in his right hand. He clicked his tongue. He looked at Mr. Anthony Allday with his black, tired eyes. The truth is, he said after a while, I really don't know, carajo. The only thing I can tell you is that, despite everything, I've not stopped searching for ways to make huacos that speak from the very dark center of their being. That's the truth. Oh, I've made lots of whimsical pottery, Cosme Salvatierra went on, now with a growing slur in his speech. Searching. Searching. A couple of years ago, I made special gorditos; you know, gorditos with no names, with no sitio, carajo; gorditos that almost spoke through their silence. Some were totally naked. Some were like the silvery fish that come down every year from the Andes with the floods. Understand? . . . Happy as could be, I showed them to my friends. They looked at them and, bam! veils of sadness covered their faces. They all shook their heads and told me I'd better go on making ordinary gorditos. . . . Puta madre. I wanted to tell them all to go to hell. I swear, Mr. Anthony. But I don't know, perhaps because of my fear of being alone in the big city, I said nothing. . . . Boy! Whiskey does go straight to your head. . . . I've not stopped searching, of course. At night, when I'm finished making ordinary gorditos, I keep on looking for ways to make real huacos. I have to. It's in my blood. You understand? . . . It's been two years since I showed these pieces to anyone. . . . But, Mr. Anthony, let me be frank: if I see my whole life as a bundle, the big city hasn't been all that bad. Look, I sell a lot of gorditos. I send money to my family—which they really need, especially since my mom and dad are getting on in years. I'll find a way, Mr. Anthony. I'll find a way to shake hands with the old huaqueros. I'll know their secrets. Someday. . . .

With the soft light of the winter sun receding on the horizon, Antonio Alday Gutiérrez allows old feelings to flood his consciousness. Peering into the shadows of his past, he has to acknowledge that Anthony Allday meant what he said to Cosme Salvatierra in his fake gringo accent. He was truly touched by the beauty of the huaco with the man-bird head rising from the black clay. And he also had to own that Anthony Allday could have shared those feelings with Cosme Salvatierra, appreciated his gift, and simply walked away, enriched. He could have left well enough alone. Unfortunately, once he had begun his act, Anthony Allday simply could not stop himself. He did not stop until, yet again, by reconstructing himself on the spot, he had closed off any possibility of a true friendship. For, as his relationship with Hannah has shown him, without a foundation of truth there can be no genuine relationship, and certainly no love. Did that inability to step out of character once the play was on lead Anthony Allday to commit murder? Was the wicked deed prefigured in the lines of his invented character?

3

Anthony Allday paused in front of a wide display window illuminated by the tenuous light of dawn. He looked past his inner turmoil and old memories. He found himself not bad looking, at forty, even in that uniform. He imagined himself even better looking in his white linen shirt, his navy blue jacket with brass buttons, his light brown Cerruti pants, and his black Fiorentino shoes. No, Anthony Allday thought, he did not have a bad life. Being a night watchman had its benefits. He could live like a millionaire, if only during the day. Looking at the whole thing as a bundle, as Cosme would say, all his sacrifices had been embedded in a fair exchange. Who would not make the same choices? And then, walking away, at 5:30 A.M., feeling bathed in the tenuous but growing light of dawn descending into the Springfield Mall, Anthony Allday touched the plastic rim of his cap with two fingers and smiled.

At 3:00 P.M. on the same day, weighing everything anew, sitting back on the yellow vinyl couch, the Peruvian notebooks strewn to one side, the soft sun of winter climbing up his wrinkled Cerruti pants, Antonio Alday Gutiérrez confesses that perhaps he has gone too far, that perhaps he has spent too much time and money acquiring the props to cultivate his Robert Wagner–Clark Gable image; that perhaps he has sacrificed far too much to cover himself well, going so far as to live in this ugly apartment in Lima, Delaware County, Pennsylvania, surrounded by cheap broken-down furniture, without even a rug, too cold in the winter and too hot in the summer. All of that *solo para taparme,* just to cover myself.

I cannot help it, Hannah. It is how I was brought up! I am an unrepentant bourgeois!

Early on, just after he discovered Tom's secret, about every three months Anthony Allday would put on his best clothes, take a train to Center City, and spend hours in the lobbies of the luxury hotels, pretending to be waiting for someone, consulting his fake Rolex wristwatch, impatiently shaking his head at the lateness of someone who would never arrive. He made his rounds through the best hotels of the city that way. He spent most of what he had saved. The concierges, waiters, and bell-boys recognized him and treated him with respect. The maitre d'hotel showed him to a table by the window and offered the list of wines from Bordeaux. In those few hours, Anthony Allday was on top of the world. One day of the good life, he would convince himself, was well worth a whole month of living like a dog.

He would never share that view with Hannah, of course. She would have considered it extravagant and in bad taste.

Thinking about her, recalling her abundant black hair, her frank smile — which for a while now, with each passing day, has been turning ever more melancholic—Antonio Alday Gutiérrez acknowledges that, up until recently at least, he has not felt the desire to better his condition. He has been quite content in the knowledge that he has already made all the necessary sacrifices in his life. He does not even feel like Alex Sosa, who strove to buy a house, raise a family, and achieve the most common version of the American dream.

It was tolerable to spend the days holed up in his miserable apartment in Lima, Delaware County, Pennsylvania, if he could save enough money to spend those few hours in Philadelphia. Send money to Peru? What for? They would only steal it. Lima was not like Chulucanas, where Cosme came from. In Lima, people were desperate. They would steal everything. They would open the mail. They would pocket the money orders. And then, whom to complain to? It would be a pure waste. Definitely. Besides, where would those cojudos be? Lost in some desert somewhere, with no address. Nah. Besides, when she was alive, the old lady had her own children. Cosme was luckier.

Feeling the silence of the morning pregnant with the anticipation of daybreak, thinking about his long-dead mother, Anthony Allday had to acknowledge an old resentment: the more she had tried to get close to him, the more she had made him feel like her stepson. Even though he was the youngest. *¡Carajo!* At least his old man did not lie to him. Don Juan had not liked him very much, but that meant the old man treated him just like he treated the others. Not her. She would take her children's side. She would fix their beds. ¡Concha su madre! Shameless old bawd! She closed her eyes. Her heart. For her dear little children. ¡Concha su madre! For shame. Cosme's situation was not the same at all. For Toño, nights of sweat. Nights of insomnia. Nights of biting his lip so as not to yell out his disgust. To hell with them! To hell with them all! And el cojudo Genaro coming here to remind me of all of it. . . .

Looking lethargically around him, in the grip of an inchoate feeling of regret, fatigued but still unwilling to close his eyes and fall asleep, Antonio Alday Gutiérrez realizes that all he has accumulated in twenty-two years of exile could fit in his two small suitcases: an L. L. Bean goose-down parka, a trench coat, two suits, two jackets, six linen shirts, two usable pairs of Cerruti pants, silk handkerchiefs, a cashmere scarf, two pairs of Fiorentino shoes, one pair of Rockports, a few leather-bound books, a bottle of cologne, two leather belts, some underwear, a fake Rolex, a gold-colored Timex, a shaving kit, perfumed soaps, and four Peruvian notebooks. In the end, Antonio Alday Gutiérrez tells himself, I ended up like my old man: *un saltaperico en la vida,* a man going restlessly through life. Fortunately, they will never know in Tacora what I have and have not done. They will never know what happened to Genaro.

4

Shifting his position slightly to show his gold-colored Timex, Mr. Anthony let Cosme Salvatierra know that he understood him completely. He had experienced a similar situation in the USA where, at the beginning of his climb to great success, everyone treated him as if he were a mere wetback or a poor soul in exile, simply because he had been born in Peru. He had paid dearly to overcome the weight of ignorance—an ignorance that for years he, too, had felt like a noose around his neck, turning him into someone else. People are always trying to fence you in, Cosme. One has to have the balls to resist that. And Mr. Anthony assured Cosme Salvatierra that in his stores, which had cost him blood, sweat, and tears but which were now at the center of the most important malls in America, he, Cosme Salvatierra, could sell not only his gorditos but also his true art, those huacos of smooth and elevating forms. Why not?

Over the third glass of scotch, Mr. Anthony told his story: He and his family had emigrated from Miraflores when he was still a boy. His father, an English merchant who had made his fortune in Peru during the rubber boom, had married his mother who was from Celendín, up in the northern Andes. They went to the USA in the sixties once the old man had made enough money from his properties deep in the Amazon jungle. That was why Mr. Anthony Allday had been educated in the most exclusive American high schools and universities. I even graduated from Wharton, at the University of Pennsylvania, Cosme. I was meant to take over the family business. But, to everyone's displeasure, I turned down the offer because I was tired of doing what the old man wanted and, besides, I was not at all interested in plastics. I wanted to do things my own way, friend. I was prepared to suffer and sweat. After years of work and struggle, things turned out all right. So that now, Mr. Anthony was not only a man of good social standing in the USA but blessed with an inner sense of well-being. He had two children. The older was studying physics at Harvard. The younger wanted to be a physician. She had always wanted to help the poor in America. Because, believe it or not, friend, there still are many poor people in the USA. Especially newly arrived Latinos and the blacks who have been there for centuries. But that is life, Cosme; everywhere it's the same.

195

Sipping his scotch studiously, Mr. Anthony confided to his friend Cosme Salvatierra that he did what he could to help the newly arrived Latinos who reached Pennsylvania dying of hunger, looking for work. Peruvians. Salvadorans. Mexicans. Guatemalans. He would support them for months at a time. He gave them shelter in his own home, a few miles west of the city of Philadelphia, in a place called Lima but which there was pronounced "lyma."

And Cosme: Was everything in the USA like in the movies? I mean, does everyone have a new car? Do they all live in houses with swimming pools and everything, Mr. Anthony?

There is a little bit of everything, answered Mr. Anthony, looking deep into himself, returning in his mind to his lovely house in Lima, Delaware County, Pennsylvania. It's a country where people only need to dream.

As evening came, Anthony Allday asked the attentive waiter for two *espresso stretto*. The new friends smoked Kents. They saw buses pass by, overflowing with people. They turned sad considering the rampant corruption in the country. They laughed remembering the old Cantinflas movies. They enjoyed the cool breeze blowing faintly from the distant Malecón. Until the lights of the big city flickered on for miles, rendering its rambling extensions menacing. It was time to find refuge.

Just then, as they were about to say goodbye, without having planned it, Mr. Anthony Allday asked Cosme Salvatierra if he could see his huacos. And Cosme, visibly moved, invited him to come up to his studio. It's nearby, he said pointing the way with his chin.

196

5

Peruvian Notebook No. 2
March 3, 1984

I'd like to write a novel from the perspective of the poor, of the weak—like in the old novelas ejemplares, only without God. Since I was one of them, I could even write an optimistic one. Showing their perseverance would be showing their marvelous humanity. I only need time. And I need to write it in English. To write about the poor in Spanish would not mean much. It would be like writing about regular folk. Hard to produce discomfort, anger, or pity. . . .

6

Since Mr. Anthony Allday was leaving Peru earlier than expected, now not so much out of disgust and scorn as because he didn't want to change his plans again, he decided to buy several huacos from Cosme Salvatierra. He paid one hundred dollars apiece. A lot a money anywhere, but especially in Peru. In addition, he promised to return every once in a while to buy more from him. I'd like to take them home with me, friend. I'll eventually put them up for sale at some of my stores which, as I told you, are in some of the most important malls in the USA.

That Peruvian winter night, in his little studio on the top floor of an old *casona,* a colonial house, Cosme Salvatierra wrapped up five huacos in newspapers and jute: a black obelisk with a glimmer of golden fish scales, a white *algarrobo* with black tangled roots for branches, a large clay jar with no mouth adorned with low-relief *cañanes,* two elongated bald heads with blue mirrors in their perfectly round eyes, and a toy whistle in the form of a sea urchin.

And Mr. Anthony: Save them for me, Cosme. I'll pick them up tomorrow, before I leave the country. I hope you don't mind. But Mr. Anthony had no intention of picking them up. Only three years later did he return to Cosme's studio in the old casona in Miraflores. He came back with greetings and excuses. El Azar has played one of its tricks on me, my friend. You know what I mean? He then bought ten more huacos for the same price. I'll come back for them on Monday, Cosme. Would you get them ready for me? But, again, he did not show up.

Another year came and went.

In 1990, five years before Anthony Allday became a murderer, he sent Cosme a letter: Due to the imponderable designs of El Azar, he could no longer return to Peru, at least not for a while. Therefore, all the huacos he had bought from him were to revert to their initial, proper owner. Mr. Anthony Allday wished Cosme Salvatierra the best of luck. May he find what he was looking for. Sell whatever you can, Cosme. The rest, keep as a token of our friendship. If you ever come this way, call me. You can look me up in the directories of the principal malls under *All Day Imports.*

198

Thinking back to when he had written that letter, trying to explain yet another bundle of motives, Antonio Alday Gutiérrez can do no more than murmur to himself that he did all that because Cosme's friendship was worth something, even if only to fill the growing empty spaces of his memory. When Cosme Salvatierra comes to the USA now, he tells himself, to exhibit his work in galleries and museums in Miami, Houston, or Philadelphia, he probably remembers Mr. Anthony Allday. He might hope to bump into him in one of the malls in one of the big cities he now travels through. He might hope to let him know that he has finally made huacos worthy of being buried in the northern Peruvian desert for a thousand years. On the other hand, Antonio Alday Gutiérrez adds with sadness, he might already know that America is a vast country. Things and people can get lost here.

7

It is not a bad life, Anthony Allday repeated to himself, proceeding with his last round on that cursed dawn. Tom had offered him a position on the day shift, in view of his years of service and his sense of responsibility. But he did not take it. He had gotten used to working at night. No one came up to him with stupid requests. He did not have to answer to anyone. Not even to Tom. He had time to sit down and read—a habit he had assiduously cultivated since his days at the Elmwood Avenue library. Besides, despite all appearances, day or night, the Springfield Mall was far from boring or lifeless. Alex Sosa was right: the whole of life can be appreciated from any one of its moments. To appreciate life, guarding was just as good as painting, if one only did it long enough. No question about it. A lot happened in a mall, even though this might not be obvious to those who did not spend enough time there to experience its internal rhythms. To Mr. Anthony Allday, the night watchman, the steady blinking of the lights, the plain or checkerboard paths, the hard corners and exit doors, the pockets of silence in the long walls were all saturated with the scent of victory and defeat nestled in the daily drama of life.

Just like the movies at the Seekonk Drive-In, in the mall the victories and defeats seemed to ebb and flow with the seasons. Only here the seasons were internal, manufactured. The worst season in the mall began just after Christmas. Stores that only days before had been decorated with holly and blinking lights would disappear in less than a night. The crews of carpenters, electricians, and painters who came to the mall in the nights following Christmas were efficient. The idea was never to give the impression that the mall was in decay. As early as the middle of February, stretches of the mall would turn into smooth walls. The painting crew would draw geometrical patterns on them, to make them look planned. An eerie silence would soon grow in those stretches. But, as with the movies at the Seekonk Drive-In, the silences eventually disappeared. Nearing November, usually a few days before Thanksgiving, the smooth walls would all be opened up again, displaying myriad new things for sale. The decorations and blinking lights would return, together with new, smiling faces.

At around this time, Anthony Allday thought, passing the Hallmark store, another significant change took place: the new mall catalogues arrived. They would make their way to the security office within a couple of days. Tom would then ask Tony to collect the old ones still lying around and toss them away. And Anthony Allday thought that, even now, he would do the chore with a bad taste in his mouth. Despite all his years in America, he had not gotten used to its throwaway mentality. He still paused just before discarding the unused catalogues into the wastebaskets. Tacora was still in him. But he was changing. He no longer felt the urge to rescue some by taking them home with him.

The catalogues of the stores of the Springfield Mall were quite beautiful. They were perfectly edged, bright, and clean. Some had only a few pages. A few were as thick as any book at the Elmwood Avenue library. They had indexes, sections identified by color, and wonderful photographs.

It's because people buy what they see, Tony. And they appear now, before Thanksgiving, because the stores make most of their money in the next two months. The rest of the year they mostly mark time. Can you believe that? Tom had never stopped commenting on that fact since they had first met, back in 1985.

Anthony Allday read most of the catalogues with care. He liked to see the beautiful models in their different poses, wearing their alluring smiles. Sometimes he would spend a long time trying to figure out what they would really be like in person. He would unfreeze them in his mind and follow them outside the pages, imagining their mundane activities. Were they like everyone else? Or were they different for being "the beautiful people," as Tom would say? Perhaps he would never know. Still, the catalogues gave him a sense of familiarity, of intimacy almost, with the things he spent most of his waking nights protecting. In a way, he had once thought holding a new catalogue in his hands, they made him feel like a valued protector of the good life in America. And that feeling was never as clear or as strong as in November of 1986.

8

That November in 1986, Antonio Alday Gutiérrez remembers at 3:05 P.M. on the cursed day, a very different kind of store opened at the Springfield Mall. It was so distinctive that, from the time it opened to the time it closed some three months later, shoppers approached it with an attitude resembling reverence. The Blue Crow was an art gallery. It was not one of those stores that sold pieces of art the way one sells candy or perfume. The store itself was a work of art. It was decorated with bright quilts, clay figurines served as door stoppers, and the trash in the receptacles on its threshold was not really trash but art bronze pieces. Inside, people could not tell whether an article was new and dirty or old and clean. In addition, the people who worked there were very peculiar. There were bald mustachioed men with ponytails, skinny ladies in bright red or pitch black tights, older men with dragging scarves, and a man at the cash register who sang out each sale in a baritone that cut through the white noise of the nearby fountain.

These are real artists, Tom said to Anthony Allday the night the odd men and women arrived at the mall to set up their store. Apparently they're coming from all over Delaware County. Enjoy them, Tony, because, believe me, this will be the first and only time these guys will ever be together in one place. Artists hate to be together. It goes against their image, you know. But, hey, it's the season to be jolly and for every Tom, Dick, and Harry to make some money. Right?

With the artists there arrived the most beautiful catalogue Anthony Allday had ever seen. It did not have smiling models. And it was not very big. But the items presented there seemed to leap off the pages. There were pictures of ceramics with uplifting lines that seemed to defy the weight of the world. There was Peruvian opal jewelry depicting fish figures that offered a mute commentary on the unhappy trajectory of humanity. There were rough, square canvases with lines so perfect they seemed to touch infinity. . . . At least that was what the notes said. The notes, written by a bald, full-bearded man from New York, were designed to place the pieces within the fluid yet recognizable context of modern art.

A few days before Christmas in 1986, Anthony Allday read and reread

202

that catalogue, learning the terms used to talk about art. Looking at the catalogue, night after night, he memorized it in its entirety. He spent time in the art gallery on his nightly rounds, comparing the advertising copy with the actual pieces, until he had learned to say, with all the sincerity in the world, that artists were sensitive souls who tried to express something ineffable, something that strives to be born, something that cries out from the very center of their being. . . . And he kept that ability hidden, like a forbidden possession, even from Hannah. . . .

Antonio Alday Gutiérrez acknowledges with a vague sense of guilt that he kept his rehearsed sincerity like a loaded Smith & Wesson .38. When he met Cosme Salvatierra a few months later, Anthony Allday was ready to impress him. His spontaneous reconstruction at Avenida Larco was based on that rehearsed sincerity about art.

And that was not all. It was also back then, in 1986, that Anthony Allday realized for the first time that not everyone felt the need to reconstruct themselves in order to express who they truly were. Seeing how the artists lived and enjoyed themselves, without caring much about the judgmental gaze of the world, Anthony Allday intuited, knew even, that there were those who had or felt something very deep and very much their own, something that had been within them from the beginning and would remain in them to the very end—despite El Azar and all the different parts of themselves they threw out into the world as their creations. He saw that there were those who did not expend themselves by living. And there were those who did not wish to change themselves at all. And thinking of Cosme Salvatierra, Antonio Alday Gutiérrez envies him. He envies him even more than Anthony Allday envied—without realizing it—the artists of Delaware County.

9

Peruvian Notebook No. 3
October 21, 1984

Went to see The Rules of the Game at the International House. Great movie. Halls with flags from all over the world. Even Peru. The Hispanos there were different. They all looked like pitucos from Miraflores. There was a fair. Books. Posters. Machu Picchu. I was nearly invisible. I like Philadelphia. I wonder what is playing at the Seekonk Drive-In. I wonder if Alex Sosa now goes there with Cheryl.

10

Anthony Allday checked his wristwatch: 6:32 A.M. Genaro would be arriving at ten o'clock. Only three and a half hours left. ¡Puta madre! Suddenly, after four long days, time seemed to have accelerated. But at least, by ten that morning, the dread that had dogged him since he had received the news would finally come to an end.

And Antonio Alday Gutiérrez remembers being so upset that he had not been able to sleep for those four days. The hum of pain in his left big toe had increased. His body ached. His eyes felt heavy. His mind seemed stuffed with wet cotton balls.

Genaro was coming on American Airlines, flight 912, like any other tourist, carajo. It did not bode well. El cojudo would want to take everything he was about to find in his new sitio as something deserved, as something he should enjoy simply because he was here and alive. Because, let's face it, that's how people take things these days: as something to which they're entitled. Peruvians are no different; they might even be worse. ¡Puta madre! Three and a half hours. Everything could end up in a mess. He didn't even want to think about it.

To chase away his worries, Anthony Allday thought that maybe he could speak to Genaro, make him understand. Or maybe Genaro would be so dazzled by everything in America that even the ugly apartment in Lima, Delaware County, Pennsylvania, would seem ample and luxurious. Who knows? Maybe some good could come out of all that waiting, after all. Had Antonio Alday Gutiérrez not been dazzled when he had first arrived in America? Of course he had been, insisted Anthony Allday, feeling the dead weight of the Smith & Wesson .38. He had been dazzled. And not only in the very beginning. For years. And by so many things.

11

In the summer of 1977, Alex Sosa took Antonio Allday to Cranston, Rhode Island, in his newly decorated hearse. On the way Alex Sosa spooked the brand-new Antonio Allday with talk of the Mafia. They're a bunch of Italians, man, who run the entire state from their little pasta places in Federal Hill. *Por la chingada.* They settle their accounts with all those who double-cross them by burying them alive in the foundations of new buildings. But they leave us pretty much alone, Tony. They have most of their problems with the blacks and Italians from Massachusetts, who look down on them because they're from Sicily, a place in Italy that's as poor as the land where I was born. That's pretty bad, chingón. That man, Mr. Stanza, whose house you're going to paint, is high up in their organization. So don't be messing around.

They arrived in Cranston at about 8:00 A.M. The house was in a pine grove behind rocky mounds covered by rhododendrons and mountain laurels. They had to leave the state road and go down a narrow, white gravel driveway bordered by a low wall made of uneven yellow rocks and white cement. There were small black lamps along the top of the wall every few feet. Alex Sosa said they hid tiny movie cameras, put there by Patriarca himself, the boss of all bosses of the Rhode Island Mafia, to keep track of the comings and goings of the people in the house. Don't you even think of peeking around, Tony! They'd skin you alive. . . . The hearse went down the white gravel road making a sound like a retreating wave. The stunted desert pines were nearly hidden by a thick morning haze. The cries of unseen crows came and went. Such a windless and heavy morning gave Antonio the shivers. . . . Alex Sosa parked the hearse by the front door. They unloaded the equipment in silence. When they finished, Alex Sosa winked at Tony: I'll come back to get you at six. Behave yourself, chingón! He got into the hearse and left. Antonio heard the sound of the car fade among the pines lost in the haze.

Close by, Antonio noticed the light of a jaundiced sun cut through the fog rising from the numerous flowerbeds, hanging pots, artificial ponds, and scattered plants that surrounded the yellowish stucco house. He also noticed that the thick fog eddied close to his body. He seemed to move in *una bruma de ensueño,* a dreamlike haze. Not wishing to remain alone on the grounds, he decided to enter the house and begin his work. As he approached the front door, it opened automatically. But there was no one there to receive him. Hello? No one answered. Not knowing what else to do, Antonio went inside.

Several tall stained glass windows filtered the morning sun into a large foyer with dark red wall-to-wall carpeting. Huge rose marble lion heads perched atop Roman columns in the corners of the room, their lustrous black eyes menacing the front door. A black marble umbrella holder containing a glass walking stick stood to one side. A full-length mirror, decorated with gold-leaf motifs, covered the left wall. On the far wall, a glass table with crystal figurines caught the stained glass glow. Beyond it, a wide curved staircase disappeared around a thick multicolored tapestry falling from the ceiling. Below the eastern window, at the far left, where the sunlight was stronger, there was a white credenza. It had bowed legs and well-defined gilded lines. On top of its narrow surface were two small boxes with gold inscriptions. Hello? Still no one answered.

The next room was larger and carpeted in pale green. Several pieces of furniture upholstered in velvet surrounded a black metal center table with a clear glass top. Three glass bowls, containing plastic bananas, apples, and white-and-purple grapes, were set in a straight line. Farther in, behind a sectional leather sofa, was a large rose marble fireplace with a shiny brass screen. In the front center of the fireplace, two small cherubs held high by long arching golden rods blew short trumpets in opposite directions. There were several large paintings of hunting scenes on the near walls: men in tall hats, red jackets, white pants, and black boots rode white horses. There were reddish brown foxes in the distance. A grandfather clock with gold chains and weights stood against the right wall near a terra-cotta pot containing blue, green, and red pampas grass plumes. Beyond the plumes there was an archway decorated with satin valances. Hello? Antonio took a deep breath.

He passed under the archway, slowly and silently, taking in the scent of the musty air. The archway led into a reading room. The rust-colored scatter rugs left large sections of the hardwood floor exposed. Rows of leather-bound books covered the left wall. On the right hung a large painting on dark canvas with a gilded frame: Roman men wearing togas and laurel crowns surrounded by listless boys and solicitous women wrapped in gowns. Directly beneath sat a television set built right into the wall. The set was on, but without sound. Near the television set there was a small bar, with glasses of several types on display. Hello?

Antonio continued on. He came upon a long corridor. Plastic plants and silk flowers hung from the ceiling in shiny, moss-filled wicker baskets. A miniature fountain, complete with black stones, windmill, and pristine shells, gurgled gently. Two wicker rocking chairs looked out onto a small inner garden barely visible through a smoked and frosted sliding glass door. Beyond the corridor, another archway led to a dark area.

Hello? Antonio stood still in the hall for a moment. He listened. But he could only hear the gurgling of the miniature fountain. He decided to walk into the dark area, where he found a bedroom. All four walls were covered with mirrors of different sizes, colors, and shapes. There was a wide bed adorned with different sizes of pink pillows, the bedstead painted some shade of blue. Large paintings hung on the left wall, but Tony could not see them clearly in the dark. Nor did he really want to see them. He had the sensation something was amiss. Hello?

Antonio started to worry about being there, alone. He felt he was being watched. He needed to get out. He circled the bed to reach the other side of the room and came upon another dark glass sliding door. He opened it. Hello?

Mrs. Stanza was lying face-down on a red chaise lounge by a pristine pool abutting the inner garden. But for her wide-rimmed sunglasses, she was completely naked. She turned and looked at Antonio from head to toe. She smiled. In that instant, blinded by the foggy morning sunlight, Antonio thought Mrs. Stanza looked just like Marilyn Monroe, with a small beauty mark near her rouged lips and everything. He averted his eyes. He then saw floating red cushions in the water and the statue of a gowned woman with a jar in her arms. She seemed suspended in midair. He heard a million insects hum. And Antonio felt Mrs. Stanza's hidden eyes on him. And he didn't know what to do. He was her prisoner. Finally, to free himself, Antonio tried floating away in the morning bruma, back into the dark room. Without raising his eyes, he reached for the sliding door in front of him, preparing to flee.

But then Mrs. Stanza called out to him: Hi! Her voice made the fog swirl and quiver. Antonio didn't know whether to answer or ignore her. Come on out! It's all right! She seemed amused now. Come on out! Antonio decided to peek outside. She had taken her dark glasses off. You can start with the ceiling, she said in the sexiest voice Antonio had ever heard: Be careful not to dirty the surfaces. You know what to do, right? Is Alex coming? . . . There's beer in the refrigerator. . . . As she talked, Mrs. Stanza walked over to the pool and plunged in. Yes! Antonio shouted, as she hit the water. I know what to do. Don't worry, Miss.

Of course, Antonio Alday Gutiérrez thinks, his tired eyes resting on his stack of notebooks, remembering the embarrassment, the self-consciousness of Antonio Allday back then in 1977, of course Mrs. Stanza lived in a world totally different from Antonio's. A world with borders he could only dimly imagine. Of course, Antonio had been dazzled by it. And yet on that foggy morning, despite the cold knots of fear, desire, and shame in his gut, Antonio knew to appreciate what Stanza the Italian had achieved. He had constructed a world to his measure. Yes, of course, only a few years later, to Mr. Anthony Allday, to the man who had borrowed books from the Elmwood Avenue branch of the Providence Public Library, to the man who had read all the catalogues that had come to the Springfield Mall with every new season, to the man who had enjoyed the life of someone with good taste, to the pituco from Miraflores, that mansion in Cranston, with all its iron-and-glass fakeness, would be nothing but the highest crest of *huachafería*, low-class bad taste. But to Antonio, the illegal Peruvian, all of that huachafería represented the realization of a dream, an affirmation of what was possible in his new sitio.

If only Anthony Allday had allowed Genaro the chance to choose. Who knew? Genaro might have seen things in a similar way. He might have been content simply to be in America. Like the rest of the world.

12

Anthony Allday saw Karen in the distance. The young Dominican woman with the pleasant smile was opening the coffee shop. She seemed completely absorbed in her task, appearing and disappearing behind the faux granite counter, bringing out little sacks of coffee and placing them all around her. Anthony Allday approached her, the first diffuse rays of the morning sun on his back. He heard the hiss of espresso machines being tested. It was 7:35 A.M. Soon the blessed smell of coffee would fill all the empty spaces of the mall. Anthony Allday closed his eyes and sniffed the air theatrically. He looked up and saw the rays of the morning sun beginning to drench the mall through its cupola. Comfort warmed his heart. And Anthony Allday decided to step out of his routine and have a double espresso before eight o'clock in the morning.

What a beautiful day! What do you say, Karen? On a day like this we ought to get married or die or something. To mark the occasion, I mean. What do you think? Don't you find the morning glorious? Would you prepare me a double espresso? Maybe its bitterness will balance the sweetness in my heart.

The young woman looked at Anthony Allday from behind her long fake eyelashes. She gave him a knowing smile. She sucked on her lips. You know, Mr. Allday, she said, leaning over the counter, the coffee won't be ready 'til 8:30, as usual. Have to weigh it and grind it yet. Now if you come back at 8:15, you and I could have us the very first cups, *pa' festeja el nuevo día, pué*—to celebrate the new day.

And Anthony Allday: *¡Magnífico!* I'll come back then. Meanwhile, keep up the good work!

Anthony Allday never went back. Only a few hours later, at 3:07 P.M., in the throes of a feverish fatigue but still trying, desperately now, to retrace all his ill-taken steps, Antonio Alday Gutiérrez wonders whether that simple omission changed his life forever. Had Anthony Allday returned to have that cup of coffee with Karen, would he have been saved from what was to befall him later that morning? Maybe it was that broken promise, that very instance of attachment to routine, that had ruined his life. And Antonio Alday Gutiérrez then thinks that, perhaps, routine does not only make furrows in one's brow and in one's soul, as his old man had warned with his dying breath, but it can also drag one back into the ruts of a cursed destiny. Perhaps El Azar had sprung the trap only at 7:35 that very morning.

13

Broken promises. There had been so many. Despite all his guarding against making promises without thinking. Or breaking them even when he had actually meant to keep them. Like the promise Toño had made to Betti. A sad story.

At 3:10 after the sinful deed, in a brief clearing of his turmoil, Antonio Alday Gutiérrez experiences gratitude: Betti taught Toño so much. All promises are lies 'til they're fulfilled, Toño, she had said with an opaque light in her black eyes. Remember that. To make easy promises is to cover oneself with layers upon layers of lies. Each one is not too significant, but in the long run they become your *mortaja,* your shroud, Toño. In the end, God only knows how many promises we can actually fulfill. Do you see, Toño?

Antonio Alday Gutiérrez has to admit that not having returned for her, even though he was bound merely by a child's promise, has affected him deeply. He has felt that lingering lie as a constant presence underneath all his transformations, like the throbbing in his left big toe—even in his sleep.

Things had changed by the time Anthony Allday came along. He knew how to set clear and early limits on any and all expectations. He promised little of consequence. That was certainly the case in his relationship with Hannah. His inventions and the sincerity with which he presented them were in large part meant to prevent future regrets. One could say, then, that they were the cover for his good intentions. That despite his best efforts he may not have succeeded in sparing Hannah any pain was another matter. He had honestly tried to protect her. Still, even after Anthony Allday came along, even after he looked at himself in the mirror and honestly promised himself never again to make or exact easy promises, El Azar worked its wiles to place him in a bind such that he was forced to make an easy promise as the best way to prevent future regrets. That was what had happened with Cosme. He never went back there, either. And that was what happened with Rosaura.

Or was Rosaura's case more complicated? Did she use the designs of El Azar to her own ends? Was that even possible? Did she risk everything she was and everything she had accomplished because of her own invented promises? Was it possible that those who promise are really the quarry of those who are eventually betrayed? Because Rosaura must have known what she was getting into. She must have chosen to tug at the webs of El Azar. She must have had her own reasons for doing so. And Antonio Alday Gutiérrez retraces his steps to recover Rosaura's face from the ruins of his past. In his fatigued and confused state, he finds it comforting.

14

If you only knew how much I love you, Rosaura whispered in his ear, playing with his hair. If you only knew how much I value you. Value you—because I am not a woman to have such deep feelings at the drop of a hat. I value and love you with the gentle sweetness I had once had, as a naïve young woman, before I married Alfredo, before life had conspired against my dreams.

¡Ay, Tony! I had buried that part of myself. I had resigned myself to have only gray feelings in my heart. But then you appeared, like a *matador en agosto,* to bring color to my life. *Me escuchas, amor?* Are you listening to me, love?

That was why she had fallen in love and now she hurt just thinking about him. Ever since that Saturday afternoon when they met.

Do you remember Tony? It only seemed like love at first sight. I confess it now so you know how much I love and trust you. It wasn't like that, darling.

She already knew him because Cristina had drawn him in fine strokes: a Peruvian who has just arrived from Philadelphia, a businessman. But, listen, it's like he's no longer Peruvian. He has a gringo accent. *Un churro,* good looking. Don Victorio met him at the Sheraton, at one of those talks they have there. I don't know, Rosaura. They've become fast friends. He asked me to attend to him personally. I'm going. If you want, get ready, *chica.* Since you got involved with Alfredo, you've done nothing but be a mother.

Cristina was always laughing at her expense. And yet the truth was that her jibes touched open wounds. Cristina knew that. That was why she continued to tease her. Luckily, they were like sisters. Perhaps even closer. But very different, one from the other. Rosaura made that clear, lifting herself slightly from the double bed and tilting her head to see him better. Cristina had decided to have a career, to cultivate a good figure, and to have fun. She, on the other hand, succumbed to everyone's expectations and married because it was the thing to do. Even so, Cristina had always behaved admirably.

When I found out that Alfredo had been cheating on me—with his own secretary, Tony, a lousy mousy woman ten years his senior!—when

I was on the brink of insanity and about to kill myself, Cristina found a way to calm me down. Cristina picked me up from the floor, Tony. Cristina spent entire days with me, feeding me, bathing me, putting me to bed, inviting evil gossip from everyone who, as the fad of the day dictated, thought us lesbians. People are awful, Tony. Awful.

All of Rosaura's other friends, even those she had known since before high school, either disappeared or became exquisitely polite. They could always find ways to feign sympathy and maintain distance. And afterwards, when Rosaura had recovered and was again ready to face the world, when Alfredo returned to her with tears in his eyes, they all came back, slinking, purring, and nudging themselves like cats in heat.

Cristina knows me, Tony, Rosaura whispered, lost in her past, drawing invisible lines on his moist belly.

Cristina remembered the Rosaura of her youth: full of life and desire. That was why she had said that Saturday afternoon, If you want, get ready, chica.

Rosaura had had no idea she was going to fall in love with Mr. Anthony Allday. She went to meet him because Alfredo was preoccupied with his business, as always; because Lima was covered with the gloomy ashen mist of winter; and because the air of her casona in San Isidro was fetid with silence. Also, she thought that a day in the countryside might be good for Robertito, who was already eight years old.

Cristina promised to get us seats very close to the dressage grounds for the *caballos de paso,* the Peruvian pacing horses which, if you can still recall our history, Tony, were the inspiration for Chabuca Granda's greatest contributions to our culture, our very being. No, darling, believe me, that day I didn't have even the slightest intention of falling in love with you.

She had asked Clara, the servant girl, to get Robertito ready in time and to make sure he wore the genuine cowboy hat his father had brought him directly from Houston. You know Houston, Tony?

And Tony: yes, I often travel there on business. An impressive city.

And Rosaura: We had to get up with the servants, before eight. Of course I was nervous. But not too nervous. I had already been to several similar events; the best of our culture, Tony. And I put on my white silk blouse, Gap blue jeans, Fry boots, also brought from Houston, Tony, my Ray-Ban dark glasses, Donna Karan kerchief and belt, and a simple gold necklace. Remember Tony? Remember?

At 3:12 after the murder, Antonio Alday Gutiérrez overcomes his fatigue to remember how, on that afternoon in August 1989, before his last departure from Lima, before he made his decision never to return, Rosaura coaxed him to review the details of their brief romance. She lived for that, he murmurs to himself, feebly. His words linger for an instant before dissolving into the soft light of the weakening winter sun. Yes. Rosaura liked to review her feelings every time they lay together, side by side, after the lovemaking. It was as if she wished for him to really see her, to really know her, and to make her real. My God! Rosaura needed someone to witness her caressing her lonely heart, squeezing her own troubled conscience. Summoning his fading defenses, Antonio Alday Gutiérrez tries to convince himself that Rosaura had needed him for at least that much. He had made her happy just by being there.

Rosaura said that, while driving her black Volvo 740 to the countryside that Saturday in August, she was thinking that, in truth, she did not have such a bad life. After all, Robertito was a healthy boy and Alfredo no longer gave her any grief; on the contrary, one could even say that after he had almost killed her, he had begun, in subtle ways, to show her he loved her more and more with each passing day.

Certainly, Alfredo continues always to be busy, involved in politics, protecting his import-export business, doing all those men's things, but, I swear Tony, with each passing day, he shows himself ever more attentive.

He brought her dozens of yellow roses on her birthdays. He arranged for her trips to Miami, encouraging her, Go, Rosaura, go and have fun. Go. I'll take care of things here. She had taken him up on his offer and had gone to Miami many times, to visit old friends who had fled Peru during the Alvarado dictatorship, to stroll along those beautiful beaches.

But no, Tony, I prefer the simple things; things like this, lying beside each other, satiated, talking about things, anything, laughing at the unpredictability of life, telling our life stories.

Driving along the dusty roads on the southeastern outskirts of Lima on that Saturday, passing by ancient ruins, the remnants of cultures now buried deep in time, Rosaura had to admit that Cristina knew her only too well. Yes, Tony, she confessed, it is true that sometimes, even when playing golf at the Huampaní Country Club or drinking piña coladas in Ancón, I feel utterly alone. It's a loneliness that devours my soul.

But she also wanted to confess that, on that Saturday, driving past dry water canals bordered by dusty grama grass, by arid fields punctuated with the scarce shade of moribund and twisted trees, by thick mud-walled ruins surrounded by the hovels of the poor, she pitied Cristina. She pitied her because she knew that poor woman would someday end up just like those places, all crumpled inside by the sheer desolation of her freedom.

It's true, Tony. We must all protect ourselves against our undying desire to taste our own sadness. Cristina does it with gaiety and fun. But that will not last. For us women, when all is said and done, the soul strives to follow the body. To fend off such decay we must find something new to embrace in order to replace the material fibers which attach us to life. Dreams work just as well as hatreds. But Cristina refuses to learn. Am I boring you, Tony? Perhaps I'm wrong. Perhaps she's right when she says that the only thing we can truly possess and truly share is our loneliness, and so there is no need for anyone to replace anything. Do you think so, Tony?

At 10:00 A.M. Rosaura reached a long and dusty callejón, a narrow lane between two mud walls. From there, when the wind swirled the desert dust favorably, the distant dove-gray mountains encircling the Lima valley looked almost blue. To her left, behind some stunted *sauces llorones,* weeping willows, Rosaura could now see an accumulation of desert mud-and-reed huts.

Time felt heavy there, Tony. The faces of the descendants of the Incas—perhaps our ancestors, no?—passed eerily by the dark windows of the Volvo 740. Quizzical faces. Astonished faces, Tony. They seemed so burdened by the desert and by time. Do you see? How could I complain about my life? Right? I was lucky, after all. I was feeling pretty rotten, really.

Luckily, a little farther on, all of a sudden, the trees turned a pale green. It was as if they had been washed by hand, Tony. The Volvo 740 turned a last corner and we came upon the green pastures of Pachacamac. The fields gleamed under the morning Andean sun. White picket fences formed perfect circles and squares on the clean grass. There was a strong smell of walnuts in the air, Tony. It was there that we first met. Right, Tony? Right?

15

The end of the shift found Anthony Allday in the security office. Tom had already left for the day and the new guards were making their first rounds. He could hear Mr. Jerome Ronstadt, the daytime chief of security, nearby. He was giving orders to someone. Anthony Allday took off his heavy belt. He hung the key ring on its hook, next to the coat closet. He took the Smith & Wesson .38 out of its holster. He looked at it with arrested attention, as if for the first time. He thought its steel blue color accentuated its power. He had often imagined himself having to use it, but, thank God, he had never had reason to. He wiped it clean with his silk handkerchief, slid it back into its holster, and placed it in the designated drawer. For an instant, he missed the gun's weight and power. But he also gained an odd sense of freedom, as if he were finally safe from temptation. He ambled to the mirror on the back wall. He saw himself looking tired. His shoulders drooped. His eyes were bloodshot. His beard was rough to the touch. No doubt about it, he thought, this has been the last of four rough nights. He needed to rest. Not so much from the work as from his memories and his worries about the future. He took off his cap. His hair was flat and greasy.

I look like a cholo de mierda, Anthony Allday cursed to himself at 8:15 that morning, the pain in his left big toe throbbing gently, witnessing his despair. I look as much a cholo as Genaro! That son of a bitch, Genaro! And, looking into the tired eyes in the square mirror on the back wall, Anthony Allday accepted that there was no way out of his predicament. He had to explain to everyone how it was that his cousin was like that: cholo and cojudo! Because Genaro, just like all those who came out of Tacora, had to be that way—even when el cholo had escaped to the desert.

Anthony Allday prepared to leave. He put on his L. L. Bean goosedown parka, adjusted his cashmere scarf, put on his Isotoner gloves, and said goodbye to Mr. Ronstadt on his way to the parking lot. Walking out through the side door, feeling the cold December air on his face, he wished he had said goodbye to Tom, patted him on the shoulder, told him to take care of his family and to say hello to his mother. See you on Monday, Tom, as usual. Don't forget to bring the donuts. But Tom had left before eight o'clock. Poor Tom.

Perhaps he wished he had said goodbye to Tom because in a strange kind of way, Anthony Allday had an inkling that his own world was about to change. He felt the weirdness and the possibility in the air. Yes. Antonio Alday Gutiérrez thinks at 3:15 P.M.: Anthony Allday's presentiment that morning did not come from within himself. It seemed to float in the air he breathed, to quiver in the light reaching his tired eyes. It penetrated him through the roots of his limp hair and the pores of his body, as if he were being touched by the invisible webs of a hidden destiny.

Did he fear the presence of his cousin that much? Had that fear distorted his already minimal sense of proportion? It could not be! Antonio Alday Gutiérrez protests with fading strength. Yes, Anthony Allday felt the full weight of that fear throughout the cursed morning, but he managed to pass beyond it. Yeah, he told himself, Genaro is going to mess up my life. I'll have to take him with me everywhere. I'll have to explain this and that to him. I'll have to be his babysitter. But, really, it cannot be all that bad. *Esta mala espina,* this presentiment of disaster is not coming from my fear but from somewhere else. Maybe I'm just too tired. And now, to shake off his despair, Antonio Alday Gutiérrez curses to himself: if he had only gone back to Karen and taken that double espresso.

Anthony Allday let the heavy metal side door of the Springfield Mall close behind him and walked briskly against the sun towards the parking lot. He was thinking that it would do him good to drive his red '77 Corvette, carajo, a car befitting a man like him, a man of the world, with an enviable past, an alluring future, a present life temporarily complicated because of his indomitable heart, his stubborn attachment to his ideals, ideals as yet uncorrupted by the wealth of his family, carajo.

La gente hace cojudeces, murmurs Antonio Alday Gutiérrez, astonished at what he has been capable of. People do the weirdest things.

16

Peruvian Notebook No. 2
February 1984

Sometimes I feel like a motherless child.
Sometimes I feel like a motherless child.

. . . . .

The black man sang alone on the stage. He had graying hair and big hands, and was toothless. This must be the saddest song I have ever heard in America. The man sings to and for everyone. There is an odd nostalgia in America. Not a nostalgia for a place or a time. Not a desire to return anywhere. A nostalgia for what it could have been. Salvation.

. . . . .

I wonder about don Luna, how he is.

17

Anthony Allday got in his Corvette and left the parking lot. He headed for the Baltimore Pike traffic light. The purr of the engine calmed his frayed nerves. At the light, he leaned back against the leather and relaxed. The sun was clear on the horizon. A thin blanket of snow reflected the rays of light to a clear winter sky. He was thinking: Why was he all of a sudden feeling trapped in the webs of his inventions? Why was he nagged by feelings of regret for having been reborn? Why such unexpected misgivings? The light changed. He turned right and took the turnpike west. Maybe it was nothing. Maybe he was just tired. Maybe all he needed was a moment to rest, to close his eyes. He still had plenty of time. The flight was not due until ten.

As he passed Media and left the heavy traffic behind, Anthony Allday felt the last, now feeble and fleeting, wave of desire to retrace his steps searching for clues that might give clarity and meaning to the tangled wattle that was his life. Had he made the right choices? Could he choose otherwise still? But, feeling drained, he drove on and let himself be soothed by the winter sun, the rolling hills, and the promise of rest.

There, recognizes Antonio Alday Gutiérrez later that day, at 3:17 P.M., there ended my first real search for the motives for what I sensed was to come. Too bad. Had Anthony Allday still had enough energy, he might yet have been able to avoid the trap set for him by El Azar. Perhaps he might have been able to change what after that moment became inevitable. Now, as the soft light of the winter sun dims slowly on the horizon, Antonio Alday Gutiérrez has to admit that what he has been doing for the past three hours—picking this and that image for scrutiny, reading from his Peruvian notebooks, remembering, divining, lamenting, cursing, wringing his hands, looking into the light to illuminate his inner shadows, all of it—was based only on the crazy idea, the hope, rather, that maybe everything was just a nightmare, a nightmare in which, in order to wake up, he needed to find, to remember, something specific, something he had not yet identified, a regret, a forgiveness, a promise.

Enveloped in a feverish fatigue, Antonio Alday Gutiérrez wants to rest. To fall asleep and wake up, yet again reborn, to a different reality.

But in the depths of his being, he knows he is not ready for sleep. He has not yet understood why he became a murderer and therefore cannot yet atone for it. Besides, he is once again too afraid of waking up to a knock on his door. And he has long since lost his ability to sleep on command.

Wishing to regain control over his fading senses, Antonio Alday Gutiérrez strains to hear the familiar sounds of Rogers Lane. But the white world outside seems laden with a heavy silence. In the house, Mr. Mozino, the landlord, is not puttering around the halls as usual. The mailman has long since moved on.

He returns to his memories.

18

It was a phenomenal day, wasn't it? Nice and warm. The horses paced. The *cúculas* sang. The children laughed. Remember, Tony? Remember?

Rosaura climbed the wide wooden stairs up to the viewing stand with Clara and Robertito in tow. Two chairs had been reserved for her in the front section. Clara had to find her own place, in the balcony. But the important thing was that she and Robertito were seated so close to the track, they could almost touch the horses. They could see their dark and mysterious eyes fixed on an invisible point in the distance. Remember, Tony? They paced round and round with their long manes waving, rising and falling, feathery under the sun. Their sinuous bodies shining, quivering. Their forelegs drawing half-circles in the air. Their hooves landing gently on the thin layer of sawdust on the moist ground. Oh Tony! The horses knew they were there to perform. They must have known they had made her feel happy, full of life.

But she sensed something else was afoot.

It was an intuition, Tony, that made me feel as if something deep inside me were about to wake up, at any moment.

It was an intuition that reminded her of the feeling she had once had, a long time ago, when she was still at the university, pretending to study literature, thinking this and doing that instead; a time when she had felt like a burst of light deep inside as she was walking down the main path that led to the chapel, bordered by gladioli and yellow roses, that she would never be happy as a nun, that God had meant for her to take another path, a path that led to marriage and the union of pleasure and responsibility.

That was when I saw you, Tony. You were at the other end of the viewing stand. I saw you, and it was as though, once again, a silent lightning bolt of recognition had lit up my inner sky. I swear it sent shivers up and down my spine. I felt faint.

What was it in him that made her feel so? She could not tell. The only thing of which she was certain on that Saturday morning in August, was that she had never seen him before.

Right, my love? We had never met before, right? You stepped into my life when I was ready for you, Tony.

Right. Rosaura could not have known then that only a few years later, before a sinking sun, in another winter, Antonio Alday Gutiérrez would remember her and think that, perhaps, it was not really Tony who had lit up her inner sky but only what he represented: someone who was not Alfredo.

But Rosaura, in his bed: I felt the chill spread all over me, Tony; even though you had not even seen me yet because you were mesmerized admiring, yes admiring, Tony, I saw it in your eyes, don't deny it, admiring the elegant *chalanes,* the Peruvian riders, with their dark and mysterious eyes fixed in the distance, their white hats shielding their dark, taciturn, chiseled faces from our prying eyes, their sinuous hands steady, their white linen ponchos waving, rising and falling, feathery, under the sun.

Startled, Rosaura began to retreat.

Because, the truth, Tony, something inside me said I was in danger of losing the happiness—such as it was, I know—the peace and quiet, then, that I had managed to secure. So I took Robertito by the hand and left the viewing stand. I wanted to lose myself among the people loitering around the stables. I wanted to disappear, dissolve completely into the strong smells of stables and food, into the dense shades of the tall green locust trees. Why did I feel like that, Tony? Rosaura was resting on her right elbow, tracing lines on his belly with her wet index finger, enjoying the aftermath of her sinful act. Why did I want to escape you? Why do you think I didn't succeed? Do you think we were destined to meet? Do you believe in El Azar?

Mr. Anthony Allday appeared from behind the gallery, accompanied by an excited Cristina, who was now calling and gesturing for Rosaura to stop and wait for them.

I had no other recourse but to prostrate myself before you, my love! *Los hilos de El Azar,* the strings of El Azar, were stronger than my will. I sensed then I could not escape you. I have come to accept that, Tony. And when Cristina introduced us I said, Enchanted! And you said, Nice to meet you! And you put out your hand! Such an unexpected and inappropriate gesture, Tony. So sweetly foreign. I fell in love with you just for that!

Remembering Rosaura's cascading laughter, at 3:20 P.M., Antonio Al-day Gutiérrez feels the need to repeat to himself: For those few days I made her the happiest woman in the world.

It was your gringo way of looking at the world, Tony. We are so proper and affected here. It's the price we pay for living in an underdeveloped country. We use our formality as a fence against the rest of the people. Don't get me wrong, my love. You were very courteous and elegant. But your elegance was different. It flowed from your self-confidence. It was genuine. Do you know what I mean?

And Tony: I guess. I have so much to learn about you and this country, Rosaura.

But Antonio Alday Gutiérrez remembers that Anthony Allday knew he had played his cards just right. He had seen the desperation in Rosaura's eyes and had acted accordingly. What was the harm in having an affair with such a beautiful and desperate woman? He was willing to cater to her desire for adventure; he would make her happy for as long as he could.

Looking into his eyes, Rosaura confessed to Tony that ever since they met, she had felt his presence spread like a blessed balm all around her, that she felt—she knew, rather—that he could see her, intimately and completely, that she knew he was capable of finding her wherever she might be hiding and could bring her out, be she frightened or angry or hurt or indifferent, that he made her present, and that he gave her life. That was why, from the very beginning, when Tony penetrated her with the light of his eyes, when he offered her the gift of his slightly crooked smile, when he spoke to her with that beautiful voice, soft yet firm, sincere, she had no other recourse but to follow him through all the labyrinths of sin he would allow her to explore.

I have just returned to Peru after many years, he said, catching her eyes. I would appreciate it very much if you would consent to be my guide. What daring, Tony! She resisted a little, as she knew she should: I don't know the city as well as Cristina does, Mr. Allday.

And then Cristina: Why don't you show him Lima, chica; that way you'll get to discover it all over again.

225

And that was that, Tony. Remember?

The next morning she came to wait for him at the lobby of the Sheraton Hotel. I came here with a strange pain in the pit of my stomach, darling; my insides were all tangled up in cold knots. You came out of the elevator like a movie star! You had on a gray herringbone jacket, a dove-gray muffler, tan gabardine pants, brown Rockport shoes, a Rolex wristwatch, and an adorable smile. You even smelled like a gringo, Tony!

They rode and walked all around Lima. She would point out for him places he might have known as a child, when his family still lived in San Isidro, on a street that no longer existed.

And he: The streets and houses have changed so much, Rosaura! La Plaza San Martín: I might have daydreamed here, Rosaura; I might have played in its fountains, now dry and dirty; I might have climbed these stone steps, now covered with dust and neglect. El Jirón de la Unión: I remember little round tables on the old cobblestones, the smell of coffee, the silversmith shops. El Hotel Bolívar: The sight of the cupola of its entry hall touches something teetering at the edge of my consciousness; perhaps I walked these wood-paneled corridors and looked up at these high crystal chandeliers. La Plaza de Armas. Lima's main cathedral. El Museo de Oro. . . . And Tony showed himself marvelously interested in that past: If only my parents had not decided to move to the USA! I've lost so much of who I truly am, Rosaura. I regret that. And Rosaura smiled at him with tenderness, happy as a schoolgirl.

Late that Sunday evening, they said goodbye. She saw him leaving her side, after a touch of hands, a kiss on her cheek. She saw him framed by the golden doors of the hotel. The doorman, in his evening livery, white gloved and red jacketed, watched him pass as if he were a true Hollywood star. And afterwards, as the hotel taxi took her away, leaning against the old leather seat, closing her eyes, she felt as if she had just sinned against everything that up to then she had held dear: her station, marriage, motherhood. But she didn't care.

I swear, Tony. I didn't. I was willing to suffer anything. I felt asphyxiated, twisted, wrung out, by a glorious desire. I swear to you.

And that was why, hours later that night, standing before her green glass windows, looking into the interior garden now hidden in darkness, Rosaura heard Alfredo's steps as though they were echoes in her mind. And when he undressed before her, waiting for her tender touch, as usual, for having worked so hard—Rosaurita, my Rosaurita—she caressed him, *de palmo a palmo,* from the tip of his head to the tip of his toes, but now thinking of the unknown, imagined, desired, remembered other body.

Rosaura must have closed her eyes with bitter tenderness, thinks Antonio Alday Gutiérrez at 3:20 P.M.: a tenderness meant for Alfredo, the man who, from then on, would never be enough for her. She deserved better.

19

Anthony Allday turned left. His car climbed up a narrow street bordered by cropped forsythias and burning bushes in full winter sleep, went around a gentle bend, crossed a small bridge, and came upon a large white house with a neglected garden and a faded blue porch. He parked the Corvette in the side carport. He turned the engine off but sat for a moment, both hands on the wheel. He was not trying to think. He was not cursing his bad luck. He was just sitting there. Finally, he opened the door and stepped out. A deep winter chill pierced him to the bone. He bounded up the stairs to the faded porch. He pushed the door open, thinking that, despite all his time in America, he had not yet gotten used to a winter where the sun, with its oblique rays, was an impotent ally against the cold.

He stepped into the small foyer and was glad to find that his landlord, Mr. Mozino, had turned the heat on. He could hear the crackling of the steam radiators. He took a deep breath and began climbing the two narrow flights of stairs to his apartment on the third floor. The wooden stairs bent and creaked under his weight. The soft echoes reminded him of the mall at 3:00 A.M. The wallpaper was water damaged, faded, and dusty. A single oval stained glass window at the first landing filtered a rainbow of light into the narrow, musty stairwell. On the third floor, Anthony Allday stopped at a slightly crooked door. He turned the key, pulled the doorknob upwards, and kicked the door in with his right foot.

The wallpaper in the living room, a grimy yellow with faded tiny white flowers, was peeling off near the ceiling and by the windows. The dark and dull wood floor was mostly covered by old newspapers, flyers, and catalogues. Pants, shirts, a belt, and a backpack hung from an old hat rack by the door. A yellow vinyl sofa and two mismatched mahogany side tables faced a small television set with broken rabbit ears. On top of the television there was a small sepia-toned photograph in a red wooden frame: two women in puffed-up white dresses and wide-brimmed hats with ribbons posed on a grassy field overlooking a distant city. They stared at the camera with playful intensity. They were Anthony Allday's aunts, vacationing in Siena, in the twenties.

Peruvians are always late when it comes to style, Hannah. The new fads come to Lima only when the people in Paris have moved on. You know what I mean? It's the price of living at the edge of the world.

And Hannah: I've always liked those dresses. They are beautiful.

On the left side of the front room there was a narrow table full of catalogues and several green Coca-Cola bottles. For my collection, Hannah. I buy them at the Media flea market. Someday they'll be worth a ton.

Anthony Allday dropped down onto the yellow vinyl sofa. He felt its familiar hard surface against his back and let himself be engulfed by the indirect soft light of the winter sun filtered by the astonishingly clear panes of the two large windows facing west. He thought he would have liked some coffee just then, to recover his energy, but he was too tired to see the kitchen, full of dirty dishes, with cockroaches that no longer scampered when he opened the ugly curtains, brown with red flowers, that Hannah once washed but he had never ironed. He was too tired to face the attached small dining room, with a table full of more flyers and catalogues, which he used to peruse in the morning when he drank his coffee, before going to bed, or in the midafternoon, preparing to see Hannah or getting ready for his quarterly trip to Philadelphia, flyers and catalogues that made him feel a part of that world, of America, even if from a distance, so he could keep on weaving the story of his past, his present, his future, so he could keep on feeling that he could, if he wanted to, purchase any and all of those things, the comfortable life, what with so much on sale, with such discounts every day, so he could exercise his willpower and save for other things, but still feel that he could buy happiness if he wanted, at night, because he no longer wanted to go to the Springfield Mall during the day, when he would then have to purchase something, he would then have to spend his money, in order not to feel conspicuous, like an idiot, since he wanted to save for other things.

At 3:22 after the murder, recalling his already frail state of mind that very morning, Antonio Alday Gutiérrez thinks that perhaps he was already tiring of the owl's life he led. Perhaps he unconsciously saw the dismal deed as an excuse to begin a new life, to abandon the life he led in Lima, Delaware County, Pennsylvania, which was already making furrows in

229

his brow, in his soul. No, he protests. Anthony Allday can't have been that blind. It was El Azar that pulled him into the life of a criminal.

Forlorn and limp on his yellow vinyl sofa, Anthony Allday pictured his bedroom: a twin mattress and box spring on a bed frame with casters, woolen blankets, a pillow. There was a small bookcase with several old leather-bound books, which he had bought when he had first arrived in Philadelphia, at the Salvation Army Store on Ridge Avenue, but had never read, except for *The Opera Goers' Complete Guide, comprising two hundred and sixty-eight opera plots with musical numbers and casts*, by Leo Melitz, director of the Stadt Theatre at Basel, translated and with commentary by Richard Salinger, *Revised and brought up to date after consultation with the librarian of the Metropolitan Opera Company* by Louise Wallace Hackney, published by the Garden City Publishing Company, Garden City, 1936, large sections of which he had read and memorized. There were two brass lamps he had bought at the Bryn Mawr Hospital Thrift Shop, where he had bought so many other things, a cardboard suitcase, where he kept his washed undergarments and, on the back wall of the room, four large rectangular pictures in wide gilded frames.

His father: a gloomy man in a khaki safari outfit, with a handlebar mustache and small, dark, piercing eyes. I swear to you, Hannah, in Peru he passed himself off as a conquistador. He was ruthless and cruel. His enemies and his servants feared him. Even his children, of course, Toño himself feared him. That is why I could not possibly return to Peru. It would mean risking my own identity. No, I have to suffer my self-imposed exile. Listen, Hannah, the old man wanted to fry me, yes, to put me in jail, because his only son had the audacity to defend the poor and go against his interests. Do you understand now why I had to escape that oppressive gaze at any cost? Do you?

His mother: flowing locks of hair, gently blushing cheeks, long curled eyelashes, big sad brown eyes, delicate fingers holding an open silk fan. Because in Peru it is truly hot, Hannah. It's so hot that people often cannot leave their homes in the middle of the day, for fear of heat exhaustion. That's why they take siestas. It's a question of necessity, you know? Of course, they loved each other very much. They would always protect each other. Still, I'm sure my mother prefers me far away, safe from the dangers of Peruvian politics and the oppressive gaze of my

230

father. It is she whom I miss the most. Because of her I've returned to Peru now and then, incognito, to kiss those ever more withered cheeks, to tell her not to worry, that I am all right, even though I sometimes feel hunger and often live in neglect, all that to avoid the grasp of my father. Yes, I rendezvous with my mother, alone, in any corner of Lima. Oh, those are happy times, Hannah, you have no idea. No idea.

His sister Cándida Esther: The poor woman could not even play the violin that she loved so much because Father forbade it. Can you imagine it, Hannah? All because at fifteen she fell in love with her instructor, who happened to be a Sephardic Jew. Something inside her died that day. She never recovered. And she never fell in love again. Can you notice the languor in her eyes? When she sat for that portrait, at sixteen, she was already resigned to lead a miserable life. She once confessed to me, with bitterness and total resignation, that she desired nothing more than to grow old. She is so beautiful, don't you think? That is Sandals, her little dog, her only companion. No, she never loved again. Not even at the university where she surely had pretenders and where she studied Egyptology, something exotic and useless, as was expected of young ladies of her standing, in that other Lima. It breaks my heart, Hannah.

Uncle Pedro Enrique: the youngest of the brothers Allday, the millionaire. He is always in the society pages. He even appeared once in *Life* magazine, in a story about the Peruvian pacing horses, which are distinctive and known around the world. He is a vain man. He doesn't care about anything. I know his weaknesses, his dark side, his secrets. Uncle Pedro Enrique could never touch me, Hannah. But all that is better left alone, buried under the weight of distance and the passing of time.

I have them all here, in this dark corner of my bedroom because, with the exception of Mother, I don't wish to see them even in pictures. They are part of a life I want to but am incapable of leaving behind. I am sorry.

Anthony Allday opened his eyes. He was about to doze off. He sat up and checked his wristwatch. It was 9:32 A.M. Almost time to leave for the airport. American Airlines flight 912 was probably already flying over Washington. He wanted to arrive at 10:15 so he wouldn't have to wait. Anthony Allday hated to wait.

Sensing all the quivering threads in the web that was his past, in the growing haze of that cold winter, at 3:25 P.M., feeling the hard yellow vinyl couch against his back, surprised by the daring quality of his fictions, turning his tired limp body to face the dark side of his bedroom, as if to make sure there was no one there rising against him, Antonio Alday Gutiérrez asks himself if it is possible that he himself bought all his fictions, that his fictions had truly become his reality. If so, how and when did it happen? When he first met Tom? When he crossed the Río Bravo? When Alex Sosa called out his new name? When he lay beside Rosaura? Why did he end up with blood on his hands? He is tired and wants to cry.

20

Antonio Alday Gutiérrez lets himself be warmed by the memory of Rosaura's voice once again. She was childlike, playful, sensual. He feels uplifted by the remembered touch of her wet index finger drawing on his body. It had been a marvelous week. A week the likes of which he had never known before and would never know again, not even counting the many good times with Hannah, who loved him so much, or the days he spent in Betti's company, so long ago now that they are only fading impressions. Unfortunately, Tony didn't know how marvelous it all was when he saw Rosaura for the last time, on the second Saturday night in the Peruvian winter of 1989. They both knew they had come together to say goodbye, of course. It was inevitable. Even though they each pretended not to notice the other's sadness. They didn't want to spoil their last moments together. La verdad es que la gente hace cojudeces, Antonio Alday Gutiérrez says in a barely audible murmur, looking into himself with astonishment, the truth is that people do the weirdest things.

21

The Sheraton Hotel in Lima was built during the Cold War, at a time when Fidel Castro's face was seen on every street corner in Latin America and John F. Kennedy was determined not to lose his backyard. Its massive cement-and-steel exterior walls give the impression they were made to withstand siege and plunder. Its vertical growth lords over the gray horizontal urban sprawl. By 1989, the hotel had lost some of its cachet to newer buildings in the big city, mostly along the cliffs of Miraflores overlooking the pale green waters of the Pacific. But the hotel continued to proclaim its position as the preeminent gathering place in Lima. To make its claim visible, it displayed on the roof of its main lobby oversized flags from all the countries of the Americas. In the winter of 1989, enveloped in the ashen shroud of Lima, the drooping flags gave the impression of an abandoned fortress.

Up on the tenth floor, however, Anthony Allday's room was warm and cozy. Its wide, draped windows faced the front of the hotel. From there, he could see a small park across the main street. On that second Saturday night the park was barely visible beyond the flickering lights of passing traffic and the dim glow of a row of streetlamps. In the drizzle the few small trees that survived there, against all odds, resembled crouching sentinels. Beyond the park the gray Palacio de Justicia building seemed to be hiding in the fog. Far in the distance, spikes of light identified the different sections of the big city. All around there was a heavy silence in the air. In view of the gloom, Anthony Allday promised himself to find a new place, in Miraflores, if he ever came back to Lima. Now he waited for Rosaura.

Anthony Allday helped Rosaura take off her baby alpaca jacket. He fixed her hair with tenderness. He kissed her lips softly. You're the most beautiful woman in Peru, Rosaura, he murmured in her ear. And she, kicking off her blue shoes on the plush rose carpet, smiled at him, coquettishly. She let herself be carried in his strong arms to the bed. She loved to be carried away like that, she confessed into his ear, with her eyes closed, to give herself entirely. And Tony laid her down. And he began to undress her slowly, tenderly, spying her closed eyes, enjoying her rhythmic sighs, barely audible, watching her soft belly, rising and falling, noticing the glistening of her down.

And she: I'm yours, Tony. Completely. And he took her, daringly, full of strength. And she: I adore you, Tony. Take me away. And he gave himself to her too, spying her closed eyes, you're everything to me, Rosaura. Everything.

How many times did they make love that second Saturday night? Antonio Alday Gutiérrez no longer remembers. And it does not matter to him now. Why remember such things? It was so long ago. But he has never forgotten that when they said goodbye, at dawn, looking out on the city, still turbid and gloomy in its drizzle shroud, they swore to love each other forever.

He had to get back to attend to his business, of course. She had so much to fix in the routine of her own life. He promised to return soon. She swore she would wait for him. He confessed he was disoriented, seized by a desire to remain in Peru for good. She gave him encouragement to depart, so long as he promised to return, having fixed whatever needed fixing back home: And when you come back, my love, we'll make a future together. I promise. I promise.

And looking into that canescent distance, Tony promised to return within a month.

Oh, Tony! I'll keep you in my smile until you come back to me. My darling! My love!

When she rides or walks on Lima's streets, thinks Antonio Alday Gutiérrez at 3:28 P.M., shaking off the rest of his memories, Rosaura probably still remembers me. I made her happy. Even though it was only for a little while. I saved her from an everlasting sadness. And I paid the price. Simulating and dissimulating before someone I cared for took away my sleep. I was for many weeks as I am now: wanting but not being able to rest, cursing the designs of El Azar, wishing they could have been different, wishing but unable to cry even for my sins.

Three-Thirty

Peruvian Notebook No. 4
August 1, 1992

For future use in a story about Philadelphia—the USA.

. . . . .

The Mystery Persists: How Did Death Go Undiscovered?
By Larson Paige
Inquirer Staff Writer

The forgotten man was found by a stranger two days after Thanksgiving, a desiccated corpse on the living room floor.

Nearby lay a mountain of evidence of how irrelevant he had become to the outside world: an untouched, unanswered pile of mail inside the front-door delivery slot, some of it more than three years old.

Precisely when and why Robert Eric Graham died will never be known for certain. Were he still alive, Graham would be 49.

It is presumed that he died peacefully, if inelegantly, in the Warminster townhouse he had bought a decade earlier with inherited cash from his cultured, accomplished mother. Olivia S. Graham was named teacher of the year by the Philadelphia Board of Education in 1982.

The body—discovered Saturday by the townhouse's new owner—was fully clothed, its bones and skin unbroken, and there were no signs of robbery or struggle.

1

At 9:30am, Anthony Allday decided to open the windows to let in fresh air and clear his head. He had to do that whenever the heat from the steam radiators made his apartment too stuffy. He usually found the clear winter air replenished his energies. This time, however, instead of helping, the fresh air betrayed him. Its scent awoke in him unpleasant traces of long ago. Pucusana.

As it resurfaced, the memory of his trip to the beach when he was still a child, back in the sixties, muddled his thoughts, dried his tongue, tightened his throat. It was a memory trace that used to come back often in the early part of his life—whenever he was in trouble, sinking into despair—but that had not been awakened in more than ten years. Now, at 9:30 A.M. on December 10, 1995, Anthony Allday was compelled to relive the moment when, oh so unfairly, he had been accused of shitting himself because he was a marica. He was compelled to remember that he had not even wanted to explain, that all he had wanted was to close his eyes and disappear, to dissipate completely, in the fresh air of Pucusana.

In the throes of this old anguish, Anthony Allday felt abandoned, but he didn't know why or by whom. He felt paralyzed, sinking impotently into oblivion, being carried away by the horror of utter forlornness. He wished to ride the waves of despair, embrace La Pelona, death, as his father had done, and follow her to the bitter end.

But then, Antonio Alday Gutiérrez recalls at 3:35 P.M., to his evergrowing bad luck Anthony Allday managed to recover his balance. He brought himself back from the brink of absolute despair and perhaps insanity to accept that, on this morning in December 1995, just as when he was still only a child, it was useless to wish for the impossible—he could not disappear by embracing La Pelona. He had to deal with things. Too bad. If Anthony Allday had lost his mind then and there, once and for all, then perhaps the deed might have gone undone.

Anthony Allday felt he had no choice but to go out and meet his cousin at the airport. Maybe on his way there it would come to him, exactly why he felt Tacora so frightfully near. Maybe he would then have a better idea as to why, since he had received his uncle's letter announcing Genaro's arrival, he had been unable to eat or sleep. Perhaps he would then understand why he was so overwhelmed by the feeling that everything he had worked for, everything he had become, was fast going to hell.

He knew, Antonio Alday Gutiérrez accepts now, finding a clearing in the fog of his fatigue: Anthony Allday knew full well, but did not wish to accept, the source of his fear. He knew he was afraid of being found out. He was afraid of being pulled down, back into a past he no longer recognized. He knew that, from this morning on, everyone, from Tom to Genaro himself, would expect an explanation, a clearing of the record, an accounting of who he really was. And he also knew he would not be able to do what they would all expect.

It would not be because he wished to continue simulating and dissimulating. Not at all. Who was he, really? Had he not developed, grown, changed, over the last twenty-two years? Who could now say he was not the rebellious son, the faithful friend, the man of principles, the man he had become, after so much effort, so many false starts, searching for the best past, a past that would fit his temperament, his ambition? Had he not changed his intimate ways, just as much as his appearance, to conform to that invented past? What more could be asked of a man? His constructed past gave him a clear orientation. It made him a useful member of society, a tolerant and trusted friend. If everyone could invent themselves as he had, by free will alone, who would not invent themselves good, faithful, just, so as to be held in high esteem, so as to make sure that the old past, which they did not choose, the past which they cannot otherwise escape, would not bring them down, back to suffering without respite, from the inherited daily routines that make deep furrows in their souls? Why should others—parents, siblings, lovers, friends, people—have veto power on the kind of life a person wants? Is not the past, which affects one so much, better invented?

Anthony Allday got up from the yellow vinyl couch unsteadily. He ambled to his bedroom, darkened still by heavy curtains, looking for he knew not what. Finding the bedroom impenetrable to his tired eyes, he ambled back towards the living room. He dropped onto the yellow vinyl couch again, cursing his bad luck.

Remembering himself that morning with feelings overflowing his heart and mind, Antonio Alday Gutiérrez has to admit that he had never before been so oddly bitter. He was bitter against everything and nothing at the same time. It certainly was not a bitterness directed against Genaro. On the contrary. He might have even pitied the poor man, who surely never had the opportunity to choose anything for himself. No. He felt bitterness against the world. Yes, Antonio Alday Gutiérrez exclaims, at 3:37 P.M., as the sun begins to sink slowly over Lima's horizon, it was then that his thick shell finally cracked and all his festering anger oozed out! It was then that he began his descent into hell.

How could he have prevented it? What had he neglected to do? Antonio Alday Gutiérrez cannot think of anything. In his feverish fatigue, it then occurs to him that perhaps if he had had the time and the desire to write down his anger and despair in his Peruvian notebooks, maybe Anthony Allday would have been able to evade the clutches of El Azar. Antonio Allday used to do something like that, back in New England, whenever he was filled with such bitterness. He spent hours remembering the past that still held him down. He spent hours rewriting it, at night, with a fine-point pen, three tight blue lines of script between two blurry red lines, to make the paper last, as if each blank page held a measured dose of salvation. But when Anthony Allday got the job as night watchman at the Springfield Mall, in Delaware County, Pennsylvania, he abandoned the practice. Peruvian Notebook No. 4 was almost blank. He became careless. He let his guard down. He wrongly believed the blue steel of the Smith & Wesson .38 made him into a true American, and hence beyond peril.

2

Anthony Allday got up and closed the windows. He picked up the L. L. Bean jacket and the cashmere scarf that were casually draped over an end table. He was ready to walk out of his ugly apartment. He felt tired but somehow better. The anger and bitterness were safely tucked away. After all, Anthony Allday was not the kind of man to walk away from his responsibilities.

Before he could reach the front door, however, the memory of Betti imposed itself on his consciousness. He had been expecting it. He knew he would eventually have to reflect on her possible questions and, in this case, her possible disapproval, if he were ever to divine her possible advice. Divine her advice. There was no other way to put it. Despite his recent denials, Anthony Allday knew he had done so before, in the early years, when he found himself in a bind. Still, this time her memory came with unusual force. It stopped him in his tracks. Betti would not be ignored. And so Anthony Allday stood, with his back against the light filtering through the western windows, suspended in time and indecision. He pictured her face. She had not aged a day. But she seemed to have grown wiser. And leaning his head against the slightly crooked door of his ugly apartment, Anthony Allday remembered what he had written about her.

3

Peruvian Notebook No. 3
September 1, 1984

Betti gets up ready to run. As usual. She likes to trot along the banks of the Seine, va y viene, as César Vallejo would say, back and forth, back and forth. She likes to think in the open air, to see the world with new eyes, Toño. That way, there is so much to see! ... Running along the rows of closed kiosks, nearing the Pont Neuf, at this time bathed in a particularly golden light, feeling the uneven sidewalk under her feet, Betti confesses to herself that she has always looked at the world out of the corner of her eyes, always searching for unexpected outlets, hidden windows, magical tunnels that might lead her to greener places, far from the twisting muddy gray streets of Tacora and their smell of rotten leather.

Tacora—during the day she maintained a studied serenity, a much admired correctness, finding happiness in the smallest things of life, greeting everyone with a smile. Tacora—at night she was a prisoner of the willed insomnia, a guard against fear, violence, shamelessness, a way to sink deep into her own heart and mind.

Nightmares.

Without a father or brother in that twisted world, Betti let things be done to her that she found at first revolting and later hateful. And her hatred spread out easily to touch anyone with a say in her life. All of them. Including herself. Afterwards, when she was a little older, perhaps when she was twelve, she learned to pity herself. She learned also to forgive herself. From then on, she gave herself up with indifference. She learned to live with the hated tufo, the offensive smell of damnation that made the hair on the back of her neck stand on end. She learned to live with the dirty traces on her body, on her soul. She learned not to cry with each threat, with each shove, with each fondling touch. Me da un pepino, Toño; it's nothing to me, she would tell her only friend in that labyrinth, her black eyes filled with disdain and absence.

She was never a child. But she became a woman when she was fifteen. She made herself into a woman by refusing to remain quiet in the bed, in the dark—Quiet! Quiet, carajo! or you know what'll happen to you. Quiet!—by refusing to let others use her body, that body that just grew and grew, pointing her out, displaying her, everywhere and to everyone.

Fifteen years old!

Betti is following the gentle bend of the river, towards the large cathedral of Paris looming in the distance.

On a winter's night, a cold and moonless night, a Tacora night, she got up from under his weight, kicking, scratching, screaming, jumped out of the bed, turned on the light and, pointing with her black eyes at the man, she cried out her shame, she vomited her hatred, she swore she would never do that again, even if she had to live on the muddy streets. Then the old hags surrounded her. Aunts. Neighbors. Friends. They patted her hand: there, there. They fixed her hair. It's nothing. It's nothing. It's going to pass. It's going to pass. What temerity! How could he! . . . As if they had never known. As if they really cared. . . . She escaped their embrace, their phony pity, their smell of darkness, their fear for their own future. And the younger women, looking at her covering herself, continued to measure themselves against her, against her face, against her body, a body that just grew and grew, obeying obscure forces. They must have hated me. Poor souls. . . . I don't know why I'm telling you this, Toño. Perhaps I just want someone to know.

Yes, acknowledges Antonio Alday Gutiérrez at 3:38 on the cursed afternoon, with a heavy heart, remembering Anthony Allday standing by the vinyl couch where he now sits, peering into his Peruvian Notebook No. 3, still searching for something that would help him face his own torment: Betti saw the world with new eyes to cleanse herself from the daily tufo of the world around her. And Antonio Alday Gutiérrez manages to refocus his eyes on his diminutive scribbles, the red lines of his Peruvian Book No. 3 blurrier than ever.

They had to kiss once, remembers Betti, trotting along, missing Toño. Don Luna decided to put on a play based on Romeo and Juliet that took place in Tacora. They kissed as an example of the forbidden: Toño was an old white man kissing Betti, a young black woman. It was in mid-February, during carnival. Unlike in the rehearsals, when they only pretended to kiss, they were now to show true passion. I mean it has to come from within, Toño. It has to be real. You get me?

Yes, don Luna . . . yes.

When they kissed, they were not merely acting. They both felt it. Betti smiles, curving with the river.

On that stage, behind the cardboard bushes, Betti felt his fear and his erect masculinity. She knew enough to help Toño overcome his shame and the sweetness woven in his fear. She smiled at him, tenderly. You know, she whispered, we can have a Coca-Cola when we're done. It's sooo hot, Toño.

Betti trots along the Seine. She feels her sweat rolling down her cheeks, her bosom, her back. She feels the sun toasting her bare neck and shoulders. She breathes in. She breathes out. She follows her shadow to the cathedral. She is thinking back.

In 1973, when Toño asked her what she thought of his decision to go north, to Los Estados, she encouraged him: Don't think twice, Toño. We've got to do anything to get out of here. Whatever it takes. You'll be all right. I'll be going away myself, someday. Don't know how, when, or where to, but I'm leaving. . . . Don't be a fool, Toño. The States or this garbage heap. What choice is there? Besides, when you become a big shot in Gringolandia, you can come back for me!

Toño and Betti made love, Antonio Alday Gutiérrez remembers with a sigh, letting an old sadness creep into his heart. They made love because they didn't want to regret not having done it and because they didn't know how to curb the attraction of their young bodies. They made love because they didn't know how to explain their desire to be together, in silence. They made love to give each other courage. They made love to say goodbye.

Did they really love each other? Years later, trotting along the banks of the Seine, va y viene, back and forth, remembering her past in her native land, Betti would not know what to say. But she was sure that on a night long ago, back in 1973, before Toño left Peru

245

never to return, among the paraphernalia of the theater she recovered her body for intimacy. That night Toño helped her to blot out some of the bitterness in her heart. He helped her to free herself from some of the dead weight that was Tacora. Forever.

When they asked if she knew anything about el cojudo Antonio, who had disappeared after selling the car, the motorcycle, books, bottles, flowerpots, everything ¡carajo! nearing the end of 1973, she said no, she hadn't seen him for days.

How could you not know where he is, since you're mixed up with him? How could you not know, when you're like nail and flesh? Why do you pretend to be innocent? Did he share the money with you?

El cojudo Ricardo and the whore Carmen wouldn't stop. But Betti didn't say anything. She didn't tell them she had even broken her piggybank to give Toño all of her two hundred fifty soles, in coins, saved over two years of deprivation. You can repay me when you make lots of money, Toño. Take it! You know how much I love you. Take it, Toño! And Toño looked at her, intensely. He kissed her, as if praying, and promised her he would keep in touch for the rest of their lives. If I make it in the USA, Betti, I'll come back for you. I swear it!

And she: I trust you, Toño. I know you'll make it. Go, Toño! Go!

They both knew those were parting words, protested Anthony Allday under his breath against the divined accusations. Those were promises designed to ease the awkwardness of the moment. Betti had given him her life savings freely. He had not asked for it. She had not expected anything in return. It had not been his fault. As for Genaro, he would do for him the best he could. With that, Anthony Allday turned his back on the light, walked to the front door, opened it, and left his ugly apartment.

Who would have known then, Antonio Alday Gutiérrez thinks, that many years later, at 3:40 P.M., reviewing his past, in Lima, Delaware County, Pennsylvania, with his chin heavy on his chest, with his eyes closed, feeling the oblique and fading rays of the winter sun on his limp body, under the full weight of sleeplessness and the confusion of that cursed day, who would have known that Toño would remember Betti, wishing he could cry?

Who would have also known then that on that very Saturday morning Antonio Alday Gutiérrez would ask Genaro, when they finally met at the Philadelphia International Airport, with a mixture of guilt and anticipation: And Betti? And that Genaro, lifting his eyes from the cement floor of the parking garage of the airport, where they were waiting for the police to arrive, would say, as if the news were utterly unimportant: She left one day with a bunch of sailors from Algeria who got to calling her Cherie. People say they sailed away for Paris. Thing is, we never heard any more about her, Cousin.

Who, twenty-two years ago, would have believed it would turn out like this? And who could explain how it was that Anthony Allday had anticipated Betti's escape, already in 1984, and had written it down in his diary! For once, it seems at last, Anthony Allday had told the truth.

4

At 9:30 A.M., Anthony Allday walked down the stairs from his apartment. He didn't have the presence of mind to ask himself why he had to go, thinks Antonio Alday Gutiérrez a few hours later. It did not even occur to him to leave el cojudo Genaro to his own devices, in Philadelphia. Who would have made Anthony Allday accountable? No one in all of America knew of his family obligations. No one in all of America cared about such things. His old Peruvian sentimentality got the best of him. Or perhaps everything was meant to happen the way it did. Genaro might have been resourceful and found him anyway. Maybe his old man was mistaken and El Azar and fate are one and the same.

Anthony Allday saw the Philadelphia International Airport on his right, as he headed north on I-95. The gray sprawling building was barely visible under the glare of the low-rising midmorning winter sun. He took the airport exit. He followed its curve and stopped at the bottom of the ramp. As he waited for the light, he cursed to himself again: Genaro was coming as a tourist, carajo. Like a prince. Whereas he had had to make his way to Pennsylvania running scared, slinking, crawling, like a cojudo. And he thought that it must be true that the world was getting smaller and that people now lived in a global village, as someone had said on the television. And Anthony Allday asked himself why he had never considered trying out as an anchorman or as a weather reporter. He could have been good at it. And he thought he could have been good at many other things as well. An actor, for example. A star. A politician. He already knew how to be sincere. Like Ronald Reagan. He knew how to act the part. And Anthony Allday again thought it would now be next to impossible to reconstruct himself one more time, what with Genaro coming and all. He had to accept being a night watchman at the Springfield Mall. That was it. Whereas Genaro could still be anyone and do anything he wanted.

Anthony Allday entered the garage in section B. He found a place on the top floor, away from the crowded spaces. He parked his red Corvette in a corner. He then took the center elevator to the bridge connecting the garage building and main concourse of the airport. He had plenty of time. But then, as he descended, Anthony Allday wondered whether

248

he had locked the car. For the briefest moment, he wasn't sure. But he dismissed the thought. It wouldn't be like him to do something like that. His doubts were a product of his fatigue. He checked the time: Genaro's flight would have landed and el cojudo might already be looking for him, desperately, since his cousin might not even recognize him. Anthony Allday got off the elevator and entered the main concourse.

Two hours later, Antonio Alday Gutiérrez would marvel at the power of El Azar to turn around so decisively and make his life so miserable. That jester had followed him, twisting his life in so many ways, from the very beginning until the very end. And even now, at 3:45 after the sinful deed, even through his feverish fatigue, he can remember, clear as day, that when he parked the Corvette on the top floor of the garage, section B, he had locked it. After all, Anthony Allday was a watchman; he knew all about locking things down. No doubt about it, Antonio Alday Gutiérrez thinks, feeling faint, that cursed Saturday in December, El Azar turned against him and nestled his bad luck in the blind knots of his being for good.

5

As the sun begins to disappear behind the hills and Victorian houses of Lima, Antonio Alday Gutiérrez feels himself sinking into a heavy stupor. He senses that the end of the man he has become, after twenty-two years of effort, is near. The police will be knocking on his door any moment. He is running out of time. He wants to continue recollecting his ill-taken steps and follow Anthony Allday to the very end, but he has no strength to relive the moment of the murder. He needs rest. Seeking respite, he turns his gaze toward the Peruvian notebooks beside him. He recognizes the newspaper clipping he has saved between the pages of the third notebook.

The Ancestral Art of Cosme Salvatierra
By Sol Saletan
Exclusive for the *Philadelphia Inquirer*

The much anticipated exhibition of pre-Columbian art and artifacts opens at the Philadelphia Museum of Art this weekend. Thanks to the tireless efforts of Dr. Richard J. Schultz, curator of the New World art and artifacts collection at the museum, the exhibition combines rare pieces from long-extinct cultures, such as the Tiahuanaco (Peru-Bolivia) and the Toltec (Yucatan Peninsula), with works by contemporary Latin American artists.

The works by Peruvian ceramicist Cosme Salvatierra are particularly noteworthy. The central pieces by this young artist, including "Chulucanas Soul" and "Wind," show a rare mastery of technique and composition. The bases and bodies of these pieces are reminiscent of the famous huacos from the Chimú and Mochica cultures of northern Peru. But Mr. Salvatierra superimposes on them highly polished and nearly translucent motifs drawn from contemporary mythology. The result is breathtaking. Pieces like "Wind" seem to defy gravity, a feature distinct in Peruvian huacos.

In an informal conversation with the native Peruvian, I suggested that his work dealt with the inevitable conflict between two distinct visions of the world: native-ancient and Western-modern. Mr. Salvatierra smiled, adding that "the combination of color and line is new. But the soul, the silence that inhabits that space, is the same." Such a comment might well be an update on an ancient philosophy. According to Salvatierra, his family tree stretches back to pre-Inca times.

The exhibition ends December 24, 1993.

6

There he was. Concourse B, Gate 6. Anthony Allday recognized him right away: blue pants too short and too tight; gaudy, multicolored shirt; narrow, dirty, brown shoes. There was Genaro. A duffle soccer bag the color of shit hanging from his right shoulder. Greasy black hair cropped short. Dark, sunken, lost eyes. Skinny, ugly hands. Narrow, drooping shoulders. Thin, short neck. Turning around. Searching. There was the son of a bitch who had come to ruin his life. Searching for his cousin. Stuck there. Fearing to leave his place. Waiting. Concha su madre. Like an abandoned orphan. Like all the cholos who come down to La Parada. And Anthony Allday: Are you Genaro Alday?

And he: Yes! Cousin Antonio? Just like that, in one swoop, Genaro threatened to put out all the lights of his world. Cousin Antonio. Son of a bitch!

With the soft light of the day hitting his closed eyes, feeling ever more disoriented and fatigued, Antonio Alday Gutiérrez continues to be accosted by unanswerable questions: Why didn't he just pretend he had never received the letter? Or afterwards, when he saw Genaro at the airport, why didn't he just walk away? Was it really because of sentimentality? Because of pity? Because he thought Genaro would be more resourceful than he now appeared? Or was it because his constructed past, the past of a just man, had left him no choice but to greet him? If he had not gone to pick up Genaro, if he had not greeted him once he saw him, would he, could he have continued being Mr. Anthony Allday?

And so: Hi, Cousin! I've been waiting for you. Welcome to the USA! How was your flight? Tired? And Genaro was impressed with his cousin Antonio. He was a true American. I'm glad you're here, Cousin. And Antonio Alday smiled at him. Patted him on the back. And led him to the parking garage. They did not have to go to the baggage claim area. Genaro had stuffed everything he had into his duffle soccer bag. He followed his cousin. A little lamb. In silence. Mesmerized by the soft brick-red carpets. Sniffing the air now and then. A suspicious lamb. A spooked goat. And Anthony Allday looked at Genaro out of the corner of his eye, not knowing whether he was choking with anger or envy.

Yes, anger and envy. Because el cojudo still had his past and therefore his future intact. Because he could still reconstruct himself as he wished. Because Genaro had reason to believe he might count on his cousin Antonio for help. Who had helped Anthony Allday in his reconstruction? No one. Who could he have asked for help in determining whether this or that detail was good or bad for his unfolding past, as it became the basis for his future? No one.

Anthony Allday was definitely filled with anger, Antonio Alday Gutiérrez recognizes at 3:50 P.M. Because when he tried to imagine for the briefest moment how they might construct a life together, he felt sick to his stomach, dragged down into an oily, briny world that left a sour film in his mouth. Oh God. And those feelings did not go away. Not until the deed.

The only life in which Genaro could possibly fit, Anthony Allday thought as they walked to the top floor of the parking garage, given the established borders of his constructed past, would be a relationship of master and servant. But Genaro would never accept that. Genaro would want to be his cousin. He would want to be coddled. Protected. And Anthony Allday felt the pain in his left big toe increase. And the hot air of the concourse dried his mouth. And his fatigue and headache also increased. And he looked at el cojudo out of the corner of his eye. And he cursed his bad luck. It would be impossible. El cojudo could not be a servant because he had all the luck in the world.

That was not all, of course. Antonio Alday Gutiérrez remembers with astonishment that things were just beginning to get out of control. The worst was yet to come. For when they got to the place where Anthony Allday had parked his Corvette, on the roof of the garage, section B, just as he felt the cold air clearing his mind, calming him down, he came finally to realize how unfairly, how wickedly, El Azar had thrown its full force against him.

7

This can't be happening! Anthony Allday yelled out, holding his head with both hands, walking around the empty spot, incredulous, cursing, trying to explain to Genaro in a muddled Spanish that cars didn't just disappear like that in America, that Philadelphia was not like Lima, carajo. While Genaro looked at his cousin chagrined, not daring to say a word, keeping his gaze far into the distance, hands in his pockets, contracting his shoulders to combat the cold. What's going on?

Anthony Allday found the yellow emergency box, picked up the receiver, and spoke with a woman on the other end of the line. She said the police would be arriving in a few minutes. He slammed down the receiver and went back to the empty spot, where Genaro was waiting. He sat down on the low cement parapet circling the top of the building. He didn't look at his cousin. He didn't say a word. Meanwhile, el cojudo Genaro seemed lost. He was standing in the middle of that cement-gray world, picking at his nails inside the pockets of his too-short and too-tight pants, pretending admiration at the little mounds of snow that remained on the roof despite the golden rays of the morning sun, a sun that must have seemed fake to him because it was so cold.

He must have been cold, Antonio Alday Gutiérrez thinks back. Cold and afraid. Poor Genaro.

When the most awkward moments had passed, Genaro went to sit next to his cousin, perhaps as a gesture of solidarity. He approached and sat down very slowly beside him. He dropped his duffle soccer bag by his feet, set his pointy elbows on his thighs, and rested his bewildered face, eyes looking into the ground, in his dark, rough hands. He did not dare look at his cousin, who was now cursing to himself, in English. Genaro stayed in that position, as if he were asleep, for a long time. Until the black policewoman came, in her blue uniform, her shoes black and shiny, a nightstick banging her thigh, notepad in hand, swaying side to side. Anthony Allday checked on his cousin. But he was not a bit nervous or concerned. On the contrary, he seemed relieved. Imagine that! he thought. The luck of the son of a bitch! He looks relieved!

254

Antonio Alday Gutiérrez remembers that for a flicker of an instant Anthony Allday had recalled his fear of people in uniform upon his arrival in America. As a child, he had seen uniformed men make old men and young women cry. But also in Houston, in San Antonio, in New Bedford, everywhere in America, everyone knew uniformed men were the eyes and ears of La Migra. To survive, he had learned to be invisible. He had escaped their grasp at least twice that way: In San Antonio he dove into the river to become one with the murky waters. He floated along the River Walk until he found a restaurant where an old man played the guitar: Nowadays la gente have to be invisible, Antonio, don Jacinto had told him then. Not like in my times, when we could still choose to stand or to run. Things have changed, little Peruvian. In New Bedford, Alex Sosa saved him by changing him to Mr. Allday on the spot. He eventually became invisible in broad daylight. The trick had lasted a long time. And now, Antonio Alday Gutiérrez accepts with sadness, he was visible all over again.

Genaro was unimpressed by what was happening around him, Anthony Allday was thinking as the policewoman asked him for details. There he was, el cojudo, with his pointy elbows resting his thighs, his wrinkled clown face between his ugly hands, his dark lamb's eyes fixed on the ground, as if nothing of importance was really happening around him. Some people are born just to show off, carajo.

When the policewoman had put away her notepad and disappeared into the elevator, Anthony Allday could not take it any longer and asked Genaro if he was even remotely worried. Genaro sat up eager to please, looked him in the eye, and answered with all the calm in the world: I knew you'd fix everything, Cousin. My father told me you're a big man around here. What would a policewoman do to a man like you? The police only mess with people like me.

Anthony Allday had been so preoccupied with his anger and his envy that he had forgotten for a while about the life in America he had constructed for the Peruvians: He was the owner of a clothing factory. He traveled to Europe to make worldwide deals. He had numerous contracts with the Pentagon, to provide the army with uniforms, tents, even bathrobes for the officers. He had made a fortune manufacturing plastics. He had stores in the most important malls in the USA. Of course. How could he be nervous in the presence of a black police-woman? Genaro wasn't crazy. He was aware of his cousin's exploits in America.

Was it at that moment, in that regurgitation of the image of Antonio Al-day Gutiérrez as the successful businessman in America, that Anthony Allday began to blind himself with hatred, with regret, with despair, all of which ultimately led him to commit the murder? Was it then that Anthony Allday began his descent into hell? Disoriented, hoping against hope for the dying soft light of the winter sun to warm his body, Antonio Alday Gutiérrez has no answers. The only thing he can say for certain is that when Genaro expressed his total trust in him, Anthony Allday felt a shiver, thin and writhing, with crystal tendrils running down his spine all the way down to his left big toe.

The success story had not been casually made. Antonio Alday Gutiér-rez's saga listed specific accomplishments: a big house in the country, with gardens and azaleas always in bloom, with dwarf cypresses forming long and even borders, with an artificial pond filled with goldfish the size of dogs; several cars: Mercedes, Jaguars, and Lincolns; the latest electronic equipment; security systems with twenty-four-hour surveil-lance; six servants; and guests, lots of guests, all year round. Nothing casual in his few letters to Peru. Antonio Alday Gutiérrez had pro-claimed his life in America as a trail of overcome obstacles with many happy endings.

Was it then, when he realized that he could never show Genaro what he had come expecting, that his thick shell began to crush him?

8

When did he start to weave the story of his life in America for his family? It had to have been back in 1986, when Antonio Alday Gutiérrez summoned his uncle Aniceto, Genaro's father, to have lunch with him at La Tiendecita Blanca, in Miraflores, around the corner from El Vivaldi, near the park.

He called Roncero's store, in Tacora, and asked doña Rosa to relay a message to his uncle that he would be calling back two hours later. The old lady said the Aldays had all moved away, to Canto Grande, some years back, but that she knew the number of the community telephone service there. They'll give him the message, Toñito. I'm sure you can talk with him. He's always around. How are you, son? How come you don't come visit? And Toñito said he would visit them very soon. Later that day, Anthony Allday called the community telephone service and heard his uncle Aniceto's voice, low and guttural, deferential, very old. And Antonio ended their short conversation: I don't have much time, Uncle. I'm only passing through. Take a taxi, Uncle. Please. I'll take care of the fare. Don't worry. Please, take a taxi. I don't want you to get lost. All right? The old man agreed, with gratitude in his voice.

Uncle Aniceto arrived shortly after noon. He had on a coarse green cotton shirt with metal buttons and a starched collar. His shoes were surely borrowed, and clearly too tight. His baggy pants were too long; the double cuffs were soiled with Lima's winter grime. He hasn't changed for shit, Antonio Alday Gutiérrez—who by then was already Anthony Allday—exclaimed to himself. He invited the old man to take a seat at one of the round tables protected from the drizzle by a wide awning. They sat facing the busy street. Order whatever you want for lunch, Uncle. We have some time. Don't worry. They have very good beef and lamb dishes here. Let's make it a true Peruvian midday dinner! But Uncle Aniceto said he only wanted a cup of coffee and a hot sandwich. It's too bad we didn't know you were coming, Toño. I'm sure your dear mother would have wanted to see you. But, of course, I understand.

Uncle Aniceto understood that if Gloria were to see her youngest son for only a brief moment, then see him depart again, she would suffer needlessly. It would be better that he, his only uncle, should tell her that he had seen her son with his own eyes, for lunch, even if only for a few minutes, that Toñito was well, that he had asked him to tell her that he loved her very much, that he thinks about you every day, Gloria. Your boy is doing fine. Of course, son, Uncle Aniceto said, folding and unfolding his cloth napkin, looking out on the busy street in Miraflores. It's better. Of course. We know how women are. She wouldn't understand. I'll make sure she knows, Toño. I'll tell her. You can count on me. And Toño stuffed five one hundred dollar bills in his uncle's pocket: For her, Uncle. The first of many installments, I swear. And as the old man shifted in his seat, the moistness in his eyes caught the weak light of the day, reflecting it.

And Toño—who was already Anthony Allday: Tell my mother that I'm always thinking of her. Tell her that I'm going through some difficult times right now because, since there are no wars these days, the gringos are less willing to buy new clothes. Tell her she should go to the doctor once in a while, that it's good to be checked out. And he bowed his head, to show his emotion. And he called a taxi, even though the old man had not yet touched his sandwich. But they both understood lunch was not the reason for his coming. Uncle Aniceto knew he needed to sink back down into Canto Grande. And then, in a departure from the script, Toño scribbled on a piece of paper and placed it in the old man's shirt pocket: My address in the USA, Uncle. Save it. Just in case.

That was the beginning of the success story Anthony Allday would then modify, little by little, over the years. And at 3:52 P.M., Antonio Allday Gutiérrez thinks that Anthony Allday must have wanted to keep in touch. He must have wanted to know about his mother, his brother, his sister, and everyone else in Tacora. Even back then, on that winter day in 1986. Otherwise, why would he have given his bewildered uncle his address? What other purpose would it have served? Of course, he was convinced there was no way his family could ever intrude into his new life. Tacora and Canto Grande were too far removed to really matter. But, deep inside, he must have known better. He must have known it is never a good idea to play footloose and fancy free with El Azar. As it turned out, in that moment of weakness long ago, Anthony Allday contributed to his eventual undoing.

The three short letters he sent later, addressed to his uncle at the community center in Canto Grande, were filled with imprudent details. He had been in Algiers, in Morocco, in Thailand, shoring up his business, feeling bad that he was unable to return to Peru. Perhaps next year. I promise to do my best, Uncle. His last letter was reckless: *How I would like for the family to be here! The thing is, Uncle, I miss Peru. I miss everyone. If, someday, any one of you would ever come to visit me in the USA, I promise you'll have everything. You have my address. My house really belongs to the family.*

Shortly after sending that last letter Anthony Allday came to regret having sent any of them. He came to regret having met with his uncle Aniceto and having said all the things he had. At 3:52 P.M., Antonio Alday Gutiérrez remembers that after that last letter Anthony Allday finally realized what he should have known from the very beginning: that from the moment he invented his success in America, he would find it impossible to return to Tacora or to follow them to Canto Grande, and that he would never see his mother again.

How would he ever have been able to look into his mother's eyes and tell her that all he had said to his uncle had been a lie? It would have broken her heart. No. But even more, despite all his anger and pain, Toñito would never have been able to lie to his mother face to face. Toñito would never have been able to be someone else before her. She would have seen right through him. Mr. Anthony Allday would have melted back into Tacora the moment he held his mother's hands and smelled her breath.

¡Me lleva el diablo! The devil take me away! curses Antonio Alday Gutiérrez, Anthony Allday had gone too far. That was why he never went back to see her. Not even when she died.

Antonio Alday Gutiérrez shifts his stiffening body on the vinyl couch. He remembers Ricardo's brief letter, dated January 15, 1993: *I don't know if this letter will reach you. But I feel I need to send it anyway. Our dear mother is dead. She died yesterday at the hospital.* And Carmen had added below: *I hope you are fine, Toño. We are finally truly orphans. You should come home.*

259

I never went back because I refused to be young and vulnerable again, Antonio Alday Gutiérrez murmurs to himself. I refused!

Perhaps due to his feverish fatigue, or perhaps because he has finally gained some insight into the world of shadows that was his past, on this cold December day in 1995, in Lima, Delaware County, Antonio Alday Gutiérrez is finally able to cry and through his tears acknowledge the pain of an old but still open wound: What he hated most about his father's death was not that he had died young, Antonio could accept that—don Juan himself had done so—but that he had died at the Hospital Loayza. That was why, two years ago, when he received Ricardo's letter, he read it over and over to convince himself she had been spared. And, indeed, Ricardo had not mentioned the Hospital Loayza. But now, at 3:58 P.M., as he revisits his fears and his pain, he feels he needs to accept what he has always denied: he could certainly have prevented it. He could have sent them money. A mere thousand dollars at most. And Antonio Alday Gutiérrez lets his tears roll down his face. His guilty hands start shaking again. He traces the path of the pain of his toe to its end. He desperately wants to find a way to pay for something.

9

What to do now? The police would take their time to find the Corvette, if they found it at all. They might have to take a taxi. What else was there to do? Genaro was already shivering, skinny arms crossed, patting his bird shoulders, watching his frozen breath dissipate in the air, like an idiot. On the other hand, a taxi would cost at least forty dollars. Way too much. It was better to take the train to Center City. They would then take the R-3 to Elwyn and walk from there to Lima. It was only eleven o'clock. Besides, Genaro might even be impressed at traveling by train.

Anthony Allday was not mistaken. Genaro's jaw dropped when he saw the brand-new coach pull up to the airport and come to a full stop. It hardly made a sound. The uniformed conductor invited all aboard. Genaro turned to his cousin for approval before climbing the black metal steps. He found the first seat and lowered himself into it with much circumspection, feeling his way down with both hands but pretending to look out the window. It was as though he wanted to make sure he was really there, in that train, going to Philadelphia. The train moved northeast. Genaro traveled sitting up straight, enthralled by the America passing by his window.

Anthony Allday gazed at Genaro's reflection in the window glass: his half-closed black eyes were taking in everything; his disheveled hair seemed to reach out from his skull to absorb the texture of the winter air; his vulgar fingers were like dragging hooks, holding on to the new vinyl seats. Anthony Allday felt the already familiar feelings of anger and envy cut through his heart. The son of a bitch! He feels protected by my hard-earned life. He doesn't show the slightest sense of uncertainty; not a trace of fear. ¡Concha su madre!

They arrived at the Thirtieth Street Station, in West Philadelphia. Genaro was impressed by the immense station hall. He stood by its tall, east-facing doors and gawked at the skyscrapers through them. The idiot went around the main hall with his mouth open, looking up at the ceiling, staring at the passengers, turning around, as if to follow the garbled words of the invisible announcer, holding his duffle soccer bag low to the ground, almost dragging, with his hooklike fingers.

But Cousin Antonio: Philadelphia is one of the oldest and biggest cities in America, Genaro. You will come to know it soon.

And Genaro: Is it bigger than Lima, even? I mean, we're about six million, I think.

And Cousin Antonio, locking onto Genaro's lamb's eyes, to keep him from gawking at everything: No, Cousin; but it is cleaner and better. Much better. And they crossed the main hall. As they reached the side entrance that led to the R-3 trains for the suburban stations. Genaro stopped to turn around and give a last look at the main hall. He touched the marble of the massive column marking the entrance. He smiled. And Anthony Allday thought, stupid cholo!

They passed through a large bronze-and-steel door. Cousin Antonio bought the tickets. They climbed the metal stairs to the platform in silence. Anthony Allday was thinking that it had been a long time since he had practiced imitating Clark Gable and Robert Wagner in front of a mirror; that Hannah might show up one of these days, unannounced, in his ugly apartment; that Tom was screwed because he could never be free to love those he loved most. And to Genaro: We need to wait for the next train, Cousin. It'll arrive in a few minutes.

And Genaro: Where are we going, Cousin? Far?

And Cousin Antonio said that it was not very far, that the weather was unusually cold, that they needed to buy winter clothes, and he showed Genaro how to warm his hands by blowing his breath into them, with a little hole for the steam to go through, Cousin, like this. He gave him the news that people did not play much soccer in Philadelphia, that it was too bad very few of his American friends were in town, that, fortunately, he did not have to go to work for a couple of days, and they could spend some time together so you can get acclimated, because things can get a little hectic in America. . . .

Until the train arrived. And Genaro saw how politely the people boarded. And Anthony Allday thought they were all enveloped in the calm routine of their lives.

Cousin Antonio motioned Genaro to follow him to the last car. He thought they might see the countryside better from back there. And Anthony Allday saw Genaro sit down in the last row of red-and-black vinyl seats, as happy as could be, as the train curved west and out of the city. Cousin Antonio was saying that it was too bad the old trains in

Peru no longer went to the highlands of Huancayo, except for once a month, when they climbed the Andes filled with tourists. And Genaro turned away from the window to confide that he had never been on a train, not until now. It's very curious, Cousin. I jumped from the car to the airplane without ever stepping on a train! And it's just wonderful! The seats. The windows. Everything. It feels like an electric current is going through my body. ¡Por mi madre! It tickles the little hairs of my shins! And Anthony Allday saw Genaro chortle, showing his uneven, rotten teeth, peeling his lips high and showing his meaty gums. Cholo de mierda, son of a bitch! And just then the conductor came to punch their tickets. And the train stopped at Yeadon, where a group of young Black men playing rap music came on board. And Anthony Allday's left big toe was killing him. And his eyes were burning from the bright light. And he remembered he had not had breakfast. And Genaro was gawking again.

10

By the time they reached Morton, Anthony Allday could not bear to be near his cousin any longer. He got up from his seat and, ignoring the sign prohibiting it, opened the back emergency door and stepped onto the narrow rear platform. He saw the steel rails shining in the morning sun. He felt the cold air of winter enveloping him. But he didn't find the open air refreshing or invigorating. On the contrary, it made him more fatigued. He panned the horizon with his eyes and thought it would be a while before they would get off the train and walk to his ugly apartment. And he cursed to himself, thinking it would be longer still, much longer, before he would know what would happen to him now that Genaro was finally there.

Anthony Allday was about to return to his seat, Antonio Alday Gutiérrez remembers at 4:00 P.M., wringing his trembling hands, listening to the faint rhythm of his guilty heart. But Genaro had followed him outside. El cojudo's eyes seemed transfixed by the blurry curtain of leafless trees passing by. He stuck out his bare head to the side and let his dingy hair dance in the wind. A total cholo, an embarrassment of a man. And just then Anthony Allday began thinking about his Corvette, which had cost him dearly and might never be found, about Tacora and Canto Grande, full of thieves. ¡Hijos de puta! And he swelled with hatred against Tacora. And God only knew where the conductor was. God only knew why the alarm had not sounded. And the shaking of the train shot through his body, sending out a million tendrils of pain. And Genaro was as happy as he could be, now with a permanent smile on his face.

The train shook and whined until it reached the faded green metal trestle at Swarthmore, which bridged a chasm made by Crum Creek many thousands of years ago. The water of the creek was a thin blue ribbon under the winter sky. On the other side of the creek, Anthony Allday could see a wide embankment. It was covered with thick grass and low-growing bushes. He leaned out and saw the train had nearly finished crossing the faded green metal bridge. Then, out of the blue, urged by something coming from the depths of his being, tricked by El

Azar, Anthony Allday took hold of his cousin by his frail, cold shoulders, as if to congratulate him for something he had done. He smiled at him, and Genaro did not know what to do, he just let himself be held, his lamb's eyes fixed on Cousin Antonio's face. Then, without saying a word, still looking into Genaro's eyes, not with anger or hatred but more like in a dance without music, he swiveled to his left. He heard the high-pitched rhythm of the rails, he felt the hard cold wind against his body, and he swiveled to the right, abruptly, without thinking, eyes closed. Suddenly, his hands let go of Genaro's skinny body, and he felt his cousin falling away, over the low rail, and he followed his cry, long, eerie, faraway, over the precipice.

For an infinitesimal moment, as the wind dispersed Genaro's cry, Anthony Allday did not recognize himself. He looked at his already trembling hands in total shock, stared at the spot where Genaro had been, looked at the emergency door with its clear red danger sign, and knew that he had become someone else—this time unplanned and not by choice. Then, with bewilderment, anger, and despair in his voice, as if to deny El Azar its ultimate victory, as if to claim as his own what he could not have possibly intended, Anthony Allday cried out: *¡Muere, carajo! ¡Muere!* Die, damn you! Die!

Before his words had dispersed in the cold air, Anthony Allday was more than willing to accept, even to demand, that he was guilty of a crime. He just didn't know why.

11

No one else seemed to have noticed the terrible deed. Anthony Allday went back into the coach, sat down on its red-and-black vinyl seat, and for the rest of the ride looked out the window in a daze. When the train arrived in the Elwyn station, near Lima, he disembarked slowly. He walked to his ugly apartment, totally unafraid. The police would come for him soon enough. He had no desire to hide. He was done with running scared. He climbed the stairs to the third floor without noticing the sunlight coming through the stained glass window. He opened his door with a kick of his right foot and an upward pull. He closed it behind him. He dropped onto the yellow vinyl couch. He let the soft light of the winter sun warm his tired body. It was high noon.

A moment later, warmed back into consciousness by the soft light of the winter sun, Antonio Alday Gutiérrez finally came to recognize what Anthony Allday had done. He now felt forlorn in a strange land. He felt guilty. He knew he had to pay for Anthony Allday's deed. And yet, at the same time, he could not believe himself capable of such an act. Antonio Alday Gutiérrez was a good man, underneath all his transformations. But how and before whom might he defend himself? To whom might he confess, to show that deeply hidden innocence? Only to himself. Only himself. No one in Lima, Delaware County, Pennsylvania, knew Antonio Alday Gutiérrez. He had only himself. And so, at high noon on Saturday, December 10, 1995, Antonio Alday Gutiérrez peered into the soft white light of the winter sun saturating his ugly apartment and began to retrace his steps, seeking absolution.

12

In the final throes of his feverish fatigue, feeling drawn into a heavier and heavier daze, wanting to sleep and, perhaps, to rest his soul, Antonio Alday Gutiérrez concedes he is guilty of a crime. There is no way of escaping that fact. At 4:00 P.M., he still wants to know what he could have done to prevent the sinful act, where in his long trail of ill-chosen steps he had made the decision that had brought him to this moment. But his mind and spirit are dimming fast. In the fog that increasingly surrounds him, Antonio Alday Gutiérrez comes to accept that the exercise of memory has been a waste of time. It has only gained him a few hours of wakefulness.

Antonio Alday Gutiérrez can still imagine Genaro's body limp among the rocks of the ravine; he can picture his too-short and too-tight pants full of blood, his lamb's eyes fixed on the blue sky, his dingy hair mixing with the thick grass, his hands clutching his duffle soccer bag. Full of pity and regret, Antonio Alday Gutiérrez wishes to cry rivers. But he is too far gone. The tears will not come. Struggling still, he tries willing himself into sadness. But his heart is too tired or too bitter even for that. And so, with the now soft, golden light of the winter sun abandoning Lima, Delaware County, Pennsylvania, feeling the faint rhythm of his heavy heart, at 4:00 after the deed, Antonio Alday Gutiérrez closes his eyes and, following the hum of pain in his left big toe, falls into a deep sleep.

Seven O'clock

Peruvian Notebook No. 4
August 10, 1994

I received the citizenship papers in the mail today. I am finally
invisible.

1

As the shadow of night grows dense and the wintry wind sweeps low across the rolling hills of Lima, Delaware County, Pennsylvania, there is a knock on the door of the apartment at 209 Rogers Lane. In the thick silence of the darkness, the knock sounds furtive, regretful. Half asleep and feeling nothing but still vaguely aware of his predicament, Antonio Alday Gutiérrez bolts upright. He smoothes his shirt. Who is it? His words flutter and die. Then, not really knowing why, he reaches for a feeble hope: Perhaps everything has been a nightmare. Who is it? He thinks he can hear Mr. Mozino's voice outside his door. His heart and his mind are now ablaze. And before anyone can answer, Antonio Alday Gutiérrez lets out under his breath: Dear God, let it be Genaro.

About the Author

Braulio Muñoz was born in Peru. Before coming to America he was a stage actor, political leader, and radio and print journalist. He holds a Ph.D. in sociology from the University of Pennsylvania and has taught at various East Coast universities. He is currently Eugene M. Lang Research Professor and Professor of Sociology at Swarthmore College. Professor Muñoz has written books and articles on sociology, psychology, philosophy, and literary criticism. *Mario Vargas Llosa: Between Civilization and Barbarism* (Rowman & Littlefield, 2000)is his most recent book on literary criticism. Professor Muñoz has also written works of fiction. His first novel, *Alejandro y los pescadores de Tancay,* was published in Italy (Andreas Lippolis Edittore, 2004). Professor Muñoz travels frequently to lecture in several languages throughout Europe and Latin America. He is currently teaching courses on social and critical theory at Swarthmore College and is working on a new book on social theory and a new novel. *The Peruvian Notebooks* is his first novel in English.